HEAD of ZEUS

THE CASE OF THE HEADLESS JESUIT

George Bellairs

HEAD of ZEUS
MYSTERIOUSPRESS.COM
presented by
HEAD OF ZEUS

WITH LOVE TO

GWLAD AND GOOFY,

MY FAITHFUL PARTNERS IN CRIME AND IN EVERYTHING

ELSE

CHARACTERS

Benjamin Hosegood and Oscar Flunder, Wardens of St. Mark's, Cobbold.

P.C. Pennyquick, Law and Order in Cobbold.

His wife and four eligible daughters.

Rev. Penderell Worsnip, M.A., Vicar of Cobbold.

Rev. Augustus Smythe, B.A., his Curate.

Granville Salter, late Lord of the Manor of Cobbold.

Superintendent Percival, of the Thorncastle Police.

A Girl in emerald green and a Man in a huge overcoat.

Ephraim Davy, Baker, of Cobbold, and his Two Women.

Phyllis Alveston, a local beauty.

Mary Ann Alveston, her mother.

Meg, Granville Salter's Old English Sheep-Dog.

The Manager and Staff of the Mitre Hotel, Thorncastle.

A Film Director and his retinue. A Film Star or two.

Lancelot Qualtrough, County Coroner.

Mortimer Whatmough, his factotum.

Benjamin Fernihough, Lawyer of the Salter Family.

Dr. Kilpheric, Police Surgeon.

The Mayor, Corporation, Chief Constable, and Football Eleven of Glebechester.

Stationmaster and Porter of Glebechester.

Mrs. Reilly: "Good beds for respectable men."

Policemen and Road Scouts.

Ex-C.S.M. Bedford, Custodian of a block of flats in Mayfair.

Deborah James, one of his tenants.

Other queer tenants.

James Cooney, alias Barney Faircluff, private investigator.

Mrs. Plucock, widow of P.C. Plucock of Carstonwood.

Her children and her mother, Mrs. Hearty.

Madeline Fothergill, a gentlewoman of Cobbold.

Felicity Grimes, her maid.

Dennis Pratt, assistant at the local Co-op., and Felicity's admirer.

Herbert Moss, Barney Faircluff's ball-boy.

Tom Sly, gravedigger at Cobbold Church.

Mr. and Mrs. Ashberry, of the Royal Oak, Cobbold.

Margaret Lacey, née Salter, Granville's Aunt.

Nathaniel Polydore, antique dealer and antiquary.

Clients in Polydore's shop.

Sergeant Dainty, Thorncastle Police.

Dr. Macduff, Nationalized physician in Cobbold.

Mrs. Whatmough, mother of Mortimer.

Mr. and Mrs. Enoch Tyle, her sister and brother-in-law.

Mrs. Pawker, who does for Mrs. Alveston and others.

Pollie Duckett, widow and grocer of Cobbold.

Sid Chapell, who is courting Pollie.

Bruno Auerhahn, a musical friend of Madeline Fothergill.

Harry Coop, a driver on the London Underground.

and

Detective-Inspector Thomas Littlejohn, of New Scotland Yard.

Detective-Sergeant Robert Cromwell, of the same.

ONE

WATCHNIGHT SERVICE

AT 11.30 on New Year's Eve, the ringers of St. Mark's, the parish church of Cobbold-in-the-Marsh, began a muffled peal for the Old Year. This was a signal for the rival congregation of Methodists over the road to start singing hymns and lamentations for days past and to praise the Lord for guiding them through life's weary pilgrimage hitherto.

> Days and moments quickly flying
>   Blend the living with the dead;
> Soon will you and I be lying
>   Each within his narrow bed.

They sang it with the gusto of eager anticipation!

In the parish church opposite they were all sitting quietly. Useless to carry on a vocal battle with the bells. Their time would come. Meanwhile, it was pleasant to sit there and look around.

The soft lights of oil lamps shone on the polished ornaments and gold thread of the altar and spread a gentle glow over the evergreens, holly and fir, which decorated the pulpit, side-chapel, and window-sills. There was a crib, lit by tiny candles, in the chapel and a large Christmas tree in the south porch. The place was almost full.

They were short of coke and it wasn't very warm. People shuffled their feet to restore circulation and their breath rose like steam. Some of the breath already bore faint traces of alcohol; a little bibbing in anticipation....

Overhead the muffled bells pealed away like soft musical footsteps on their way to heaven. People could hear them for miles across the Marsh, where, in the vast silence, they sounded like the stealthy fore-runners of death, heralds of coffins and funeral processions.

Benjamin Hosegood, people's warden, sat side by side with Oscar Flunder, the vicar's elect, in their little wardens' pew at the very back of the church. Sitting solemnly there, with their silver-topped staffs of office standing beside them, they looked like two medieval figures of the carnal sins of Greed and Gluttony, for Ben was thin and parsimonious and Oscar gross and fat. Hosegood's mean little eyes flitted from one to another of the congregation, sizing them up with pleasure or hate. His jaws kept rotating as though he were chewing a quid. Any time you expected he would spit on the floor. Flunder, on the other hand, was half asleep. It must have been the old port which now lay, like aromatic balm, on his stomach. He went through a regular routine of movements. First a nod, then his eyes would close and he would cast up a mild snore which awakened him. Then he would look sheepishly around to see if he were observed and begin the cycle all over again.

Among the motley gathering of heads and headgear in the body of the building could be seen the pink, shiny dome of the constabulary head, that of P.C. Pennyquick, celebrating, in mufti, the advent of the New Year, thanks to a dearth of malefactors. He had his wife and two daughters on one side of him and two more daughters on the other. The girls wore party dresses under their coats, for this was a brief interlude in the season's merrymaking and they hoped to continue where they had left off. The eyes of several village beaux fell with pleasure and longing on the four young and comely ladies and with resentment on the bobby, whom his fair offspring always seemed to prefer among men....

Pending the arrival of the clergy and choir, the meeting took a secular and social turn. People chattered, hobnobbed, turned in their seats to exchange gossip and greetings, or, in behind-hand whispers to comment, carp or pass slanderous remarks about something or someone. But, taken as a whole, the gathering was one of good will, for Christmas wasn't far behind and the nearness of the New Year filled most of them with awe and a fierce or feeble desire to do better than last.

The shining brass plates which commemorated generations of dead-and-gone Salters, one-time lords of the manor of Cobbold, looked down on the assembly and reflected the lamps on the countenances of rich and poor alike. Marble plaques let in the walls to the memory of this and that village or local notable still recited the innumerable virtues and accomplishments of the deceased.

Sacred to the Memory of

Thomas Proudfoot, L.M.S.S.A.

for over forty years beloved physician of this parish who laid down his task on October 25th, 1832. Of a benign and kindly disposition, a scholar and one skilled in the arts of healing, he

… etc.

P.C. Pennyquick's youngest read it over and over again, wondering why she did so, what the doctor of a hundred years ago looked like, why he died at the age of sixty-three and how he qualified so young, whilst a young admirer gazed at her in rapture and pondered whether or not to commit some fearful crime and, by her father's attentions to him, bring himself to her notice.

The effigies of armoured knights with crossed feet, lying in cold marble with their ladies beside them in alcoves on either side of the chancel, slept unmoved by the passing of the years. The Salters' family pew stood empty and forlorn. The last of the family had removed to a flat in Mayfair and sold the Hall to a doctor for a private asylum, which had not been successful and resulted in the great house now being empty and for sale. The death-watch beetle was in the rafters of the church which, now and then, as the bells shook them, sprinkled the soft brown dust of decay on those beneath. The place smelled musty from dry-rot and old stone.

Mr. Hosegood and Mr. Flunder still sat silently together. They were not on good terms and each behaved as though the other weren't there. Mr. Hosegood had tried to celebrate the passing of the year with an indigestible meal which was now beginning to ferment and cause a painful effervescence in his inside. He gripped his breast-bone and gently pressed the spot where the pain hurt him most; at the same time he grimly eyed the fur coat worn by Mrs. Pennyquick (Christmas present) and wondered how much it had cost and where the constable had got the money from. He found himself wishing he had a grown-up family to earn money for him. He was a tailor on the verge of bankruptcy and he had borrowed from his fellow-warden, a butcher and reputed to be up to his ears in the black market.

Hosegood eyed his sleeping neighbour with the hatred of the unlucky debtor for his successful creditor.

As the sound of the bells waxed and waned, the joyful strains from the chapel opposite rose and fell, invading the quiet church and then, met by the muffled swelling of the peal, retreated and fell silent like a brawling intruder.

Who of us death's awful road,
  In the coming year shall tread ...

And the chimes, though mourning themselves, seemed unable to bear the rest and chased it out of doors.

A deaf old man who could hear nothing of what was going on, was being kept posted in dumb-show by a benevolent maiden lady in the pew behind. She kept pointing upwards as a sign that the bells were still at it, and he would nod with satisfaction as though assured, by the finger raised to heaven, that

Providence was still watching over him. Even at that unearthly hour, a number of children, protected by special dispensation, had come to church and were seated in the children's pew at the very front. Whenever they manifested any signs of slumber or boredom, they were quickly set right by the ferrules of the umbrellas of two elderly ladies who, being hard of hearing, had perched themselves as near the chancel as they could.

At ten minutes to twelve the choir and clergy entered, the Rev. Penderell Worsnip, M.A. (Cantab.), rector, the Rev. Augustus Smythe, B.A. (Dunelm.), curate, six little boys and two hulking men, all in surplices. Mr. Smythe was late wherever he went and was seen hastily joining the procession, fiddling with his vestments and adjusting his stole, which he reverently kissed, as he came in step. The white linen, the vicar's silver hair, Mr. Smythe's pale, apologetic face, the boys' polished red cheeks and the livid noses of the blacksmith and the cobbler bringing up the rear in squeaking shoes, gleamed under the lamplight.

The bells padded on in their courses. Mr. Hosegood looked peevishly at his watch, wondering if the ringers, forgetting themselves and already well-fortified for their tasks at the local, would carry on their funereal ringing far into the New Year. He held his watch in his hand for a moment, bitterly contemplating it. It was of gunmetal and had, since last watchnight, replaced the gold one given to him by his father when he was twenty-one. He wondered what would happen before the end of next year.... Then the bells ceased. The youngest ringer could be heard, racing upwards to the belfry from the ringing-chamber to remove the leathers from the clappers. The vicar commenced his battle against time. A brief word, a few responses, an abbreviated hymn, with all the time vociferous competition from over the way. So, they said good-bye to the Old Year.

A half a minute to twelve, and then a hush. The congregation fingered and shuffled their prayer-books and selected the first hymn for the New Year. The two churchwardens continued to ignore one another. Old or New, it was all the same to them. They had no time for each other and so long as Hosegood paid his interest, Flunder was content to leave things as they were.

And then, just as all the people were holding their breath waiting for the first stroke of midnight on the clock, shuffling footsteps sounded in the porch and a tall, lean man entered the church. He was deathly pale and young, too; on his head was a black slouch hat, which he did not remove. With one hand he held close to him the folds of a heavy frieze-cloth overcoat; with the other he groped in the air of the aisle as though seeking support. The worshippers all turned their heads and a concerted gasp of recognition rose like vapour in the building. Mr.

Granville Salter, formerly of Cobbold Hall, now of Mayfair, London … and drunk!

A brief second or two seemed like eternity. It was as though someone had laid a curse on the assembly and turned them all to stone. The vicar, with silver hair, his open book in his hand … the curate beside him, one hand raised as though to fend off evil, the choirboys with open mouths above the ruffles of their surplices, the smith and the cobbler looking as though they'd seen a ghost. All the congregation, on their feet, turned towards the intruder with their breath caught in horror, Mr. Flunder still sitting, asleep. And the memorial tablets, the brasses, the effigies, unmoved, as though, having passed through life, or recorded all that was in it, this last little surprise did not catch them unaware.…

Before anyone could do anything, the clock struck midnight. The Methodists over the road were first off the mark and began to sing.

The year is gone beyond recall,
With all its hopes and fears …

Between the lines of the Nonconformist hymn, you could hear a fusillade of shot-guns being fired all over the Marsh, where it is the custom to shoot-in the New Year with blank cartridges.

Cobbold bells rang out, and Mr. Granville Salter fell sprawling to the ground.

The shining dome of the Law rose majestically from the middle of the gathering and, seeming to shake off its attendant women, proceeded solemnly to the scene of the commotion. Other men emerged to help, whilst women twittered, tut-tutted and wondered whether or not fainting were merited. The clergy descended to minister and Mr. Flunder, awakened by the clamour of bells, Methodists and congregation, opened his eyes, took in the scene of confusion, closed them again momentarily as though wondering if he were still dreaming, and then, ponderously rising to his feet, stumbled to join the constable.

P.C. Pennyquick first removed the hat of the newcomer. He might be drunk, but let there be no irreverence in church! Then he and Mr. Flunder tried to raise the body which, however, lay a dead-weight in their arms. The constable started, opened the greatcoat, gasped, and then closed it again. Like a mental message, the news flashed round that something was wrong, though no word was spoken. There was a momentary hush. Everyone grew rigid again. The white of the surplices, the colours of the women's clothes, the ring of clean, anxious faces, the bright holly berries, the candles on the altar and Christmas-tree.... And over all, the clashing of the joyful bells and the tumultuous welcome to the New Year from the Methodists opposite.

"Have they started yet?" quavered the deaf, old man, querulous from neglect, and, living in a silent world of his own, unaware of all that was going on.

"If they have, somebody wish me a Happy New Year...."

But they were all too busy.

They carried Mr. Granville into the vestry and there, those who had thought of drunkenness repented. For, just below the heart was a nasty knife-wound, the blood from which the victim had been holding in check with his coat. It was then that the vicar observed that his surplice was stained bright red, and, in the way we have of thinking the most trivial things in the gravest situations, his mind flew to how his housekeeper would make it clean again and what she would say when she heard it was soiled with the blood of another human, a dying man. He knelt beside the stricken man and tried to make him comfortable and prayed for his soul. But, with a great sigh, Mr. Granville Salter died without saying a word. His lips just moved and, for a second his eyes lighted and he tried to smile at the vicar, who was an old friend. The Rev. Augustus Smythe went into the open air and was violently sick, and P.C. Pennyquick, after warning all not to touch anything, although everything possible had been already violently disturbed, rushed to the nearby kiosk to dial 999 and to call a doctor. The hymns and bells continued and the vicar again found his thoughts wandering to the problem of what happened when someone was murdered in church, or died violently in it. The bishop …

Thus the New Year came to Cobbold-in-the-Marsh and gave Inspector Littlejohn, of New Scotland Yard, his first case this year.

TWO

THE DANCING CURATE

"THEY'VE not wasted much time," said Cromwell to Littlejohn as they sat back in the train taking them from London to Thorncastle, the county town of Mereshire. It was Sunday and the sergeant was dressed in his best clothes. Instruction from headquarters had suddenly withdrawn him from the bosom of his family, which he was about to conduct to the home of their grandparent to celebrate the New Year.

"No," said Littlejohn, who, worse still, had been called from bed where he was sleeping off the previous night's festivities. "It seems they've one unsolved murder on their hands already and can't risk a second. The message came by phone and, as they say trains don't run on Sundays from Thorncastle to Cobbold, where the crime occurred, we're to meet the police at Thorncastle. Is there a diner on the train?"

"Yes …" said Cromwell, removing his bowler hat and carefully placing it on the rack. There was a livid weal across his forehead where it had been supported. The thought depressed him. He compared the frugality of railway meals, even at the Special Season, with the festal menu already recited in advance by his wife's mother. It was a bit thick murdering people on New Year's Eve. The thought added zest to the angry enthusiasm he already felt for bringing the criminal to justice.

"I wonder …"

The words died in Cromwell's throat. Littlejohn was already asleep.

"Must have had a thick night," said the sergeant to himself with a lugubrious chuckle. It wasn't as he thought, however. Unexpected revellers had descended upon the Littlejohns and the Inspector had spent what had been left of the night on the couch in the lounge. The springs weren't too good....

The attendant wakened them both for lunch and by the time they'd finished soup, rabbit, and sour plums and custard, they were almost at their destination.

The train leaving an undulating, industrial district, suddenly plunged into a tunnel and emerged into the heart of Mereshire. The change was almost miraculous. Ahead there was not a hill to be seen. The land was flat, intersected by dykes, with farms and pumping-stations dotted here and there, and in the far distance they could see the twin towers of Thorncastle cathedral riding high in the air. As the train sped along, the great church gradually seemed to gather around it larger buildings and then smaller ones, like a hen collecting a brood at her feet. Then, with an extra spurt, the express slid through the scattered outskirts of the city, past goods-yards and cattle-pens and into the station.

"Here we are...."

There was no mistaking the man who had come to meet them. He was dressed in uniform and as clean as a new pin. He was anxiously watching the train for his new colleagues. They liked him at once. He was called Percival, Superintendent Percival, and he looked relieved when he found them. He was over six feet tall, well-built and cheerful. Rather a long, craggy face, with a Roman nose and a strong chin. Sparkling blue eyes, too. Neither shy nor self-assertive. All the promise of a good collaborator. They all wished each other a Happy New Year and then drove to the police station in the Superintendent's car.

"It's growing dusk," said Percival. "I guess you won't want to start in Cobbold to-night. So, I'll tell you what it's all about and then take you to your hotel. I've booked you in at 'The Mitre', a good old place here, and I'm sure you'll be comfortable."

The police had quarters in the Guildhall opposite the Cathedral. The close looked very green and peaceful in the mild evening and you could see an illuminated Christmas tree to the left of the church porch. As they talked the bells began to ring for evening service and flung a sweet chain of sound in every part of the police station.

"Cobbold has worried us of late. We've another murder on our hands there."

"So they told me at the Yard. Has the second any connection with the first?"

"We've an open mind on it, as yet, Inspector. The first was one of our own men. The village constable from Carstonwood, the next village to Cobbold, who was found drowned in one of the dykes between the two places. He'd been hit on the head first and drowned whilst unconscious."

"Nasty," grunted Cromwell.

He felt more eager than ever to get to work and find the killer. The death or injury of "one of us", as he called them, was always added stimulus to him, and to every other policeman. It marked out a particularly ruthless type of criminal....

"Yes, very nasty. And we haven't been able to get a line on it at all. There'd been nothing suspicious in the locality and Plucock left home on his usual daytime patrol. He was seen at noon. At dusk they found his body in the dyke. Not long dead. Not a sign of any strangers. No apparent motive.... A poor Christmas for his wife and family. He'd four youngsters, too."

"Beastly business. And what about last night."

"I thought I'd better get help at once. The two might be connected and murders on the Marsh are unusual. I'm a native of these parts and this and Plucock's death are the first two I remember. It happened at the watchnight service at St. Mark's Church, Cobbold...."

"Murder in church!" interjected Cromwell mysteriously.

"Not exactly. They were just going to see in the New Year when in walked a man who'd been stabbed, and collapsed and died in the aisle. Somebody must have knifed him outside and he'd made for the first lighted place he could see. Where it was done, we can't tell. Our men have been there all day, but not a clue so far. He couldn't have walked any distance with a wound like that. How he kept his feet so far is a mystery to us."

"Was he a native?"

"Had been. Although at the time he was living in London. He was a fellow called Granville Salter. The Salters used to be Lords of the Manor at Cobbold. Family there for generations. Then they fell on bad times. The death of Mr. Gregory Salter, Granville's father, finished it. Death duties took what moneylenders hadn't had already and the Hall was sold. Mr. Granville got some sort of work in London and took a flat there."

“What was he doing back in Cobbold then? Had he connections, or something?”

“He hadn’t been very well, I gather. An attack of ’flu; and he came back to Cobbold for a rest and a good old-fashioned Christmas. He was staying with an old nurse of the family, Mrs. Alveston, who married the one-time bailiff, now dead. She owned her own house and Mr. Granville was always welcome there.”

“I guess you haven’t had much time to get down to things yet, but we’ll have to find out if there were any other attractions there as well as Mrs. Alveston.”

“Phyllis …”

“Eh?”

“Phyllis Alveston. Mrs. Alveston’s daughter. A very pretty girl with half the lads in the district after her. Granville was very fond of her. They’ve known each other since they were kids. But for some reason things didn’t get any forrader. I don’t know why. We’ll have to see into it.”

Littlejohn didn't feel like work. He sat sprawled before the fire in the large old-fashioned grate with his legs stretched out. He bore the traces of Christmas. A new pipe and some special tobacco, a present from his wife, and a pair of brown socks she had knitted for him, which went admirably with his grey tweeds and mellow brown shoes. Cromwell eyed him approvingly, noticing in particular the pipe and deciding to buy one exactly like it.

"How was the wound inflicted?" asked Littlejohn suddenly.

"Just under the heart, by this...."

Percival opened a drawer and passed over the weapon. Littlejohn took out a pair of black-rimmed glasses, put them on and examined the object carefully. It was murderous. A cruel, bright steel blade about six inches in length, fitted in a heavy black haft. On the blade an inscription: "Wilh. Gruber."

Littlejohn passed it over to Cromwell, who examined it efficiently and carefully.

"A German prisoner's knife...."

"Maybe," said Littlejohn. "Maybe not. There are quite a lot of them about. Storm troopers and black-shirts carried them as part of their make-up in Germany in Hitler's time. A lot of our boys got them as souvenirs and brought them home. It might be anyone's."

Percival took the knife back.

"That's right," he added. "As far as we know, there are no German prisoners about here. We'll have to check up more carefully, but I think that's a foregone conclusion. There were no fingerprints on it, either. The murderer must have worn gloves."

"Or wiped it afterwards...."

"I don't think so. You see, we found it in the church porch. Our theory is, that Salter was stabbed and the knife left in the wound. When he reached the church, he drew out the knife himself, dropped it, and covered the wound with his overcoat. He was pressing the coat over the wound as he entered the building."

"And died almost at once."

"Yes. A fearful wound. You must see the doctor later. Well, I think that's all. I'm almost ashamed to say it. It seems so little after all our work to-day, but there it is. It's as big a mystery as poor Plucock's death."

They sat in silence for a while, the bells still ringing and footsteps of churchgoers passing on the pavements outside.

"A good start for the New Year in Cobbold. Who's in charge there?"

"Just the village constable, a fellow called Pennyquick. The man practically died in his arms. It's upset him. He's not far from retiring and, so far, has been used only to drunks and poachers. But he knows all that goes on in the village and he's furious that this affair has been sprung on him without warning. You'll find him useful for local colour and information. A good, sound, village officer."

"Right. And now about 'The Mitre', I suppose. A good meal wouldn't come amiss. You join us?"

"Well … no, sir, if you don't mind. I've a family, you see, and they'll be expecting me. My son's home on leave from the forces. He's eighteen and just doing his service. And my girl's down from Cambridge. So, there's to be a sort of family gathering if I can make it. I don't feel much like merrymaking with all this on our hands…."

"I guess you don't, but there's nothing we can do till morning. Have a good time."

Their bags had been sent on to the hotel and Littlejohn and Cromwell joined them at "The Mitre".

The place was decorated for the season and the dinner was in keeping. The inn was crowded with drinkers and diners. Here and there a family party on a special table.

"Home from home," said Cromwell, carefully opening a mince tart and pouring in rum from a small jug.

"The next best …"

It was difficult not to surrender to the general feeling of warmth and merriment and make a night of it. Cromwell, usually a bit lugubrious, thawed out considerably and wondered to himself how far expenses sheet would stand it.

"I feel like a glass of port just to top off that lot," he chuckled hopefully.

But he didn't get it, for the argument was cut short by an intrusion. It was a clerical one, too. A parson, quietly dining at a single table by the fireplace rose and approached them.

"Please pardon me, gentlemen," he said. "My name is Smythe. I'm curate at Cobbold. I saw you earlier to-day with Superintendent Percival and I wonder if you are engaged on the Cobbold murder case…. Are you?"

Cromwell eyed the parson up and down. A pasty, slim, dark young man in the middle twenties, with pale eyes and thinning, streaky hair. He was shy and nervous and had to screw up his courage whenever faced by a problem.

"Yes, sir," said Littlejohn. "We're from Scotland Yard."

The curate assumed a look of awe and he clasped his hands before him in that clerical fashion which, according to its accompanying facial contortion, can signify reverence, surprise, fervent glee, or simple resignation.

"Are you? Well, sir … I take it you are the one in charge …"

He addressed himself to Littlejohn, carefully stretching his neck and seeking an answer in the Inspector's expression. Cromwell looked at Smythe with contempt and surprise.

"Of course he is.…"

A gramophone began to blare in the next room, which embraced a dance-floor a little larger than an average door-mat. Couples rose and, crushing themselves in the small polished rectangle, began to shuffle and sway. There was hardly room to move a foot, but the promiscuity seemed to please them and each pair, lost in the rhythm of the music and movement, solemnly performed the ritual, oblivious of all else. Then, the music changed and the heaving mass broke bounds. They pranced and tramped from the polished to the rougher timber of the floor and then, over the carpet and among the tables, greatly to the consternation of those trying to eat.

"It's New Year," explained one young executant, his upper lip decorated with a huge moustache and his partner almost tucked under his arm....

"I wanted to mention a matter to you, or to the police here ..." Smythe was saying. "It may be trifling and unimportant and I don't wish to waste your time...."

He looked like excusing himself for the rest of the evening.

"What is it, sir?"

"Well … I'd been to a New Year's Eve party before the watchnight service.… A little family gathering, you know, games and so forth, the season, you know … and had to hurry to get to church in time. I'm afraid I was almost the last there.…"

"Yes.…"

Two newcomers arrived. They looked to have fortified themselves at the bar already and were in merry mood. A man and a girl. He wore an enormous frieze greatcoat, so large that he resembled a walking overcoat. He divested himself of it and flung it, with an effort, over the back of a vacant chair. He looked small and insignificant without it. His companion was a tall, well-built fair girl, with a huge mass of golden hair, sleek and brushed, and falling to her shoulders in what must have been a modern fashion. Fifty years ago, they'd have said she'd let it down ready for bed. She wore a large tweed coat, too square at the shoulders, too close at the waist. Both saw Smythe, hooted at him, pointed to the dance-floor and in pantomime urged him to participate.

"A-b-b-b," said the distracted and blushing curate to Littlejohn.

"I beg pardon...."

"I was—er—saying, as I made for the vestry door, I saw what must have been the murdered man. It couldn't have been anyone else. It wasn't pitch dark and I could make out his outline on the path which passes the main gate of the church. There was someone else with him ... er ..."

"Who, sir?"

"I don't know. They were standing, apparently talking, face to face. All I can say is, it was a man about the same build as the dead man, in a soft hat and overcoat. I was in such a hurry I didn't see more.

Only later I remembered it … I wonder if the information … er … is of use to you.…"

He looked earnestly at Littlejohn, and then across at the dance-floor where the new arrivals were performing, locked in a close embrace and cheek to cheek. The girl had removed the badly fitting coat and was now resplendent in a frock of emerald green. The couple signalled impatiently to Smythe, who smiled thinly back at them and then thinly at Littlejohn.

"It's most important, sir. You must have been the last man to see Mr. Salter alive and you probably saw his murderer, too."

"Oh.…"

Mr. Smythe, blushing at the attentions of the good-looking girl, now turned chalky white at the revelation.

"Had I spoken, or intervened, he might not.…"

The poor curate looked as if he'd committed the murder himself.

"Maybe. But you can't blame yourself for that. If anybody'd passed, spoken, or intervened, there may have been no crime. You have nothing with which to reproach yourself, sir...."

"I'm so glad.... If you want me ... I mean, if I can be of any further use, anyone in the village will tell you where to find me. I think I told you, I'm curate at Cobbold...."

"Yes, sir. Thank you for telling us this. It may prove very useful...."

"Will that be all, sir ...?"

"I think so, thank you...."

Mr. Smythe's friends were still indicating by signs that they urgently needed his presence. Still pale, he rather hesitantly left to join them. The man who owned the overcoat eagerly surrendered his partner to the parson and, nonchalantly separating another girl from her companion, clutched her closely and passed into a state of agitated trance. The fair girl took Smythe into her arms without more ado in a delighted embrace and began to steer him around. The curate looked rather sheepishly over his shoulder at the detectives, who were now making for the bar for a nightcap or two.

"Must be mother-love," said Cromwell, without moving a muscle of his face.

"He seems to need it," chuckled Littlejohn. "If you care to take a turn on the dance-floor yourself, it's all right to me."

"Me?" yelled Cromwell, and, looking down at his regulation boots, from which he was almost inseparable, he laughed, too.

THREE

THE MAN WHO BROUGHT THE NEW YEAR IN

THE wind changed to north-east during the night and, dispelling the damp and murk, sharpened the outlines of the trees and buildings in the cathedral close, cleared the sky of rain clouds and replaced them by high flying bundles of fleecy white. Littlejohn felt better for a good sleep. Cromwell joined him morosely at breakfast. In the course of performing his morning exercises he had biffed his head on one of the beams of the bedroom. He had an angry, concussed expression as he caressed a lump almost the size of a pigeon's egg at the line where his thinning hair receded from his forehead.

"Give me modern places," he grumbled. "Those damn' beams are too low...."

Percival called for them early. He looked smart and efficient and was anxious to start. Cromwell gingerly covered his lump with his bowler.

Outside the town the road became a causeway, about two feet above the surrounding fields. In bad weather they became flooded and formed a large lake with just the road to connect the towns and villages. The dark soil of the Marshland looked hard and cold. Some had been ploughed and stood up in sharp rows; and some still held the relics of the autumn crops, winter greens, stray cabbage stalks, sprouts and kale, straggling and frostbitten. Thin sunlight fell on the wintry fields. Everything stood out in keen distinctness; smallholdings and farms, bare trees and hedges, hens and geese picking and trooping about the yards and gardens of cottages and holdings. Clusters of houses and even the farms hugged the road, as though afraid to venture far across the reclaimed land. Now and then along the route the car passed stretches of water covered with thin skimmings of ice. A few men with guns prowled the fields and the sides of the meres, after the waterfowl. It was still holiday for some; others were working in the fields or driving carts of manure and turnips along the road.

They passed through two hamlets and then the outskirts of Cobbold began to appear. The church had been visible almost the whole way from Thorncastle, gradually growing larger and larger as they approached, its tall tower, with four slim pinnacles, one at each corner, and crooked iron weathercock sharply etched on the skyline. They made straight for the police station, where Pennyquick had been advised by telephone to await them.

The police-house was a double-fronted cottage standing back in its own garden. Beside the wrought-iron gate, a wooden hoarding covered with old posters. Recruiting appeals, parish notices, official orders … "Swine Fever …" "Quarter Sessions …"

and, alien and frivolous: "Whist Drive and Dance … Christmas Eve … Village Hall … Admission 1/–."

P.C. Pennyquick had been in the village almost all his constabulary life. At one time, the fecundity of Mrs. Pennyquick had threatened to dislodge him, for she bore him four daughters in rapid succession and there were only two bedrooms. The problem was solved, however, by the building of a small wing, holding an extra bedroom, with a cell on the ground floor. The latter was used for garden tools, produce, and coal, greatly to the benefit of local malefactors, mainly drunks and poachers, whom the constable took home or cautioned rather than move his implements and fuel. Nobody seemed to bother and crime was not increased by the arrangement.

The bobby greeted his superiors on the doorstep. He had one of the front rooms for an office and had been sitting at the window on the look-out. The visitors entered. The room was really Mrs. Pennyquick's parlour, used only for solemn police or social occasions. When the latter took place the constabulary impedimenta, papers, thick ink, corroded pens, huge charge-book and police notices, were piled on the official table and carted into the cell.

Pennyquick was tall, bulky and bald. There was a cheerful roundness about him; large, round, kindly, slightly protruding blue eyes, round snub nose, strong round chin, all in a solid, round, red face with a heavy grey moustache sprouting from the upper lip.

Percival was a man of tact. Pennyquick was normally overawed by the visits of his Superintendent. It wouldn't do to overdo it. So Percival, saying he had a call to make elsewhere, left the Scotland Yard men with the constable.

"I'm very put-out about all this, sir," said Pennyquick apologetically. "Looks as if I'm not doin' me duty properly. Plucock, our man from Carstonwood, was by way o' being a pal of mine, too.

If I could ’ave found out who killed him, maybe I’d have stopped the second murder. As it is …”

The bobby’s face was a study in gloom and humiliation.

“You can’t take the blame for either crime, Pennyquick,” said Littlejohn. He was sitting in a cold, old-fashioned leather armchair with an antimacassar on the back of it.

“No. But …”

His further doubts were silenced by the entrance of his wife bearing a tray. She was a suitable partner for her husband. Large, round, comfortable and quiet. She cast a proud look at her man. Strange for such a pacific and kindly soul, she loved crime pictures at the Thorncastle cinema, which she visited once a week religiously. And now, here was a real murder—nay, two!—in the village and her Andrew was going to solve them. She was hot from brewing tea and warming pastries, her face shone, and she performed the feat of balancing the tray on one hand

and capturing an errant lock of hair and skilfully imprisoning it in a bun at the back of her head with the other. From the room behind came the chatter of voices. All the girls were at home for the holidays and the house seemed to teem with them.

"Thought, maybe, the gentlemen would like a cup o' tea and a mince tart," she said to her husband, questioningly, waiting for the royal assent.

"Of course, luv," said Pennyquick.

The Law rose, took the tray, passed a huge paw over it like a conjurer about to make it all vanish.

"'Ome made," he said proudly.

"That's very nice of you, Mrs. Pennyquick," said Littlejohn.

The good lady was delighted. She had been wrestling with a moral problem. On the films the detectives always seemed to drink beer at bars.... The advice of two of her girls, one a student at the Academy of Music in London, another a mannequin at Thorncastle, had decided her. They had assured her that detectives, like the rest of folk, would enjoy her mince tarts....

But Mrs. Pennyquick, having resigned the commissariat to her man, was making clucking noises over Cromwell.

"Whatever 'ave you been doin' to yourself?" she asked anxiously, indicating the protuberance on his head. Maybe, "they"—the criminals—had already been "at it", as shown recently in *Soho After Midnight* at the Palace, Thorncastle.

Cromwell blushed.

"Oh, it's nothing.... Bumped my head on a beam in the bedroom at the hotel. They oughtn't to have low beams in bedrooms...."

"No, they oughtn't, sir. You're right...."

And she scuttered out, only to return bearing aloft on the end of her index a large blob of vaseline, with which she gently anointed Cromwell's lump.

"It's all right, Mrs. Pennyquick.... Don't bother ... I'll be all right...."

The good lady, having performed her ministrations, executed a diminutive curtsy and vanished to tell the girls all about it. Sounds of pity rose from the adjacent room.

Pennyquick ate two mince pies. It was like feeding the elephant at the zoo. He placed them solemnly in his mouth, chewed twice, and the load vanished and was assimilated without a further move. Then, he elevated his moustache with his forefinger and drank his tea. As a rule, he used a "moustache" cup, the mouth of which held a miniature porcelain bridge to hold his whiskers, but, on state occasions, this did not appear.

"The whole thing baffles me ..." he said, as if to his conscience.

"We must do what we can together. I gather that there's not a sign or a theory about what or who caused Plucock's death."

"No, sir. I can't think it 'ud be a poacher. Besides, it was broad daylight. I'd seen Plucock the afternoon before. We used to meet on our bikes where our beats crossed, you see. If there'd been anything worrying 'im, he'd 'ave told me. We used to exchange information, of course. A *nice* chap, too. If only ..."

Pennyquick stretched out his huge hands, with fingers like large bananas, and made strangling movements.

"I believe Mr. Salter's been in the village some time."

"Yes, sir. More than a week. Staying with Mrs. Alveston over Christmas. Now that's a bit of a mystery to me, too. I grant you, sir, she was 'is old nurse, but why should a young chap like Mr. Granville, with all his friends and liking what you might call 'high life' and excitement in London, come and tuck 'imself away in Cobbold for the whole of the festive season? I ask you, sir, why?"

"Something was said about Mrs. Alveston's daughter. Was Salter keen on her?"

"Aw … women's talk," said Pennyquick, with the air of experience and profundity of one from whom, from long familiarity with his five women, no feminine secrets were hid. "Women's talk. They can't bear … *can't abide* … a man and a woman to 'ave any sort of relationships together without wantin' to make a match of it. Phyllis isn't Mr. Granville's sort. They were children together, although he was a year or two older than her. Always friendly … but rowmance … rowmance … rubbish! Female talk…."

He passed it off with a contemptuous sweep of his paw.

"If there'd been anything 'cooking' … expression used by my daughters, sir … if there'd been anything cookin', I'd have known it, not alone from 'earing gossip in the village, but from my family. Not much goes on on the female side of the village that my family don't know. And I flatter myself I 'ave their fullest confidenks…."

"I'm sure you have, Pennyquick."

In the room adjoining, one of the girls was singing in a clear, uncultivated soprano. They were always singing in the Pennyquick home.

"That's one of my girls. The youngest. The eldest is in London at the Academy. Pianner. Won a scholarship. All good musicians. Take after their mother. In the Chapel choir for years till she met me. . . ."

Cromwell smiled a wintry smile, which faded before Pennyquick's look of humble pride.

"No, sirs," went on Pennyquick. "In my opinion, Mr. Granville came down here out of the way of somethin' or somebody."

He said it in a hushed and awful voice.

"You mean he was in trouble?"

"Ask me, I'd say yes, sir."

"Did you meet him before he died, Pennyquick?"

"Yes, sir, I did. Just stopped a time or two to say howdedo, and ask about him, like. He didn't look well. Like somebody recoverin' from serious illness. I asks him if he weren't well, or had he been ill. 'No, Pennyquick,' he says. 'Why?' But he gave me a queer look, as if I might be gettin' at somethin' he didn't want me to get near. 'I'm livin' in London, now,' he says. 'Miss the breezes o' Cobbold. Nothin' to put the colour in my cheeks.' But it wasn't his cheeks I was lookin' at, sir. It was his eyes. He looked scared, sir."

"Did Plucock say anything about having met him?"

"Yes. He'd seen him over in Carstonwood. Part of the old Salter estate stretches there. Mr. Granville no doubt went over to see some of the old tenants. Most of them bought their own farms when the estate was sold. A friendly lot, the Salters. Always on good terms with their folk...."

"Plucock wasn't suspicious about anything? I mean, he had no special comment to make on the appearance of Mr. Granville?"

"No, sir. He agreed with me that he didn't look himself."

"Have you questioned Mrs. Alveston about the matter?"

"I 'ad a word with her yesterday, but she wasn't much help."

"I must get along and see her myself. Had Salter much luggage?"

"No, sir. Two cases. I didn't touch them. Mrs. Alveston was took queer, like. Had one of her attacks. Heart's bad. Well … one can't go searching about the house with a sick woman there. And, in my case, it was a bit difficult. In a manner o' speakin', sir, they're all my family the people in this village. They expects help in time o' trouble, if you get what I mean. It would 'ave ill become me to make Mrs. Alveston more distressed than she was. Phyllis was lookin' after 'er, so I let 'em be, for the time being."

"I understand. Is Mrs. Alveston ailing, then?"

"Well … yes and no. Poor in spirit, I'd call 'er, sir. Poor in spirit. Had a lot of trouble, like."

"What kind?"

"She was a maid at the Hall, sir. Then children's nurse. Alveston was one of the hands at the Hall, too. Sort of bailiff and trainer of their horses. They kept 'unters and did a bit o' steeplechasin' in the old days. My missus was at the 'all, too. A parlourmaid. That's where I met 'er."

"And Alveston died?"

"Not exactly. He and his wife didn't hit it. There was some trouble. He left her.... Ehlisted and never come back. Some said he got killed or missin'. Others said he just didn't come back."

"What was the trouble between him and his wife?"

"I can't exactly say, sir. There was rumours, though. They do say Phyllis wasn't his. He wasn't 'er father, if you see what I mean, sir. My missus always swears he wasn't."

"Why?"

"Well ..."

The bobby stroked his chin and coughed.

"Well, sir.... This is all surmise, as you might say. Not a shred of proof, although my wife swears it. She says Phyllis's father was one of the Salters. Says the girl has the Salter features, specially the Salter nose. And come to think of it, sir, she is like 'em. See her beside Mr. Granville and you'd know. But you can't go about sayin' things like that about an honest, respectable woman and as nice a girl as ever walked down this 'ere village. Can you?"

Pennyquick looked ready to burst into tears on behalf of the poor women.

"No, you can't. But it may account for the relationship, kind of blood tie, between Granville and Phyllis, and for the situation. Even if he loved her, he couldn't very well marry his own sister, or half-sister, could he?"

"No, he could not, sir. And that's what it 'ud amount to, come to think of it, because Granville's father was the only male Salter left in these parts."

"Was he a bit of a rip?" asked Cromwell, finding tongue.

"Oh, no. Never heard nothin' o' that sort about 'im. But mistakes do 'appen in the best regulated families, don't they, sir?"

"They do."

"When the thing was breathed to me, sir, I remember thinkin' how thankful I was I heard it so long after my missus was there. If I'd known when I was courtin' 'er, I'd have spent a few sleepless nights, you may be sure."

"How long had the Alvestons been married when this happened?"

"I can't say, sir.... Wait a minute ..."

Pennyquick passed into the next room, whence whispering could be heard. Then the whispering grew into a concert in which several voices joined. Finally laughter and then the chiding voice of the constable.

"Look 'ere, Annie. I won't have you speak that way. While yo're 'ere, speak respectable...."

"I'm sorry, dad. But you are so funny and old-fashioned. There's no need to whisper in corners to mother. We're women of the world, you know."

"Well, you can keep that sort of world outside this house, my girl. I *am* surprised at you, Annie. I am reely...."

The constable returned, very red-faced.

"Sorry, sirs. But really, I don't know what girls are comin' to these days. Our Annie, of all girls. Brought up like a lady by my wife who knew what ladies were. My wife says Phyllis was born six months after the weddin'. Annie must have overheard. 'Jest in time, or born in the vestry,' she says. I never heard the likes of it!"

"So, the Salters may have arranged for Alveston to marry the girl."

"Yes, sir. On the other hand ..."

"Of course. They may have made Alveston marry her even though they didn't hit it."

"Yes. You never know. All the same, my missus says …"

"Just so. Well, I'll call to see the lady and have a talk. Not that we can discuss village gossip openly. Though, I guess, most of the village will know if it's true."

"Be sure, sir. Mrs. Alveston took queer after her husband left her. Never went out in the village again. Sort of ashamed to meet her old friends. I don't even suppose she's a pension for Alveston. She's made her living by bakin' stuff. Confectionery, boiled 'am, when you could get it, meat pies, and so on. A good cook and made stuff a bit better than the local baker, old Davy. Funny thing, that. People could call at her house for the things, but she wouldn't go out. Guess she felt safer at 'ome. Spends her time bakin', doing the house, and readin' the Bible. Very religious.…"

"What does Phyllis do?"

"She's in a gown shop in Thorncastle. Good job, too, by all accounts. Bit of a hand at designin'. Our May, who's a mannequin at another fashionable shop, says she's quite good. The cathedral set like 'er things. Our May would be a mannequin, sir, in spite of me and her mother…."

This came a bit apologetically and Pennyquick's large, sympathetic eyes sought those of Littlejohn for approval.

"Well, Pennyquick, we'll get along and see the lady, if you're ready."

"Yes, sir. She'll be up and about now, I guess. I don't think there's anythin' else to report so far."

The constable thought heavily….

"Oh, yes. One thing. I was speaking to the village baker this mornin'. Mr. Ephraim Davy, sir. He's a big man at the local Wesleyans. The church is right opposite Saint Mark's, the parish church. Well, sir, they've a peculiar custom, there. They hold a watch-night service, and just before twelve, one of the deacons goes outside and when the New Year arrives he lets it in the chapel. You know, sir, like you do at home. Walks in, right up to the pulpit, shakes the parson by the 'and, wishes all the congregation Happy New Year and God Bless, so to speak, and then offers up a little prayer. It was Mr. Ephraim's turn to do it this year…."

"Yes …"

"Just as he got outside, he saw two people talkin' at the church gate of St. Mark's. Now, he says he's sure one must have been Mr. Granville Salter. Ephraim wishes he'd gone over and wished 'im all the best. Might have prevented the crime, sir."

"Who was with Granville?"

"He couldn't rightly make out, sir. It wasn't pitch dark, but you couldn't see anybody's features. However, it was somebody short and stocky, Mr. Davy says…."

"But Mr. Smythe said …" interjected Cromwell.

But Littlejohn interrupted.

“Will you get your helmet then, Pennyquick, and we’ll be getting along.”

“Certainly, sir.”

Mrs. Pennyquick arrived, ostensibly for the tray, but to find out how they’d enjoyed her good things.

“Thanks very much for the tea and the lovely mince tarts, Mrs. Pennyquick. I must beg the recipe for my wife, if you don’t mind....”

The good woman glowed.

“Certainly, Inspector. With pleasure. Come again and welcome, any time....”

Cromwell, too, had been trying to get in his words of thanks and congratulation.

“You jest watch that lump, sir,” said the bobby’s wife to him. “You never know what a knock’ll do. A cousin o’ mine once got a knock on the ’ead, like you, sir, and they never did any good with him after. Backward, it made him. Never did a day’s turn after it....

Cromwell wilted and Littlejohn gave him a wry smile.

"Now, now, mother. None o' yore tales. Frightenin' the sergeant; I won't 'ave it. You know as well as I do, your cousin Jonah *retired* on that knock on the head. It didn't turn him soft at all. It was others as it turned soft."

"Well, Andrew Pennyquick, I never …!"

But the police force was already on the march, followed by the smiling eyes of the constable's four pretty daughters, peeping round the curtains.

FOUR

THE STRAY DOG

NEW YEAR'S DAY is an established holiday in Cobbold and, as it had this year fallen on Sunday, the natives sought recompense in taking a day off on the Monday.

Pennyquick and his two detectives therefore encountered many of the villagers parading the main street, clad in their finery, the girls without swains showing themselves, the youths eyeing them over, appraising them, calling and whistling to them, attracting their attention by showing off before them and halting their haughty progress to talk and dally with them. Families, too, were abroad in their fulness, enjoying the winter sunshine and going to a meal to one another's houses, a ceremony very common on holidays in Cobbold. To-day progress was not so good. Everybody stopped in the course of promenading to discuss the murders. Agitated knots alarmed by the criminal in their midst and seeking consolation in making suggestions and comparing notes on matters of public safety, festooned the pavements.

Moving from group to group, the police encountered Mr. Ephraim Davy, the village baker, a pillar of the Methodist Church. Having warned his customers that there would be no fresh bread during the feast of New Year, Mr. Davy was free to perambulate the village until five o'clock when he was due to commence again his nocturnal kneading and baking for the morrow.

Mr. Davy was a small, fat, puffy man with the etiolated complexion of one who worked by night and slept by day. He had protruding greenish eyes, a snub nose and a fat chin which repeated itself in folds until it vanished below his collar. He was wearing his best blue, double-breasted suit, a billycock hat and a large brown overcoat, and he aired a pair of very light brown boots, which, curling at the toes, gave him the appearance of rocking his way about. With him were his two women; that is, his wife and his sister-in-law.

Mrs. Ephraim's sister had lived with them at the shop since the very day they were married. It was even jocularly remarked in the village that she accompanied the pastrycook and his wife on their honeymoon! In contrast to their pale companion, the two women were almost alike in chubby, shapeless build, dark, Spanish features and eyes, red cheeks, quick tongues. They dressed alike, too, and paid to the man of the trio equal deference and tender care. The bold ones said the baker married them both and did not discriminate between them.

When Mr. Davy met the police he raised his billycock to them, revealing a bushy head of white hair, the colour of his own flour, with a bald, monastic tonsure on the crown. Then he removed the curved briar pipe from between his teeth.

"Good hafternoon, gentlemen," said Mr. Davy, who was, greatly to the admiration of his two women, a bit of a scholar and liked to throw about a few aspirates to show his learning. He had a complete set of a somewhat out-of-date encyclopædia in his parlour and would recite to himself as he kneaded his dough in the night the cryptic inscriptions on the backs of the volumes: A-Cab; Cac-Dub; Duc-Eek; Eel-Faff.... This *Om mani padme hum* gave him great comfort and inspiration in the small hours.

"Good mornin', Mr. Davy and ladies," said Pennyquick, saluting the party deferentially. "This is Detective-Inspector Littlejohn, of Scotland Yard, and Detective-Sergeant Cromwell, of the same. They're here on The Case...."

Every eye of the outdoor villagers was cast in the direction of their distinguished visitors, whispering ceased, and there was a hush of great expectation as though Littlejohn were about to pronounce judgment and single out the culprit right away. Mr. Davy seemed to grow in stature, so great was the honour of being selected for questioning.

The detectives spoke words of greeting and satisfaction at meeting the party.

"The Inspector would like a word with you, Ephraim, about the man you saw at midnight when the crime occurred."

The two Davy women almost fainted at the sudden revelation that their man was to become a part of the investigation, but he cut short their satisfaction.

"Emma, luv," he said. "You and Fanny go 'ome. This isn't for your ears and best said in private. . . ."

Nonplussed, the two women looked ready to burst into tears, controlled their emotions, said good-bye, and sadly turned about and made off.

The onlookers, anticipating an arrest, drew a pace or two nearer.

"It's just a matter of identifying the man you saw talking with Mr. Salter on the night of his death, sir," Littlejohn began.

"Oh, in that case, I'm hafraid I shan't be much 'elp," said the baker, rolling his head from side to side with regret. "It was dark, you see, sir. I just saw the dark figures together and then, it bein' my turn to let the New Year in the chapel, I turned my thoughts to my dooties…."

"But you told the constable, I understand, that one of the figures looked like Mr. Salter…."

"Yes, yes. That's right. Just like him."

"And the other?"

"Well … a bit taller than me, I'd say. Stocky, not so fat…. All I could make out in the bit of light there was."

"Did you see Mr. Smythe, the curate, going in the church, Mr. Davy?"

"So that's who it was! Somebody went in at the wicket gate just as I got outside. Five minutes to midnight or thereabouts. Yes. . . ."

Pennyquick intervened.

"But, sir, it couldn't have been. I've checked the times carefully, being at the church service myself. The clergy came in at about ten to twelve. Mr. Smythe was with them. It couldn't have been 'im."

Mr. Davy looked annoyed. He wasn't used to having his statements challenged either by his women at home or at the chapel. "I didn't say it *was* the curate. 'Ow was I to know? It was dark. Maybe, it was some latecomer to service. Any'ow, he went in by the side gate."

"You're sure of the build of the man you saw with Salter, sir?"

"Sure as I'm 'ere."

"Thank you, sir. I think that's all for the time being. I wonder if Mr. Salter was on his way to service when he met whoever killed him."

Mr. Davy looked pleased and wise.

"I'd say not," he said mysteriously.

"Wasn't he that sort?" asked Littlejohn.

"Oh, he was connected with the church. His family have the living—sort o' patrons, you know. There's a family pew there. But, for another reason, I'd say he wasn't on his way to church."

Pennyquick looked nettled.

"Look 'ere, Ephraim," he said portentously. "If you've got information for us, give it at wunce. No time for beatin' about the bush."

Mr. Davy made consoling, flapping gestures with a soft, podgy hand, in the nails of which still adhered the flour of his last baking.

"All in good time, Andrew. You see, he set out from 'ome with his dog. Now, he wouldn't be likely to take a dog to watch-night service, would he, now?"

Poor Pennyquick looked nonplussed and reddened painfully.

"Dear me!" he muttered apologetically. "I'd quite forgotten the dawg. Well, well...."

He turned to Littlejohn.

"Mr. Salter had his dog with him. A prize Old English bobtail sheep-dog, which he was very proud of and never left behind. Let's see, what was she called?"

"Meg," said Mr. Davy, closing his eyes and opening them again with great profundity.

"Meg; that's it. I'm sorry, Inspector. I quite forgot. Where's the dog now, Ephraim?"

"Roving about. Won't let anybody near 'er. The Alvestons tell me she went out with Mr. Granville on New Year's Eve and didn't come 'ome. Must know wot's 'appened. Hinstinct."

"Funny she didn't come with 'im in the church, Ephraim...."

"Either she was druv off by whoever did it, or else scared away by what had 'appened. Anyhow, people

’ve seen ’er hanging round the edge o’ the village but she wouldn’t come near.”

“Well, shall we be getting along to the Alvestons’ then, Pennyquick?” interposed Littlejohn. He filled his pipe, lit it and puffed out a cloud of smoke. The party broke up and Mr. Ephraim Davy went off to tell his brother, Silas, who was a farmer, all about it.

The police went on their way, their breath rising in vapour. There was a drop on the end of Cromwell’s beaky nose. He wiped it away and stamped his feet as he walked.

The Alvestons lived in a small double-fronted house at the end of the village. At one time it had belonged to the Salter family and had been the home of estate workmen. Now Mrs. Alveston owned it. Pennyquick knocked on the door. There was a little delay and the radio, which they could hear playing faintly, was suddenly cut off. Pennyquick knocked again and Phyllis Alveston opened the door. Fear came into her eyes when she saw Pennyquick and his companions.

"Good afternoon, Miss Phyllis...."

"Good afternoon, Mr. Pennyquick. I'm afraid mother can't see anyone, yet. She's still very upset."

Phyllis was tall, dark and well-built. There was an air of good breeding about her which might have confirmed the local view that she was a Salter, born on the wrong side of the blanket. Her eyes were fine, her arched nose and well-cut lips refined, and she held her head with a trace of arrogance.

"Can we come in for a minute? These two gentlemen are from Scotland Yard and would like a word with you about Mr. Granville, if you don't mind."

Pennyquick was deferential in his manner, as though he were, in very fact, speaking to one of the ladies of the manor. It was evident that the Alvestons, or at least, Phyllis, was regarded as above the average.

"Very well, Mr. Pennyquick. But I don't want mother bothering. She's taken all this business very badly...."

They followed the girl indoors. There was a faint, pleasant smell of baking about the place. The retained aroma of hundreds of cakes and good things cooked there in the past. They followed Phyllis down the dark, narrow passage to the first door on the right. She ushered them into the parlour which seemed little used. Then, from above, came the bumping of a stick on the floor, the signal that whoever was upstairs was wanting attention and, maybe, wanting information.

"Excuse me...."

Phyllis left briskly and they could hear her running up the stairs which led from the passage. She was a bright girl, well-dressed and sophisticated. She was quite capable of handling the situation.

The parlour was coldly furnished in an out-of-date leather-upholstered suite and chairs. There was a heavy sideboard, too, holding hideous old-fashioned ornaments. Marble clock on the mantel-piece. There was one finger missing and the clock was stopped. On each side of it, more hideous ornaments. A bamboo plant-stand under the window with an anæmic plant in an ugly pot on it. Over the fireplace a framed portrait of a handsome bullet-headed man, with a dark moustache, impudent eyes and an unintelligent face. His hair was thin, with a calf-lick across his forehead.

"That's Alveston," said Pennyquick in a whisper as though imparting a vital secret.

The room smelled stale and damp. There was no fire in the grate, which held, instead, a large green fan, fully spread to cover the blackness of the back of the fireplace.

It looked as if Mrs. Alveston was mistress in her own home, at least; otherwise a modern type of girl like Phyllis would soon have swept away the ugly contents of the sitting-room and modernized it.

"My mother is in bed, but will see you. . . ." Phyllis returned and said it in a surprised tone.

"Very well, Miss Alveston," said Littlejohn. "We could call again when she's more in the mind to talk, if she wishes. . . ."

"She insists. . . ."

They climbed the narrow stairs. Two bedrooms gave on to the landing and there seemed to be a bathroom at the back.

They entered the larger of the two bedrooms. Mrs. Alveston was sitting-up in bed. She wore a knitted pink bed-jacket, and her eyes looked red as though she had recently done some weeping.

The room smelled smoky. There was a fire in the grate, burning fitfully and every now and then puffs of smoke belched out and, recoiling, went back up the chimney, leaving behind flecks of soot which settled about the place.

"I'm sorry to bring you up here, but I must talk with you seeing you have called. You must excuse the smoky room. The fire always does this when the wind's in this direction. I'll have to have the chimney seen to...."

Mrs. Alveston had a thin, puffy face and the large appealing eyes of the persecuted. If life does not unduly persecute them, they persecute themselves.

The furniture of the room was heavy and outmoded. Large wardrobe, chest of drawers and marble-topped washstand in mahogany. Patterned wallpaper repeating a rose-in-basket design linked by ribbons *ad nauseam*. There was a patchwork quilt on the bed under a pink eiderdown, and by the bedside a table filled with medicine bottles, beside a large Bible, devotional tracts and a pair of spectacles. Mrs. Alveston spent a lot of time in bed. Her happy days at the Salters' home before misfortune overtook her, were ever in her mind and, comparing them with the unhappiness which had befallen her in later life, filled her with ever-present sorrow and a sense of having been wronged. Genuine grief for her husband's desertion had stricken her mentally, and, physically, her sufferings had brought upon her an obscure feminine complaint which walking aggravated. This kept her indoors and, with the exception of the visits of customers for her cakes and pies, she was a voluntary recluse. Quite impossible, too, for her daughter to run the household or even assert herself now and then. Any show of will on Phyllis's part brought upon Mrs. Alveston one of her "attacks", immobilized her in bed, turned her to her devotions with renewed fervour and multiplied her lamentations and weeping for her miserable state.

Pennyquick introduced Littlejohn and Cromwell.

"I'm sorry to intrude on you, Mrs. Alveston," said the Inspector. "I wanted a word with you about Mr. Granville, who, I understand, was staying with you.... It can wait, though, if you don't ..."

Mrs. Alveston wept softly and her nervous state caused a tremor of her head and neck, like the palsy.

"I might as well get it over, sir," she said. "No use putting off the evil day. There'll be more troubles tomorrow and it's no use saving to-day's till then, is it?"

"No.... Well, shall we get this over quickly?"

Phyllis stood in the doorway first, then, when her mother began to weep, hastened to give her a clean handkerchief and smooth her forehead.

"Don't start crying again, mother, please. It'll only upset you more. Shall I get you a cup of tea, dear?"

"No, not now. It wouldn't do me any good till I'm quiet again. Give the gentlemen some chairs. Don't keep them standing about. It's bad manners, Phyllis, and you haven't been brought up that way."

The girl drew two cane-bottomed bedroom chairs from corners and, hurrying out, brought in another of the same kind from her own room.

"You needn't have seen the men, you know, mother. I could have told them all they want to know...."

"Well! … I like that! I'm quite capable of looking after my own affairs, madam."

Mrs. Alveston alternated between petulance with her daughter and self-pity. She drew her new bed-jacket around her and indicated that she was ready by drying her eyes and blowing her nose.

Littlejohn drew his chair up to the bedside.

"First, did Mr. Salter always come here for Christmas, madam?"

"No, not always. He came several times a year, though, to see his old nurse. I brought him up, sir, and he never forgot his old nurse."

"What brought him here this Christmas, then? Have you any idea?"

"He'd not been well and nobody could look after him like me, although I say it myself. Could they, Phyllis?"

"No, mother."

"Did he seem worried about anything—besides being run-down by his recent illness?"

"No, not that I'd say...."

"Why, mother ..."

Phyllis interrupted in surprise.

"Be quiet, madam," cried her mother. "This is my business and I'll thank you not to interfere. You know Mr. Granville had no worries here. He was perfectly happy."

Littlejohn let it go.

"Do you think he had any enemies who might have wished him ill, Mrs. Alveston?"

"No. Why should he? Mr. Granville couldn't have had an enemy in the world. He was a fine young gentleman...."

"I gather the family sold the Hall some time ago and Mr. Granville went to live in London. What did he do for a living there, do you know?"

"Yes, the Hall was sold as a convalescent home. A shame, I call it, after being theirs all these hundreds of years. Mr. Granville earned his living in London, he said, by buying and selling antiques...."

“He got in contact with several dealers when the things at the Hall were sold, and as he was always interested in stuff like that, they persuaded him to enter the trade, I think,” added Phyllis, who was sitting now on the foot of the bed.

“I was coming to that,” said Mrs. Alveston, petulantly. She wanted to hold all the interest and could scarcely bear her daughter to speak.

“I understand that Mr. Granville was the last of the family.”

“He has a cousin somewhere, but seems to have lost track of him. Then there’s his aunt, Miss Margaret. Mr. Granville’s father had a scrapegrace brother....”

“Scapegrace, mother....”

“That’s what I said, isn’t it? This brother ran away when young and went abroad with some actress or other ... married, she was. And he died away. They had a son, I believe. Mr. Granville said he met him once or twice in London, but he never came near here."

"You didn't know the cousin, then?"

"No. I said he never came near here."

"I see. And now about New Year's Eve. Was Mr. Granville going to meet anybody when he left here for the last time?"

"No, not that I knew of. He went out about half-past nine, saying he'd like to walk round and see the village and then bring in the New Year for us.... A fine New Year it's been so far...."

Whereat Mrs. Alveston began to weep again. She soon settled, however. She seemed, at bottom, to be enjoying herself and her misery.

"And he took his dog with him?"

"Yes. And that reminds me. Phyllis, has Meg come home yet? I can't understand it at all. Such a nice, obedient dog, who never went away from home. He could leave her with me and go anywhere and she as good as gold. And now, when she might be a comfort to me and a companion in sorrow, away she goes and isn't seen again. Have you heard where she is, Phyllis ...?"

"Yes, mother. She's been seen sneaking about by people, but nobody could get near her. She just turned tail and off."

"Somethin' must have 'appened to scare her good and proper," said Pennyquick judicially.

"All the same, why couldn't she 'ave come here? We'd 'ave given her a good home."

Mrs. Alveston had taken umbrage at the dog's ingratitude.

Littlejohn had formed a pretty good opinion of Mrs. Alveston. A hypochondriac, full of self-pity, yet close with her own affairs. If any family trouble caused the murder, he wasn't going to get very far with her. She was loyal and would protect the Salters with all she'd got. Any help the police wanted would have to come from Phyllis and it was up to him to get her on their side as quickly as possible.

"Well … we'll not disturb your rest any longer, Mrs. Alveston. I'll call again when you feel better and we'll have another chat."

"I don't enjoy very good health, sir. And this business had got me down. Seems as if misfortunes never cease coming my way. I don't know what I've done to deserve them. Still, it says in the Good Book, 'Whom He loveth, He chasteneth.' There's comfort in that…."

She groped for her glasses and one of the devotional books on the bedside table, and with that the party left her.

"I'd like to see you again, very soon, Miss Alveston. I don't like upsetting your mother and I guess you know as much about things as she does."

"Yes, I think I do."

Phyllis smiled a knowing smile.

"Very well, then. You work in Thorncastle, I believe."

"Yes…."

"Do you get out for coffee in the mornings?"

"I could do...."

"Well, suppose you join me at my hotel, 'The Mitre', for coffee to-morrow. Is it far from your place?"

"No. A few doors away. Shall we say ten-thirty?"

"Yes, that's all right."

Cromwell had turned to look through the window to hide his smiles. A nice girl, Phyllis. He wouldn't have minded changing places with Littlejohn for a bit....

"Here," said Cromwell suddenly. "There's that dog. Look!"

They all crowded round the window.

Across the way, dejected and bedraggled, stood Meg, Granville Salter's bobtail sheep-dog. Her coat muddy and hanging in shaggy tails, instead of fluffy and clean as of old. The white of her face was smoky black and her rump, where other dogs have tails, was almost on the ground with misery. She looked with anxious liquid eyes across at the house. The hair which usually covers the eyes of the breed was held back by a device of Mr. Granville's, a pipe cleaner twisted like a woman's curling-pin.

"Poor Meg," said Phyllis, and flew to the door to bring her in. But the dog, taking one despairing look, fled again and was lost in the rough cover and bushes of the common across the way.

Littlejohn, who was fond of dogs, and who had only recently lost his own, felt his heart turn over, but said nothing.

The police prepared to leave and gathered their hats and coats and Pennyquick assumed his helmet which made him look more of a policeman again.

"And by the way, Inspector," said Phyllis as they parted at the door. "Granville was worried about something. Mother didn't know, but he was...."

"So I guessed from your interruption," said Littlejohn. "We'll talk about it to-morrow. So, for the present, good-bye...."

"Good-bye, Inspector."

"You two go on and find Percival. I've something I want to attend to," Littlejohn said. "I'll join you in a little while."

Cromwell eyed his chief quizzically. Maybe he'd fallen for Phyllis! Something unusual with Littlejohn.... He stifled his own questions and led Pennyquick away puzzled.

Littlejohn crossed the road and took to the common. Brushing aside the rough branches and treading down the bracken, he made his way to the thick part. Then he whistled. He walked another twenty yards or so and whistled again. In a clearing stood the dog. She looked at him warily. Gently he approached her, stretched out a hand to her and talked to her comfortably. She stood stock still, graceful in every line in spite of her bedraggled state.

"Sit," he called.

Meg looked at him and then sat down.

"Stay," he shouted.

And she stayed there, trembling but obedient.

As he neared the dog, she did not move, but in fear, slowly bared her teeth. Then she made as if to rise.

"Stay," he shouted sternly. And she did.

He reached her, knelt and gently touched her head, then her soft ears, then her muzzle. She whined and turned upon him her sad, stricken eyes.

Then and there, having lost one master, Meg found another for the rest of her life.

FIVE

THE HEADLESS JESUIT

AT first the manager of "The Mitre" made it plain to Cromwell that they didn't serve coffee in the middle of the morning. There were cafés in the town for the purpose. Why not try one of them? Cromwell, previously fortified by a perusal of the Innkeepers' Act from one of the volumes in the portable library which he always lugged around in his suitcase, gently, but incorrectly, began to quote chapter and verse. Then, rather more loudly, he spoke of writing to the R.A.C. and having the manager's many stars removed from the handbook....

When Phyllis Alveston met Littlejohn in the lounge, an obsequious waiter, attended by an acolyte in a white jacket, served coffee from the hotel's best silver service....

Phyllis was wearing a very becoming loose red coat with a Robin Hood hat to match. The clear, sharp weather had flushed her cheeks and made her comely. The members of a film company, who had, on the previous evening, invaded the hotel, halted their to-ing and fro-ing, part of their campaign of publicity and exhibitionism, and looked hard and admiringly at her. The dashing star, Ronald Rainod, straightened his tie and deliberately crossed her path, flashing her one of his sure-fire smiles as he passed. Phyllis didn't even see him, but hurried to join a smart, middle-aged man, sitting near the window and reading the morning paper.

Rainod pursed his lips in the sibilant whistle of modern wolves on the hunt.

"The old 'uns get all the luck," he drawled. "Who the hell's he?"

"That's Detective-Inspector Littlejohn, of Scotland Yard."

Cromwell threw it at him tersely and vanished up the huge carved staircase. The rest of the company held their sides, for Rainod was, in his new film, featuring as a Scotland Yard detective himself....

"... I won't keep you long, Miss Alveston," Littlejohn was saying. The flunkeys had departed deferentially leaving them with what looked like troubled tea, but which tasted faintly of toasted acorns. "But there are one or two things about which I didn't want to trouble your mother...."

The girl's face showed little animation. Superficially, she looked a picture, but deep down something was wrong. Her eyes bore a fixed, stunned look and she held her lips in a frozen artificial smile.

"Are you in trouble yourself?"

"Well, Inspector, a thing like this ... I mean, a murder in the village and of one ... one to whom we were very attached.... I hardly feel like jumping for joy."

"Ah, yes.... Granville Salter. You've known each other for a long time?"

"Yes.... As long as I can remember. We even played together sometimes at the Hall when we were kids. And he came down to all the gatherings in the village. And then, after the Hall closed, he stayed at our place when he came back to Cobbold...."

"This recent visit. Was it true he came for a holiday after an illness? I heard that was the case...."

"I ... really ... He wasn't very well.... And he liked the old place at Christmas time. It held happy memories for him...."

Phyllis played with her gloves and stirred her coffee.

"Do you take sugar? I didn't put any in...."

"Oh ... I ..."

"Look, Miss Alveston ... I wish you'd be quite candid with me. There's some mystery surrounding the visit of Mr. Salter to Cobbold. Some say this and some say that.… If you know what it is all about, I'd be grateful if you'd tell me. It will save a lot of trouble for us and, whatever you withhold, we shall find out eventually. So …"

The waiter was back again.

"Coffee all right, sir?"

"It will do, thanks.…"

The man withdrew with a puzzled frown on his face. Outside the room he started to mutter rebelliously.

"Granville came to see mother about something. That was the main reason."

"What was it?"

She had laid aside her gloves and was now fussing with her handkerchief. She caught Littlejohn's eye and smiled wanly.

"He wanted to marry me.…"

Just like that, in a dull voice. No tears. The girl was simply stunned with grief.

"I'm so sorry, Miss Alveston. I'd no idea. And he'd called for your mother's consent. Was she surprised and willing?"

"Neither. You see, he'd asked her several times before. We've been in love for a long time. Granville had a little money of his own and now he'd got a job. But the thing seemed to upset mother terribly. Every time it was mentioned, she had one of her attacks."

"What sort of attacks?"

"Nervous attacks. She's had them for years. She's had a lot of trouble, you see, and it has worn her out. She starts to tremble and cry out and sort of passes into a faint, but with her eyes open. . . ."

It sounded like hysterics to Littlejohn!

Phyllis seemed to read the Inspector's thoughts.

"The doctor said it was mainly hysterical; but that wasn't fair. You can help yourself in hysterics, but mother seemed past that. The past has not been kind to her."

"But why should a good fellow wanting to marry her daughter upset her so much? You'd have thought she would be glad to see you settled and happy...."

"Yes, wouldn't you? But she wouldn't hear of it. She wouldn't be persuaded to give her consent."

"Why?"

"Said I mustn't marry above my station. You see, in her young days she'd been a servant at the Hall and so had my father. The Salters were in another world and the very thought of one of her class marrying the family would have been as thinkable in those days as reaching for the moon. She just wouldn't admit that times have changed. And another thing. She said we wouldn't be happy once the first flush had worn off. She said the Salters were always a fickle lot, who didn't treat their women very well. I had a row with her about it. There was nothing of the kind about Granville, or his father, for that matter. It was just an excuse. She didn't want me to leave her, that was it. I don't blame her, really. She is very helpless and has little pleasure in life, or ever had, for that matter. All the same … I'd my life to live."

"Of course."

Outside, the film director was marshalling his forces. They'd been waiting for months for these shots. The cathedral with a background of clear sky and high clouds, in a frame of old, leafless trees. The great man was posting his cameras, moving them here and there. He was in a bad temper. He wanted to shift the church two yards to the right to make a wizard shot and couldn't. As a rule, he got his own way, thanks to a pocketful of cash, but here was something he couldn't pay for.… "Why does it always have to happen to me, blast it?" Mr. Rainod was in a bad mood, as well. He wouldn't do as he was told. There had to be children playing, too, as the criminal went to ground in the crypt. Just to set guilt against a background of innocence. The director passed a fistful of notes to a flunkey. "Round up some kids. Give 'em a quid apiece, and tell the little devils to bring their skippin' ropes and balls.... Go on.... Get cracking...."

"And what did Mr. Salter say to all this?" Littlejohn was asking. He pushed the coffee apparatus away.

"He was very mad about it. If he pressed it, mother just started to cry. He wanted me to marry him and run away, but I just couldn't. How could I leave her as she was?"

"Very difficult. And was that all? Just an impasse?"

"Yes. At first, just after the war and when he was demobbed, he said ..."

"He served in the Forces ...? Excuse the interruption; it's important."

"Yes.... In Burma...."

"Just Burma.... Not in Germany at all?"

"No. Why?"

"I just wanted to be precise. Please go on."

"When he came home, his father had died and there wasn't enough left to keep up the Hall. We'd written to each other all the time and then he suggested our getting married and living in the village at the small dower-house."

"And your mother objected?"

"I'll say she did. She seemed terrified."

"And then the battle began. All the trouble and argument. . . ."

"Yes. Then, mother had a long talk with Granville without me. He seemed to cool off after that. Mother must have been so pathetic that it moved him. He went off to live in London."

"Did you see him much after that?"

"No. Once, I think. He came up on business and called."

"Had he changed much?"

"Yes. He looked awful. Pale and thin. And with me, he was very strange. As though he still loved me, yet something held him back."

Littlejohn remembered what Mrs. Pennyquick had said. No wonder Salter's attitude had been changed and mysterious if Mrs. Alveston had told him he was in love with his half-sister! Apparently Phyllis didn't know about it, or, if she did, she wasn't admitting anything. One couldn't very well ask her.

"What made him change his mind this time? He came and stayed with you again for some days, didn't he?"

"Yes. A few days before he arrived, Granville wrote to me. He seemed very excited. He wanted to start where we'd left off. There'd been no leaving off for me. I could never love anyone else...."

You could have heard a pin drop. She just sat silent. No emotion; simply a sort of stunned resignation, as though, all the time she'd been expecting things to turn out badly. Outside, you could see the film unit at work. The sound and cameras were "on", the murderer was sneaking to the church, followed by the whole circus on wheels, and the director was pantomiming for the children to play harder. They skipped and bounced their balls frenziedly, thinking of the pound notes to come.

"What do you think Mr. Salter was excited about?"

"I don't know. But he said in his letter he would like to come to us for Christmas and he thought that, at last, he'd be able to make mother see reason."

"And did he?"

"As far as I could see, he didn't. He said he thought things were going to be all right, but by the time he was … he died … he hadn't spoken to mother. He said he'd something to do before he tackled her again."

"You've no idea what it was?"

"No. But he said he was going to be sure it wouldn't upset her again before he spoke."

"H'm. And your mother has never taken you fully into her confidence about her objections?"

"I don't understand you. What more could she have to tell me?"

"Nothing, maybe. I just wondered, Miss Alveston."

Time was passing. In the dining-room opposite you could see the waiters laying the tables for lunch. The chef in his white cap and uniform was having an argument with the manager and doing most of the talking. Outside, the director was re-taking the whole business and shoppers were looking in the windows and entering the very select establishments of the cathedral close.

"I hope I'm not keeping you, Miss Alveston."

"It's all right. I asked off for an hour."

"I'm very grateful to you for your help. And now rather a delicate question. Can you tell me anything about your father?"

"Not a thing. I hate him. I can't see why mother can bear to speak of him or keep his photograph up in the house. She won't hear of taking it down. You'd think he'd died loving her dearly, instead of leaving her in the lurch."

"Have you ever seen him?"

"Not to remember. He married mother during the first war, in nineteen-seventeen, and I was born soon after...."

It was difficult to think of Phyllis as over thirty. She looked young and fresh, in spite of her troubles. Yet, she had the poise and sophistication of one of that age. And all the time, she'd waited for Granville Salter and just when happiness seemed within their reach, someone had ...

"I was born soon after. Father, if such I can call him, father served with the army in occupied Germany and came home on leave until he was demobbed. Then he disappeared. He just left mother in the lurch."

"And what did she do?"

"She had a little money.... I don't know how much or where it came from. She's very close on her private affairs. She started baking cakes and bread and the like. Built up a nice little business. But she seemed stunned and afraid by what had happened. She just wouldn't go out and about any more."

"And she's more or less stayed indoors ever since?"

"Yes.... Except when she goes to see her sister at Barewood-le-Fen...."

"Where's that?"

"About three miles the other side of Thorncastle from Cobbold. She comes by train to Thorncastle and goes on by bus."

"But why this sudden trip?"

"Well, you see, my aunt has been totally bedridden for years. They were very much attached and she's mother's only living relative. She goes twice a year to see her."

"Alone?"

"Yes. She insists. I bring her to Thorncastle on my way to work and put her on the Bareham bus. Then, she sits and waits for me to pick her up in the afternoon when she returns and she goes home with me."

"And she stands the trip after being indoors all the rest of the year?"

"Yes. Funny, isn't it?"

"It is. Returning to your father. Did Mr. Salter ever mention him?"

"Casually. Why?"

"How casually?"

"Just casually, that's all."

"I mean, he never suggested tracing him or trying to get him to help with your getting married."

"Why should he? He may, of course, have spoken to mother about him when I wasn't there. I don't think he ever met father, although he was once a bailiff or something on their estate."

"Did your mother ever try to trace him?"

"No. She always said she believed in leaving well alone."

"A strange remark."

"She mustn't have been happy with him. They had to get married, you know, because of me. You may as well know it."

Littlejohn didn't answer. He was watching the film scene. Just as the villain entered the church for the retake, someone came out. A familiar clerical figure. It materialized into Smythe, the curate from Cobbold.

"There's Smythe from Cobbold coming from the cathedral."

Phyllis followed Littlejohn's direction without much enthusiasm.

"He's often around. Sometimes calls at the shop, to ask me out for lunch. I used to go now and then, but it got too frequent."

"He's keen on you?"

"Yes. But I'm not that way. Besides, he's a bit of a lady-fancier, I hear. Moves in a rather swift social set in Thorncastle."

Littlejohn remembered the dancing incident of the first night at "The Mitre."

Smythe drifted from view, vacantly looking in the direction of the shop in the close where Phyllis worked.

"Will you do something for me, Miss Alveston?"

"I'll try. What is it?"

"Borrow a photograph of your father, if you have one about."

"How strange. What's that for?"

"Just in case we wish to trace him."

"Surely, he doesn't come into this. You don't think he …?"

"No. But we must explore every angle."

"Very well. He had a photograph taken in khaki. Mother had two copies. I'll get one. It's a group. Four pals of them, I guess—an awful-looking lot. But mother won't part with it. I'll get one of them."

"Thank you. Do you know what regiment he was in?"

"No. I'm not interested. As far as I'm concerned he never existed."

"I see. Your hour's up, I'm afraid. I mustn't keep you any longer. By the way, did Mr. Salter go much to the Hall after it was sold?"

"Yes. He loved it. So did I. We were very happy there in the good days. Granville used to say that one day he hoped to make enough money to buy it back and then we'd be married and start the family there all over again. Now ..."

"I'm very sorry to keep raking up this unhappiness, Miss Alveston. But you understand."

"Of course. If I don't remember he's dead, I like talking about these things. Granville was always around the Hall whenever he returned to Cobbold. You see, it's been empty for a while. It was a sort of home run by a doctor for a time and wasn't a success. The military took it over for a bit. Made an awful mess of it, too. It's been empty since, though I believe the County Council are thinking of buying it for an asylum or something. Poor Granville.... He used to talk of finding the Salter treasure and starting all afresh. But that was just our fun."

"The Salter treasure ...?"

"Yes. There's an old part of the Hall dating to Stuart times. They say the Salters fought for the King and when the Parliamentary troops were reported nearing Cobbold, Sir Thomas Salter, the then lord of the manor, put all his wealth, said to be very great, in a chest and hid it in a secret place. He was killed, shortly after, at Naseby. His wife, who shared his secret, went mad at the news. The only other who knew where the gold was, was a Jesuit, the family chaplain. Somebody told Cromwell's troopers about the treasure and they came and tortured the priest to tell them where it was. He wouldn't, so they beheaded him in rage and flung his body in the river. The place has been haunted ever since by a headless Jesuit...."

"You seem interested in all these things, Miss Alveston."

"I've a natural interest in them somehow. You see, Granville talked so much of the family and its history. After all, if his dreams had come true, I'd have been lady of the manor myself one day...."

She laughed, a short, overwrought laugh, and looked out of the window without seeing anything. Littlejohn noticed, for the first time, that tears were flowing.

"All right, Miss Alveston, have a good cry. It'll do you a lot of good."

"I can't. It's all pent up inside me like a heavy stone in my heart."

She dried her eyes and tried to change the subject.

"I'm not telling you tall tales. The headless Jesuit has been seen often. Ask anybody in the village. They won't go near after dark. Granville wasn't scared, however. He said the priest was a faithful family friend."

"I wonder how the Jesuit went on when the army were in occupation."

"I wouldn't know. But I've heard of his being seen lately. They always say he's around when one of the family's going to die. He must have known about Granville. . . ."

"I must have a look around the Hall. I'm interested in such places. Especially when they're haunted. . . ."

"Yes. You should go, Inspector. There's a man lives in one of the lodges, looking after the place in his way. Fred Brown, he's called. He'll let you look round. Maybe you'll find the treasure. Or, at least, one of the priest-holes."

"So, they have priest-holes, too?"

"They say so. I never saw any. But the family was Catholic until Victorian times and always had a chaplain or other hidden about the place in days when Mass was forbidden."

"How interesting. Do you know the time? It's nearly twelve. I don't want you to get the sack, you know."

"No. I must be off at once."

"Thanks for all you've told me. Most interesting about the family and the Hall."

"And you will find out who did this, won't you, Inspector? They are saying already that Granville was mixed up in some racket and fell out with his associates. I want his name clearing, if nothing else."

"I'll do my best. Good-bye, for the present, then."

"Good-bye for the present. And thank you for the coffee."

"Coffee, did you say?"

She laughed for the first time.

Littlejohn watched her out of sight through the window. As she neared the shop, Smythe emerged from somewhere and joined her. He looked delighted.

Littlejohn ordered a bottle of beer and sat thinking over the information he'd just gathered. But he didn't have long to himself. He was disturbed by the arrival of Cromwell, who had, it appeared, been giving the film director a tip or two on how they shadowed a suspect.

"He seemed grateful, too. Put me in the film, he did, by way of reward, so to speak. I walked round the cathedral as a sightseer. He wanted a few, he said. Gave me a pound for doing it...."

"Well, well. We are coming on. Film-star now. You'll be leaving the Force, I guess, soon."

"Not ruddy likely. But I must take the wife and family to see the film when it comes our way. I won't tell 'em I'm in it. That'll surprise 'em.... Any luck with Miss Alveston?"

"Yes. Quite a bit about the Salter family and her own. I want you to try and find out where the father is. He ran away soon after she was born. She'll get us a picture of him and we'll try to trace him through his regiment and pals, if we can find out the regiment."

"Tall order."

"Chicken-feed for a detective like you. Adviser to film companies...."

Cromwell blushed.

"I think I'll just walk round the close for a breath of air before lunch. See you soon, Cromwell."

And with that, Littlejohn left his colleague buying himself a beer from the proceeds of his technical advice.

SIX

INQUEST

MR. LANCELOT QUALTROUGH, County Coroner, sat in his private room in the Thorncastle courthouse, waiting for something to turn up. He always came half an hour before the scheduled time for a quiet attack on the crossword puzzle in the *Daily Trumpet*. If between nine-thirty and ten o'clock when the business of the day began, Mr. Qualtrough had not polished off the mystery, he was in bad form for the rest of the morning.

The Coroner was a distinguished antiquary and a member of many learned societies. He had an obsession for puzzles of any kind, be they coins dug up, ruins laid bare, relics found in strange places, or rebuses, enigmas, anagrams, unsolved crimes, or bones discovered in spots where you wouldn't expect to come across them. Every Sunday morning at eight, the *Observer* and the *Sunday Times* were placed on Mr. Qualtrough's bedside table. If, by breakfast time at ten o'clock, he hadn't solved both crosswords, Lancelot fasted for the rest of the day.

When Percival knocked on the Coroner's door, Mr. Qualtrough was just dealing with the last clue.

"Black queen's ablutions lead to royal seduction."

"Bathsheba ..." shouted the Coroner in contempt. "Too easy!"

"Beg pardon, sir," said the surprised Percival.

"Good morning, Percival. I hope I find you well."

"Good morning, Mr. Qualtrough...."

Mr. Qualtrough raised a protesting hand.

"It is pronounced Qualtrock, not Qualtrow, and, in the dying Celtic language of its origin, means Foreigner or Stranger. Most appropriate seeing that I've lived here all my life...."

And the Coroner burst into a wild cackle at his own wit. He was a small, bald, bird-like man with a large head, which, one would have thought, he had vigorously polished with furniture cream after shaving and cleaning his teeth. Percival didn't, as a rule, have much to do with Mr. Qualtrough. He usually left it to his subordinates. But this was a case of murder. So …

"I just came for a word on procedure before we begin, sir, if you don't mind."

"Of course."

"We'll only require identification, medical evidence, and then adjournment for further investigation, if you please."

"Of course, of course. Why not?"

It was difficult to tell Mr. Qualtrough outright. But the truth was that at the inquest on poor P.C. Plucock, the Coroner, excited when confronted by a new and novel mystery, began in his court to try and unravel it. It had taken the police all their time to stop him.

"Shall we go in, then. Where's Whatmough?"

A lugubrious figure, as tall and thin as his master was short and plump, materialized from somewhere like the genie of the ring.

"Here, sir," fluted Whatmough, the Coroner's factotum, in a high voice which seemed to come through a reed as it left his throat.

Littlejohn was sitting in the well of the court with Pennyquick, who was one of the star witnesses.

"A very clever man in his way is Mr. Qualtrough—insists on being called Qualtrock, don't know why. As I was sayin', sir, he's very clever. Knows all the ancient 'istory of the city and of the county for miles round here. Come Saturday afternoons, you'll find him leadin'' a crowd of professors and the like, off to dig up some ruin or look over some ancient monument. He's written books, too. Very clever ones for those as likes old coins, buildin's, and such like.

There's an old boat in the city museum that he dug up. Made from a tree trunk, hollered out. Found it near Cobbold where the Marsh used to be before they drained it. Said to be 'undreds of years old...."

"Indeed!"

"Yes, sir. I'm not very interested. But I must say his book on Salter Hall's worth readin'. Tells the whole history of the place."

"Now that's worth knowing, Pennyquick. Maybe Mr. Qualtrough will be able to help us there."

Pennyquick didn't quite know how the Coroner could help, but the arrival of that gentleman in his pulpitlike perch prevented further conversation.

Mr. Fernihough—pronounced Fernihuff this time—the Salter family lawyer and Phyllis Alveston identified the body of the deceased in the absence of any relatives. Mr. Fernihough called the Coroner Mr. Qualtruff and was corrected, and Mr. Qualtrough then gave the lawyer "Fernihock" and was himself put right. Whereat they both laughed like a pair of schoolboys, for it was their little joke. The Mephistophelian Coroner's clerk looked on with bilious disapproval.

P.C. Pennyquick then gave evidence of how the tragedy occurred. As many as could safely postpone their work in Cobbold had left the village and now were sitting packed together in the courtroom. The bulk of them had been at the fatal watchnight service and punctuated the constable's recital by grunts of approval or concurrence, or groans of sympathy and dismay. On the seat nearest the door sat Mr. Ephraim Davy, his loaves for the day already baked and sold. Now and then the baker left the room for a smoke. He was an inveterate pipe-smoker and couldn't go for long without a puff or two. He would parade up and down the pavement outside smoking like a chimney, then, his appetite appeased and his pipe rendered harmless by the insertion of a cork in the bowl, he would return for another dose of horror.

"… At first, I thought he was drunk, sir. Then, Mr. Flunder and me, we picked 'im up and found that …"

Mr. Flunder, who had fallen asleep, jerked awake at the sound of his name and the groan which arose from the audience. He had been dreaming he was at school again.

"Adsum!" he shouted as he opened his eyes, thinking it was roll-call.

A woman fainted and was carried out.

"Let me see the weapon," said Mr. Qualtrough.

Percival handed it up to the pulpit with a sigh.

The Coroner handled the gruesome knife with relish. He tested the blade for sharpness and the whole for balance. Then, he took out a lens and read out the name.

"Willh.… that will be short for Wilhelm … Wilh. Gruber … I see. A German knife.… Brown or Blackshirt presumably. Quite a modern affair.…"

He sounded disappointed; maybe at the fact that it wasn't an antique or a flint axe.

"Are there any Germans about, prisoners or such like?"

"No, sir," chimed in Percival, and gave Mr. Qualtrough a very reproachful look.

"Aye … ahem …" said Mr. Coroner, realizing what the look implied. "Thank you. Very nasty. What have you to tell us, Dr. Kilpheric?"

The police surgeon, an Irishman, who might have been the twin brother of Mr. Qualtrough, except that his eyes were green instead of blue, said the wound could have been inflicted by the knife.… He'd say it had been. It had been delivered with an upward thrust and pierced the heart.

"And would the victim live long enough after that to walk in church and die there, doctor?"

Another woman went off into hysterics this time. Her cries were stifled by someone ramming a handkerchief half down her throat and she was hustled outside in the wake of Mr. Ephraim Davy, who uncorked his pipe again and had another smoke.

"Oh yes, yes, yes, sir," answered Kilpheric. "It has been known … soldiers and the like … when the great vessels have not been pierced."

"Ah!" said the Coroner, who didn't know a thing about it, but tried to look as though he did. He turned to his diabolical assistant and told him to make a note of it. With that, Mr. Qualtrough looked sadly at the assembly, the police, the knife, and the record of crime before him. He longed to start questioning everyone and, armed with a lot of clues, try to solve the mystery then and there by ratiocination, as he called it. He whispered to Mephistopheles, who looked as though he hated his master, but really was utterly devoted to him, even to the extent of digging deep among ruins for him when requested.

"No," said the clerk in firm, restraining tones.

"Inquest adjourned, *sine die,* then," said Mr. Qualtrough rather plaintively. "Further investigations by the police.... Thank you all for your help and attendance."

The crowd filtered out, feeling they had rendered the law a great service. There was a stampede for places on the Cobbold bus.

Meanwhile, Percival was introducing Littlejohn to Mr. Qualtrough. The Coroner's eyes lit up.

"I'm very pleased to make your acquaintance, Inspector. I'm a mystery addict myself and maybe could be of use to you."

"Thank you, sir. There is one little matter you might help to clear up...."

Mr. Qualtrough rubbed his neat little hands together.

"Already! Good. Good. Pray tell me what it is. I'll be delighted."

"I am told that you are an antiquary, sir, and the historian of Salter Hall, at Cobbold...."

"Yes, I am, Inspector.... Pray sit down."

"You won't need me, sir?" asked Percival, anxious to be about his business.

Mr. Qualtrough looked dismayed. He hoped Percival wasn't annoyed with him about the knife.

"No, no. Don't go...."

"It's all right if you're busy," interposed Littlejohn. "I won't be long. Join you at the police station."

The Superintendent hurried off.

"I do hope I haven't worried Percival at the inquest. He seems ..."

"He's worried about the murder and very busy, sir. We were talking about Salter Hall. Have you ever heard the tale of the headless Jesuit?"

"Of course. Who hasn't in these parts? It's a legend, you know. As far as I can tell you, there has been no manifestation of the haunting in my time, and such as is recorded, is from unreliable sources, mainly hysterical servants. They once had a poltergeist there, I believe. Threw things about in the kitchen. But that was, I'm sure, one of those strange phenomena which sometimes accompany hysterical kitchen-maids. Remember the affair at Epworth Parsonage?"

"I think I do, sir. The Wesleys, wasn't it? But that's not what I'm after. I've been told by a perfectly sensible person that people have seen the headless Jesuit there of late. For myself, I think it's probably some intruder, a tramp maybe, taking a free night's lodging. They do say that the villagers won't go near at night."

"You're probably right, Inspector. Of course, the legend had a true foundation, but it doesn't go back to Cromwellian times. It concerns one Simister Salter, a Regency buck, and lord of the manor for a while. Shall I go on …?"

"Please do, sir."

Mr. Qualtrough rubbed his hands and settled down cosily in his chair. The cadaverous clerk popped his head round the door to see if his master was there and in order.

"Sorry," he fluted and withdrew.

"That's Whatmough, my clerk. Strange.... He calls himself Whatmow. I'm Qualtrock and the Salters' lawyer is Fernihuff. All with O-U-G-H. Isn't our language funny?"

Mr. Qualtrough was settling down on his pet hobbyhorse, surnames.

"About the Jesuit, sir. You were saying ..."

"Ah, yes. The Jesuit. Well, it seems there was some sort of a tale from Stuart times about a Jesuit getting himself maltreated and losing his head for not disclosing the hiding-place of the Salter treasure. There may have been a Jesuit. They were Catholics, of course. But there never was a treasure."

The Coroner delivered judgment with a snap and an air of scholarly finality.

"No, Inspector. No treasure. They were a poor family until the Marsh was drained and they made farms for themselves. Their rent-roll in Stuart times was paltry. Something and nothing. I've seen the manorial records. The tenants were all copyholders, and many couldn't pay their dues. Furthermore, the family at the time made no rich marriages. What girl would want to marry an impoverished squire of a lot of fenland? I mean what girl of any wealth? They just allied themselves to the local gentry like themselves. You always get tales of that kind about old families. It adds a touch of romance and, I might say, power to a house when there's a haunting or ghost about it."

"But you said, sir, there was some foundation to the story."

"All in good time. I'm coming to it. I was mentioning Simister Salter, or Saltaire, as they were once called. He was a wild one. He treated his wife shamefully. He gambled, drank and wenched all over the countryside and left illegitimate offspring all over the place. The bad blood of the family came out fully in him. There have been splashes of it here and there on occasions, but Simister had the whole bucketful. In the end, his wife ran away in the night with the estate steward, a young, and from all accounts, good-looking man. The pair were never seen again. The following morning Hosegood, the body-servant of Simister—he still has descendants in the village—was found in the park. He'd been shot through the heart. It's thought he tried to intercept the runaways and met his match. . . ."

The tale looked like continuing indefinitely. Suddenly, Whatmough's emaciated face appeared again.

"You won't forget, sir, you've an appointment at the barber's at noon and, after that, a lunch date?"

A french polisher rather than a barber seemed indicated by the Coroner's shiny pate, but there it was.

"All right. All right, Whatmough. What time is it?"

Mephistopheles consulted a huge timepiece which he drew with difficulty from his fob-pocket.

"Quarter to twelve," he said testily and replaced the watch, which slid with a thud to the bottom of the pocket again.

"I must hurry. Well, Simister was hardly ever sober again after that. He was not a religious man and with him the Catholic side of the line died out, because—and this caused many quarrels with his wife—he insisted on sending his only son to Oxford as a member of thc Establishment. But on his deathbed, the devil turned saint. He sent for the parish priest, a fellow named Tranter, who kept a diary and left us a record. Simister was dying when he arrived. He'd had a stroke and was bereft of speech. He took little heed of the religious ministrations but made it obvious that he wanted to tell Tranter something. He couldn't articulate. Then, just as the throes were upon him, he made a terrible effort and with his last breath cried, 'The Headless Jesuit,' and died."

Littlejohn looked bewildered at the rigmarole.

“I see you are puzzled, Inspector. Well you might be. All I was trying to show is that the Headless Jesuit cropped up again. Tranter must have told about it, for, from then onwards, the legend revived. It got about that the death of Simister was due in some way to the Jesuit. Punishment for his sins and for renouncing the Catholic religion. Now they say that when a Salter is due for death, the Jesuit is seen. That, of course, is nonsense. Folklore …”

“I see. And what is the theory about Simister’s dying cry, sir?”

“You know as much as I do. Maybe it was delirium. Whatever it was, it gave renewed fillip to the old wife’s tale.… Oh, dear, I must get my hair cut. Excuse my rushing off.…”

And, with that, Mr. Qualtrough bowed himself out and hurried to the barber’s. Littlejohn remained sitting as he filled his pipe and turned over the Coroner’s tale, trying to make some sense out of it.

Mr. Whatmough appeared again, presumably to tidy up and lock the place.

"Excuse me, sir," he said, and sniffed. "I couldn't help overhearing. The Headless Jesuit, sir, I think it was about. I am myself, thanks to Mr. Qualtrough's interest, something of an antiquary. I am a member of the Thorncastle Antiquaries Society, etcetera, and have written a small monograph on Urn Burial in the Cobbold Marsh...."

He paused for breath and sniffed again. Littlejohn wondered what it was all about. Was the pale shadow of the Coroner about to refute or increase the strange information already given by his master?

"Whilst I confirm everything Mr. Qualtrough has told you, Inspector, I have something to add. Mr. Simister Salter had also a reputation as a punster, practical joker and hoaxer. It's strange that Mr. Qualtrough should have omitted to tell you this, because, whilst he has none of Simister's cruelty and vindictiveness, he likes his little puzzle and his little joke himself.... He, he, he...."

Whatmough tittered shrilly at the thought of it. His breath smelled of peppermints and he looked like a walking corpse.

"Maybe, he forgot in his haste to get to the hairdresser's...."

"Where is this leading to, Mr. Whatmough? I must be going. It's lunch time...."

"I was only going to say, it is on record that Mr. Simister, like many of the bucks of his time, was addicted to joking. What if the story of the Headless Jesuit and his last words mentioning it, were a cryptic reference to some secret in his life, a clue to the solution of some puzzle ...?"

"Well? Where would that get us?"

"It is a theory of mine. I do not believe that the Salter Treasure was a myth. I know Mr. Qualtrough dismisses it on quite logical grounds. I have not dared to argue with him, but I have my own views. I grant that at the time when the Treasure was supposed to be hidden, the Salters were not a wealthy family. That has been established. But they were of high repute for loyalty and honour. We know that the King's men accumulated treasure for his cause. They contributed their gold and jewels to a common purse. Cobbold, in its marshes, as they were then, was one of the last Royalist strongholds to survive. What if the King's Treasure were hidden in that vast old house and what if a poor priest held the secret?"

Mr. Whatmough's eyes glowed. He prodded Littlejohn on the chest with a long, bony forefinger.

"… What if Simister Salter found the secret of the Treasure and on his deathbed tried to impart it to a village priest? Why did he send for a priest? Because he was the man he could trust…."

"Interesting theory," said Littlejohn.

"A theory which I shall always pursue till it's refuted, sir. I hope to find the Treasure one day. Then, as Mr. Qualtrough holds his Crowner's Quest on it, I shall be the principal witness, instead of a humble scribe. . . .”

The man’s mad! thought Littlejohn.

Whatmough was almost dancing with excitement.

“And I tell you this, too. There are places in that Hall not yet laid bare. And the Headless Jesuit does exist. . . . I’ve seen him!”

“What is all this? When?”

“Last night! I called at the lodge to inquire if Mr. Granville had been around there before his death. As Coroner’s officer, I feel interested in these things. It’s my duty to get to know everything. There was nobody in the lodge. I thought the gatekeeper might be at the Hall and went to see. It was locked up, but there was a dim light showing through the leaded window, the long one on the staircase. I knocked on the window and tried to peer in. There was a terrible cry, and next I saw a figure in a monk’s Habit running across the lawn and vanishing into the woods. It was dark and, though I followed, I lost him. . . .”

“It must have been a tramp or intruder you scared.”

“No. It was a monk and *there was nothing where his head should be*!”

Another great blast of peppermint!

“You must be mistaken. Such things don’t happen, Mr. Whatmough. You must have been deceived in the bad light.”

Whatmough peered cunningly into Littlejohn’s face and wagged his head to and fro.

“Before this case is ended you’ll know some strange things. The strangest you’ve ever encountered. Good morning. . . .”

Mr. Whatmough put a high-crowned bowler on his head and thus looked more elongated and sepulchral than ever. He made for the door and then, turning in his steps, delivered a parting shot.

"There is some dispute about the pronunciation of the Coroner's name, too. And mine. But he insists on his own way. He is Qualtrow and I am Whatmuff. Good-day to you, sir...."

Littlejohn stayed for a moment at the door of the courthouse where Mephistopheles had left him. And there Cromwell found him, laughing to himself.

"It's good to see somebody sane at last, old chap," said Littlejohn.

Cromwell smiled, too. Old chap! Things were looking up.

"Why, sir?"

"Qualtrow and Qualtrock, Whatmoow and Whatmuff, Headless Jesuits and King's Treasures.... They're all going mad!"

Still laughing, he told it all to Cromwell, who did not laugh. He took it very seriously.

"They're ruddy-well trying to spoof us! What the hell do they think we're here for? Well, we'll see who laughs last. Meanwhile, I've something to tell you, sir."

"Fire away, then."

"I made my way to the court, but found you'd finished. But Miss Alveston was waiting at the door. She said she wanted to see you; she had something for you. I asked if I would do, as you seemed busy. She said yes, and gave me this."

Cromwell produced a photograph of a group of men in khaki, with the tight puttees of long ago and, of all things, proudly wearing their stiff-looking, old-time privates' hats. It had been taken by a professional man and the features of each were quite clear.

"That's her father...."

A stocky, stiff-looking man, obviously posing for his picture, and, judging from the looks of the rest, the life and soul of the party. He had a broad, crafty face and a cynical, cocky smile under a heavy, dark moustache. All set against a back-cloth got up to look like the Rialto at Venice, with palms in pots at each side.

"She told me to tell you something else, too. She took the picture without asking her mother for fear of upsetting her. But last time she looked at the back of the album where it's kept, there were two copies in the same envelope. Well, one of them's gone."

SEVEN

THE TRAIL OF JERRY ALVESTON

"WE'D better find out what happened to Alveston," Littlejohn said to Cromwell. "Nobody seems to know properly."

There seemed to be something queer underlying Jerry Alveston's behaviour after 1917. From Pennyquick and then from Mrs. Alveston herself it appeared that the ex-bailiff of Salters' estate had volunteered for the army a year or two after war had broken out. His conduct since then had, to say the least of it, been very eccentric. He had not joined the Mereshires with the rest of his pals, but gone off to a distant place, enlisted in a regiment there, turned up twice on leave in khaki, during one of which visits his wife had helped herself to two photographs of her husband and comrades, and then, instead of returning home when he was demobbed, he had disappeared.

What was the cause of it all? Had he tired of his wife and previous existence and determined to start afresh, or had he, during his absence, come across some strange information or opportunity to make money and taken himself off to improve the shining hour; or, to think the worst, to hide from or shake off some threat. From past history, too, mainly recorded in mouth-to-mouth gossip, it turned out that his wife knew little about his movements whilst he was in the army. He hardly ever wrote and then only when he wanted something.

Cromwell, therefore, started from scratch to find out what had happened to the runaway.

Mrs. Alveston had even forgotten the regiment which Jerry joined. A magnifying glass and the photograph revealed, after inspection of hat badges and consultation with experts, that he had served with the Glebeshire Yeomanry.

Cromwell, always ready for a jaunt, arrived in Glebechester early in the day. The place was decked in bunting and flags flew from every building. As his train drew into the station, Cromwell found the platforms banked with flowers and a red carpet laid from the ticket-barriers all the way up the approach to the street. Outside there were huge crowds, including a band, a guard of honour, a children's choir and His Worship the Mayor in gold chain and red gown, with a mace-bearer and bewigged town clerk at his side.

"Gangway! Clear the way. The train's signalled," shouted a portly official, and Cromwell was forcibly wedged among the throng around the station entrance.

"What's going on?" asked Cromwell of a large woman by his side. But the band was beginning to play and he got no answer. It must be Royalty, he thought. The Mayor gathered his retinue and his scarlet robes around him, a small procession formed, and with stately steps vanished down the approach and into the station. A shrill whistle, and a train drew in.

A biting east wind blew down the street, but nobody heeded it. They were all warmed-up by fervour and anticipation. Down below on the platform, something was happening. Thin cheers rose on the wind from the nether regions of the station, then a swelling to a full-throated roar. The band played again, the children waved flags, the spectators flailed their arms above their heads and bellowed, and the juvenile choir began to sing. The loyal Cromwell removed his hat, clicked his heels and drew himself up like the good soldier he once had been. Then the Mayor and Corporation emerged, smiling and proud of themselves, followed by the Glebeshire Rovers. They'd won the cup!

The guard of honour presented arms, the Mayor doffed his cocked hat, flags fluttered in the wind, the Glebeshires' colours were flaunted and eleven sturdy men and a reserve, after seeing-off the mayoral Rolls Royce, piled themselves in an open-topped charabanc and, with the trophy held aloft, drove through the frenzied crowds to the Town Hall for the victory feast. Cromwell, carried away by the emotions of the mob, yelled his head off with the rest.

Then, as if by magic, the concourse melted away and Cromwell was left standing alone amid the remnants of the fury. Broken banners, torn flags and bunting, toffee papers and cigarette packets, empty bandstand, and dead microphone from which the Mayor had made his speech of welcome which nobody heard for cheers. The sergeant pulled himself together and recovered his poise.

"Nothing doing to-day by the looks of it," he grumbled.

A porter emerged from the station and slowly and irritably began to roll up the sacred carpet.

"Local high-jinks and holiday?" asked Cromwell cheerfully.

"Lot o' ruddy nonsense, if you asks me," said the official. "All this fuss about a soccer cup. Give me rugger any day. Now, that's the game...."

"Are the Glebeshire Yeomanry barracks round here?"

The man removed a cigarette from a battered paper packet, stuck it in the corner of his mouth, lit it, and ejected a cloud of smoke. He drew so hard at the tobacco, that Cromwell imagined the whole of his inside enveloped in smoke clouds.

"Aye. What do you want with 'em?"

Just as if the sergeant were a saboteur, ready to blow up or carry off the blessed place!

"I want to see the officer in charge."

"Fat lot o' good you'll do to-day. He's out with the ridgiment, guard of honour for the victors and at the banquet after, too. Banquets! With things as they are. You'd think the food 'ud choke 'em...."

The man spat in the road and kicked the carpet, which emitted a cloud of choking dust.

"Old Colonel Muspratt'll be as mad as an 'atter about it all. Always ready for a banquet is the Colonel ... and now he goes and gets himself gout and carn't turn out just on this of all days. Serve 'im right. The old devil...."

"Who's Colonel Muspratt when he's at home?"

"Led the Regiment in the 'fourteen-eighteen war. Proper devil he was, too. I know—I was there...."

"In the Glebeshires?"

"Aye. Much good it done me. Look at me now. Rollin' up ruddy carpets as others 'as wiped their feet on...."

"Remember a fellow of the name of Alveston in the Glebeshires?"

"Ask me another. There were 'undreds of us and it's thirty years or more since.... I must be gettin' on.

If the boss gets back and finds this carpet still out ’e’ll play merry ’ell.”

“Wait a minute. Recognize any of these?”

Cromwell took out the photograph and passed it to the porter who thumbed it roughly and held it close to his eyes.

“Where you get this? Seem to recollect them faces. . . .”

And with that the porter broke into malevolent chuckles. He pointed a grubby finger at one of Alveston’s companions.

“’Im. ’Im. See ’Im. You ever seen ’im afore?”

“Can’t say I have. Why?”

“Where was you when the team came out?”

“Here.”

“That’s a good ’un. You seen ’im then. Not like that, though. Too ’igh and mighty for an ordinary Tommy now. That’s ’is Worship the Mayor o’ Glebechester. . . .”

The man kicked the carpet in a frenzy of mirth. He coughed and swore horribly in his glee.

"Show it to 'im. Print it in the paper. That'll get 'im. One 'ud think he'd been Field Marshall instead of a ruddy private.... Private Enery Widgett, that's wot he was. Turn agen Widgett, Lord Mayor o' Glebechester. And wot did I get? Rollin' up the ruddy carpet 'e's wiped his big boots on...."

Cromwell had had enough. He'd made the first step. Now it was up to Mister Mayor. He bade the carpet-roller a quick good-day and made off for the town centre.

The Superintendent of Police welcomed Cromwell like a long-lost brother. Always glad to see and co-operate with Scotland Yard. What could he do to help? His breath smelled faintly of port. He'd been toasting the conquering heroes and had just popped into his office before the feed to attend to matters, mainly the deploying of his men to clear the streets of drunks after the day's holiday.

"It's going to be a bit difficult getting at the Mayor to-day. Anyhow, we'll see what we can do. It'll have to be after the luncheon...."

He was rather on the small side, and portly with it. His round, flushed face beamed in anticipation of the victuals to come. He liked his food!

"Tell you what we'll do. I'll take you in with me to lunch. One, more or less, won't make any odds. You can have a feed—and it'll be a good one, I can tell you—and it'll find you something to do till we can get His Worship aside for a little talk. Eh?"

Before Cromwell knew what was happening, he was being shoved by the elbow to a place at the high table among the Mayor, Corporation, Borough officers and footballers.

"My friend Cromwell, of Scotland Yard. Here on business...." The Superintendent introduced him all round. It caused quite a commotion. It wasn't often they had a man from Scotland Yard among them. It filled some of them with awe. You could see people eyeing Cromwell rather fearfully, as though he might be Sherlock Holmes or a mind reader.

"He really wants a word or two with you, Mr. Mayor, when you can manage it."

Mr. Widgett turned pale and fiddled with his robes as though weighed down by them. He eased his huge gold chain too as though it irked him.

"What is it?"

He couldn't wait!

The waiters were serving soup to the fifty guests, so, instead of learning his fate, the Mayor had to fall-to with the rest. He hadn't much appetite.

Cromwell sat down and left His Worship to entertain the footballers. He ate a splendid meal and listened comatosely to speeches of congratulation and thanks. They drank several toasts and the Superintendent, after granting Cromwell official indulgences, declaring him off duty and urging him to be matey, pressed drinks upon him. They were, therefore, all rather merry when they met at length in the mayor's-room during the intermission.

"Come to arrest me?" asked the Mayor with a titter.

"No, sir. Just for a little help to trace a man we want to question. Alveston was the name."

The photograph was produced again and Cromwell pointed out the man he was seeking. The Mayor looked at it, grew even redder than he already was, and hastily returned it before anyone else should see it.

"Yes. That's me. But the man you mention isn't Alveston. It's Jimmy Grigg."

"Jimmy Grigg?"

"Yes."

"But Jerry Alveston's wife gave me the photo. She said that was her husband."

"Wait a minute.... Wait a minute. It's a long time ago, but it's coming back to me...."

Mr. Widgett sat quietly pondering as though allowing his memory to tick-over and produce the necessary information.

"Yes. I've got it. His real name was Jimmy Grigg. But he enlisted under another name. Yes, it was Alveston that he enlisted under."

Cromwell felt a little light-headed from the lager he'd consumed, but surely this wasn't right!

"His real name was Alveston, but he called himself Grigg. That what you mean, Mr. Mayor?"

"No, no. Other way round."

Then it dawned on Cromwell. His allowances to his wife would have to be paid under Alveston's name. But he wanted to be known as someone else for some reason or other. So he said his real name was Grigg. He told the Mayor.

Mr. Widgett patted Cromwell's knee affectionately.

"We're gettin' all mixed up," he said fruitily. "Less leave it at that. What does matter is, what d'you wanta know about him?"

"Did you go through the war with him, sir?"

"Yes. We were demobbed together. Good chap. Found him a job when he came out. As a matter of fact, we were partners for a time."

"His Worship is a builder in the town," explained the Superintendent.

The room was cosy and warm and the padded chairs lulled you to sleep. Especially after such a good meal and drink. Cromwell decided it was time he was moving. He'd a lot to do and at this rate he'd be nowhere at bedtime.

"How long were you together, sir?"

"Six years. Then Jimmy got restless. Said he felt like a change. I didn't want to lose him. He was a good worker and knew his stuff. Very secretive, though. Never said where he'd learned his trade."

"He left you in the 'thirties then?"

"Early 'thirties, yes."

"Do you know where he went, sir?"

"Yes. Glencastle. Started up on his own. He wrote to me a time or two, but then it all stopped. I heard he was drinking."

"Where's Glencastle, sir?"

"About twenty miles north of here on the main line."

"Do you happen to have Grigg, or Alveston's address there, sir?"

"No. It's so long ago. Why? What's happened about him?"

"We're on the Cobbold murder case, if you've heard about it, sir. Grigg was a native of Cobbold and we want to find his whereabouts...."

"Jimmy didn't do it, did he?"

"No. We just want to question him...."

"I thought ... He was a good sort. Didn't know he came from there."

"He must have kept it dark."

From the banquet-hall a dull chant was sounding:

"We want the Mayor.... We want the Mayor.... We want Widgett ..."

Mr. Widgett sniggered.

"Sounds as if I'm wanted.... Must be going. The party's starting again.... Anything more, Sergeant?"

"No, sir. Thanks for your help."

"Don't mention it. Glad to help any time. You coming in with me?"

"No, sir. I must be getting on. Thanks for your hospitality. I've had a very good time...."

"Very glad. Well ... good-bye. Sign the visitors' book. Don't forget. See he signs, Superintendent...."

With that, Mr. Widgett again became Mayor by putting on his gown and chain of office and departed.

"Good ole Widgett...."

The footballers greeted him like a long-lost brother.

"Seems very popular...."

"Yes. He's president of the club. Used to play for them, too, I believe."

At Glencastle, Cromwell was very lucky. He descended from the slow train at tea-time and forthwith asked the stationmaster if he knew anyone called James Grigg.

"There was a man of that name hereabouts for years. We used to deal with his timber on the railway. A builder in rather a big way."

It was only a small branch line and the stationmaster was general factotum as well. He was busy unloading baskets of pigeons from the van of the train. As he talked he read the labels on the wicker cages. Inside the birds clucked, purred and ruffled their feathers.

"If that isn't the limit. We loose these at nine in the morning. That means I've to give 'em food and water.... As if I hadn't enough to do."

"Keeps you busy, eh?"

"I'll say it does. I'm fond of 'em though. This is one of the main centres. We release hundreds from all over the place in a year's time."

He was tall, cadaverous and stiff in the joints. As he bent to view the birds, his limbs creaked and groaned, and he placed his hands on his bended members as though fearing they would fly apart.

"About Grigg.... Doesn't he live here now?"

"No. Went bust. Left the place about five years since."

"Any idea where he went?"

"No. What you want to know for?"

The stationmaster, still on his knees with the pigeons, turned a curious suspicious look on Cromwell.

"Just a friend I'm looking up. Together in the first war."

"Can't say I admire your choice of friends."

"Why?"

"He was a drunkard. I'm strong T.T. myself. If you know the number of men I've seen ruined by drink …"

Cromwell excused himself. He felt, after the banquet he'd recently left, he couldn't bear a lecture on temperance. The stationmaster was by this talking to the pigeons….

"There, there, my beauties. Uncle Oscar'll get 'em some corn and water. Hungry, my pets? Uncle Oscar …"

At the post office they took a long time looking up the change of address forms. The postmaster was away and his deputy had been there thirty years. He remembered Grigg all right, but had forgotten where he went. Luckily, the official forms were still preserved, though deep in the archives. It took an hour to lay them bare.

"James Grigg … c/o G.P.O. Latchbury."

"Many thanks…."

At Latchbury, Cromwell found more traces of the decline and fall of Jimmy Grigg, alias Alveston. He was known to the police. In fact, he'd done time for receiving stolen goods. And he'd been in the lock-up for other short spells on charges of being drunk and disorderly and using violence when arrested.

"Where did he get to eventually?" asked Cromwell of the sergeant-in-charge. The senior officers had gone off to a funeral.

The huge bobby rang up places, turned up records, questioned his subordinates. Grigg hadn't returned to Latchbury, but, luckily, one of the constables, sent on a message of serving a writ to a nearby town, had seen Grigg there. They'd been repairing war damage and Grigg had been foreman on the job.

"Always a good workman, but a fool to himself," said the sergeant.

The name of the town in question was Barby, and the Latchbury police, who were a friendly lot, took Cromwell there in a patrol car.

"He looks dead-beat," said the sergeant sympathetically to the road-cop. "Take him to Barby and bag one or two speed-merchants on the way."

They made Cromwell some strong tea and packed him off in the natty little M.G. By way of a little diversion, they gonged and booked four unlucky motorists on the highway.

"Brought me luck," said the speed-man as they parted in Barby. "I don't usually get more than two."

He might have been out rabbit-shooting!

At Barby the Town Hall was closed when Cromwell arrived, but the police station proved a port in a storm again. Yes, they'd heard of Jimmy Grigg. A good chap, but fond of the bottle. He'd worked for the corporation for quite a time and then got the sack for irregular timekeeping. They hadn't seen him about since.

"Was his home here?"

The Inspector seemed to know all about everyone and everything.

"He was in rooms. Somewhere down Poortown...."

"Poortown?"

"A working-class district of the place. Not as bad as it sounds. I'll find out where ..."

The Inspector took Cromwell in the telephone room and there the man on the switch flashed the Poortown police-box. The man on the beat had a reply pat.

"Lodged with Mrs. Reilly, 23 Orchard Street...."

"I'll run you there if you like, Sergeant...."

"Thanks ..."

The name of Scotland Yard acted like magic!

The diggings were clean and respectable and the woman a decent little elderly body. She looked alarmed at the sight of the police.

"Has Jimmy Grigg been here lately, Mrs. Reilly?"

"No. He got stopped from the Corporation a fortnight since an' came home drunk. I told 'im I wasn't havin' that sort of carryings on in my house. I've my good name to think of...."

"I'm sure you have. Where did he go, Mrs. Reilly?"

"I don't know. But he left his things here. Said he'd send or come for 'em later. I was wonderin' what to do with them. He's not been back nor sent even a post-card. I can't keep two cases lyin' about here for ever. I want to let his room, too, though he paid up till this week-end...."

"May we see the room, please?"

She led them up a narrow flight of stairs, carpeted in thin cokernut matting. The room was clean and bare. An iron bedstead, a painted chest, a cheap table, long lace curtains at the windows, and a stuffy smell. The place had been tidied up and the only signs of an occupant were two battered fibre suitcases on top of a rough wooden wardrobe. The old lady protested a bit when the police examined the cases.

"What am I goin' to tell 'im when he finds you've been rummagin' 'em?"

"We'll be responsible."

One case was almost empty. Nothing but a clean shirt, some collars, soiled ties and dirty pyjamas. The other was the same. Toilet articles, razor, soap, ration book in the name of Grigg, a clothes brush and other odds and ends not of much use in the investigation.

"Did he take a case away with him, Mrs. Reilly?"

"No. He said he'd be back. When he was drunk, he said he was going abroad. Starting afresh. He was fed-up, he said, with the old country. Though he couldn't complain much, if you ask me. He did well at his job. It was the drink did it.... He told me when he was drunk he was goin' to where he could lay hands on some money and then he was off...."

"And when he was sober?"

"The next mornin' he ate his breakfast and went away, sayin' he'd be back and to keep his room."

"And he didn't come back?"

"No."

So there the trail ended. The police helped all they could. The railway station, the bus depot, the local taxi drivers.... Nobody remembered Jimmy Grigg's leaving town.

That was the report Cromwell gave Littlejohn, when, tired and hungry, he got back to "The Mitre" at past midnight after just catching the night mail.

Things were very wide awake, however, in the cathedral city. The film unit was taking some night shots. To-night it was a try-out. A number of adventurous citizens, at two pounds a time, were dancing round a bonfire in the cathedral close. In the script, it was supposed to come on rain, spoil the celebrations and lead up to a dreadful scene in the dark and another murder. The local fire brigade, in the absence of obliging nature, were providing the rain.... There was a terrific hullaballoo going on outside, the director yelling through a microphone and supers shouting and dogs barking.

"What do you say about moving out to the pub at Cobbold, sir? Anything rather than this...."

Littlejohn agreed, and next day, with the benevolent help of Pennyquick, they took up quarters at the "Royal Oak", Cobbold, a few minutes' walk from the scene of the crime and not far from where the Headless Jesuit was said to prowl to the discomfiture of all who saw him.

EIGHT

THE FLAT IN MAYFAIR

DURING Cromwell's absence on the track of Alveston, Littlejohn returned to London. He'd one or two things to square up at the Yard and, more important still, he wanted to visit Granville Salter's flat in Mayfair and find out what he could about the dead man's affairs at home. He made the journey, there and back, in a day, with time to spare.

The place was in a second-rate neighbourhood behind Curzon Street; a tall, bomb-scarred house let off as small flats and housing a motley assortment of tenants.

Littlejohn didn't need to ring the door-bell. The charwoman, who was cleaning the step, gave him a disinterested look when he arrived, and moved her pail to let him enter. He stood for a minute wondering what to do.

"Yes?" shouted someone from below-stairs.

"I want to see Mr. Salter's flat...."

"Why? Come down. I can't be shoutin' and bawlin' all this distance."

Littlejohn descended the narrow flight of steps which led from the once elegant, now dingy hall, and found himself in a cosy room with an enormous fire burning in the open kitchen grate. Talk about fuel shortage!

The room was neat and tidy, very stuffy from the heat, and smelling faintly of coffee.

A large sideboard covered one side of the room. Photographs of all kinds, mainly military groups in frames, and a large marble clock littered the top. There was a camp bed in one corner and oddments of furniture, looking like the salvage of evicted tenants, scattered about. By the fire a large, worn arm-chair and in it a large fat man.

"What do you want now ...?"

The words were hardly out of his mouth than the man saw Littlejohn. He recognized the official class at once, sprang to his feet and apologized.

"I'm sorry, sir. I thought it was the lawyer's clerk again. He's never away. Servin' writs mornin', noon and night. What a lot o' tenants we got these days! Now pre-war ... it was different.... Real gentry then...."

A tall, heavy man, gone to seed from idling about at his job as caretaker and yet bearing the marks of an old regular soldier.

"You from the police, sir?"

"Yes."

"I expected you.... Mr. Salter, isn't it? I read in the paper about 'im. Pity...."

He shook his head and clicked his tongue against his false teeth, which fitted badly and slipped down as he talked.

Littlejohn showed his warrant-card.

"What do you know about Mr. Salter … er … what's your name?"

"Bedford, sir. Late Company-Sergeant-Major in the Buffs. Now ekin' out my pension lookin' after this lot.… Wot a come-down …!"

"Well, Bedford, could you please tell me what you know about the late Mr. Salter? His reputation, friends, occupation … and so on.… As much as you know."

"Won't you sit down, sir?"

Littlejohn did. It was obvious that Bedford liked sitting by the fire better than work or anything else. The ex-C.S.M. sagged in the arm-chair again.

"Hope you don't mind the big fire, sir. Got a touch of the old fever in me bones again.… Relic from active days abroad.…"

"Carry on."

"Mr. Salter was a good tenant. Quite a gent. Must have been a bit short of ready, though, to take up in a place like this. Not his class. But I will say his flat's nice. Done it up, he did. Quite the best of the lot now, though it is top-floor."

"What did he do for a living?"

"That I can't say, sir. Spent a lot of time out and came home late. Left just after breakfast. Kept himself to himself. It's not hard makin' friends with these sort of tenants. Cadgin', spongin', and the women hunting for blokes to take 'em out.... But he kept out of it all."

"Did he ever have visitors?"

"Very few, sir.... Men they were, and I never knew any of 'em."

"I see...."

From above, the charwoman's strident voice filled the hall.

"I'm goin', Mr. Bedford. I've done...."

"'Ave you mopped the stairs?"

"What d'yer think I'm here for? O' course I done 'em. The milk's 'ere, too."

“Put it in the usual place. That’s all. I’m busy now.”

“All right … saucy!”

“Mr. Salter paid his rent regularly?”

“Yes, sir.…”

“I’d better see his flat, then.”

“Mind if I don’t come, sir, seein’ as you’re the police? My limbs ache with this old fever.…”

“Very well. Which one is it … and is it open?”

The C.S.M. wasn’t going to labour up and down four flights of stairs if he could help it. He’d got everything nicely organized on a labour-saving basis and directed operations from a chair by the fire.

“Here’s the key, sir. There’s only one flat on top. Was a studio once. Mr. Salter made it nice.…”

He certainly had made it comfortable. After toiling up the steep stairs, which gradually grew rougher and narrower as they ascended, Littlejohn was glad to sink in one of the cosy arm-chairs and look around as he rested. On the way up he’d run the gauntlet of a number of inquiring fellow-lodgers of the late Salter. A fat man, like a decrepit company-promoter gone to ground, with his face half-lathered, hurrying from the bathroom; a woman clad only in a soiled wrapper and with tousled bleached hair, leaning out from a half-open door for a small bottle of milk and baring her opulent bosom in the process; a small shabby man taking out a bad-tempered Pekingese for an airing; two scruffy, bearded youngsters in dirty flannels and seedy sports-coats trying to look like artists.... A motley crew.

Salter's room smelled fresh and clean after the fug of down below; stale smoke, airless bedrooms, dirty linen. The walls had been distempered off-white and held a good picture or two. There was a large Indian rug on the floor of the living-room, cosy chairs, a small mahogany round table, a gramophone and a chest of drawers. All apparently picked-up cheaply here and there. Overhead, the bare rafters and beams, also distempered. The place was lighted by large windows in the roof, perhaps added at some time by a tenant who saw the possibilities of making a good studio there. Salter had evidently tidied up the room before leaving; there was nothing out of place.

At the far end, another door. Littlejohn rose to investigate. This led to a small kitchen, little larger than a good-sized cupboard. There was a food cabinet and a gas-ring, with a sink with a dripping tap in one corner. This, too, was spick and span, evidently tidied after the last meal. Littlejohn opened the food-safe. A piece of mouldy cheese on a plate, a packet of breakfast cereal, some dog biscuits, half a bottle of milk, turned sour and solid. Nothing more. Plates, cups and saucers, a dog's bowl, and a few odds and ends of cutlery on an open shelf. Under the sink a refuse bucket and an old-fashioned hip-bath. You got hot water from a gas-geyser connected to a shilling-in-the-slot meter. A small mirror hung on the wall. Evidently the bathroom as well.

Next door, in a glorified boxroom, was a single bed, made and tidied, too. Salter seemed pretty thorough in his housekeeping and liked an orderly home. The bedroom held a cheap chest of drawers and a washstand with a ewer and basin. There was water in the ewer and two soiled towels on a rail....

Littlejohn heard the door of the next room open and turned to greet the intruder. It was the woman in the soiled wrapper. She held the latter closely to her and a cigarette dangled from the corner of her mouth.

"Oh ... I didn't know.... You a new tenant?"

"No. I was just looking round. Can I do anything for you?"

"No. I just wondered if you were anybody connected with Mr. Salter.... Pity about him.... I saw it in the papers...."

Her profession was evident. She spoke with a drawl in a "refined" voice, with an echo of the streets beneath it. Probably quite a decent sort, but with an eye to the main chance.

"He borrowed five pounds from me before he left and I was wondering …"

"Sorry, I can't help you. That's a matter for his lawyers. I'm from the police."

"Thought you'd be round. Bit of a mystery, Mr. Salter. Quite a gentleman, but a bit on the rocks, I'd say."

"Why?"

"I was thinking of the five pounds he borrowed.…"

"Did you know him well?"

"Not reely. Very reserved. We met on the stairs now and then and had a bit of a chat. Can't say we got far. Literary bloke, I think he was."

"What makes you think that, Miss … er … er …?"

"Deborah James.…"

"My name's Littlejohn—Inspector Littlejohn."

"Pleased to meet you."

Miss James took another loose cigarette from the pocket of her garment and lit it from the stub of the first one.

"You were saying, Miss James, you thought Mr. Salter a literary bloke. Why, pray?"

"I once saw him coming out of the British Museum and when I asked him whatever he was doing there, he said a bit of literary research."

"That's interesting."

"Yes.... And it must have been something historical, maybe a novel or scenario he was on. I remember coming up to borrow some milk and he had the table littered with books and papers. When he went for the milk I just took a peek at them. They were old books, smelled of must and dust and had old bindings and queer lettering. F's for S's, you know, kind of thing."

"Yes. I know what you mean. What were they all about?"

"I haven't the faintest. He was back with the milk and I never saw them again. Besides, I'm not interested in the dim past. Quite enough with the present if you ask me."

Miss James stubbed out the lipstick-stained butt of her cigarette in an ash-tray and began to search her person for another. Littlejohn supplied her with one and lit it for her.

"Ta. Well, if that's all, I'll toddle. By the way, I only made up the tale about the five pounds. I was curious about what was going on and wanted an excuse to come up. Salter was murdered, wasn't he?"

"Yes, why?"

"I don't know. There's been something funny going on here for months. He's been shutting himself up for days at a time with his books and papers and writing to places. I know that because I've seen him rushing out to post letters at the post-box. You mightn't see much funny in that. But in this place we're all interested in one another. We mayn't even be on speaking terms, but we watch one another and put two and two together and make five from it. We know one another's little habits and we know a hell of a sight more about one another than each of us thinks. See what I mean?"

"Yes.... Well?"

"It's just that Granville Salter suddenly changed. From an ordinary come-day, go-day tenant like the rest of us, a bit bored and browned-off with life, he suddenly got very busy and excited, as though he'd got on to something. That's the only way I can describe it. Maybe, some crooked dodge of making money, or a girl, or his luck on the horses changed. Come to think of it, his sudden spate of letters might have been to his bookie. I wouldn't know...."

"Did he have any visitors?"

"Not that I recollect. He seemed very quiet that way. I do remember one thing, though. He took me out once. Matey, like; nothing else. It was my birthday and I'd met him on the stairs. I was a bit down in the mouth and told him so and why. He took me to a place behind Russell Square for a meal. We had some wine, too, and we got a bit maudlin. I started to talk about the old days and the old folks at home. I've got to have it bad to get that way."

"And so …"

"He got a bit talkative too. Started to tell me about a girl he was fond of. He was a bit pickled or he wouldn't have talked the way he did. It just didn't make sense. Something about his happiness depending on his family. But he hadn't got any family, he said. So what? His happiness depended on his sorting out the family. Not long after, he started the hectic ways I told you of. Then, he went away and didn't come back, and the next thing I heard he was dead. He wished me a Merry Christmas when we met on the stairs and said he'd be back, and maybe things would be better for him in the New Year if what he thought was true. It's all just a mix-up. I can't make head or tail of it. Who'd want to do him in?"

"That's what we've to find out. By the way, Salter was a very neat and tidy chap, wasn't he? This flat's spotless."

"To tell you the truth, I did it. Thought it would be nice for him to get back to a clean place. I owed him a good turn."

"How did you get in?"

"Bedford let me in. I told him I was going to clean up. Bedford's not fussy."

"So it seems."

"Well, if you don't want me any more, I'll go and get some clothes on and a tidy up. I haven't eaten yet. Care for a cup of coffee with me?"

"No, thanks, Miss James."

"I thought not. Be seein' you."

With that she walked right out and Littlejohn heard her enter her own flat and slam the door. What had she been up-to in Salter's flat in his absence? Maybe foraging for food, or something more worth while....

There was no desk in the place, so Littlejohn turned to the chest-of-drawers, an old-fashioned article with old-fashioned locks, but every drawer fast. He took out his own bunch of keys and encountered very little resistance, except that in the intricacies of the ancient levers he had difficulty in withdrawing the keys which worked.

In the top drawer, collars, ties, handkerchiefs and other odds and ends of clothing. Beneath the lot, a service revolver. He'd not taken that with him; apparently not anticipating the need for it. That was good. His mission perhaps didn't involve anything dangerous. The next drawer also held collars, shirts, underclothes and other light articles of clothing. No more than that. Finally, the bottom one, very heavy and difficult to move. Its contents took Littlejohn an hour to go through.

Books, papers, deeds, manuscripts, records. Scores of them, all jumbled higgledy-piggledy. Notes on scraps of paper and addresses of various people in

Cobbold and elsewhere. The lot smelled musty with age and damp. Heaven knew where Salter had got them all. Presumably the family papers and a lot of other references. Salter looked to have been preparing a book or a detailed family history. But to Littlejohn, it seemed to mean more than that.

Granville Salter had been trying to satisfy himself whether or not the girl he loved was his own close relative or not! It all seemed plain. Family trees, parchments and diaries. What could he hope to find there? One book-mark revealed the tale of the Salter Treasure. Another, the legend of the Headless Jesuit. Where did it all lead to? Surely, Salter had not been intent on restoring the family fortune by finding the mythical treasure and, at the same time, clearing the way for marrying Miss Alveston, who some said was his sister!

All this stuff, Littlejohn told himself, must merely have been the husks of the game. Salter would have sorted out what he wanted from the mass of material and taken it with him to Cobbold. If so, they might find something in his luggage there. He bundled all the papers back in the drawer, retaining only the rough notes for perusal in the train back. Then he turned to the bedroom.

Two suits hung behind a curtain across one corner; a dinner suit and a shabby lounge one. The cheap chest-of-drawers was unlocked. It held more underclothes, some towels, some toilet odds and ends. And an old wallet. Littlejohn turned the latter inside out. It contained nothing but a card. Maybe Miss James had seen to the rest. Maybe, not.... The card was grubby and significant.

James Cooney,
Private Investigator.
2C King's Weighhouse Lane,
London, W.C.2.

Littlejohn picked up his hat and put on his overcoat....

Mr. Cooney was in. Four flights up a dirty staircase, with his name alone painted on the dingy door.

"Come in…."

Mr. Cooney was sitting at a battered table in a frail battered chair. He had his hat on.

"Just in time…. Huuuullllo, Inspector."

"Well, well, well. Just imagine you a detective. I *am* glad to welcome you to the fraternity."

"Now, Inspector, don't get sarcastic. I'm on the level these days, doing a nice, steady job."

"I'm glad to hear it, Barney."

"Not that! Barney's buried with the murky past. Now I'm Jimmy Cooney, at your service. Reduced terms to the force."

Before serving time for buying a car with a dud cheque and selling the same car before the cheque bounced, Mr. Barney Faircluff had described himself as an Agent. This had included the turf, finance, black market, and, the police suspected, stolen goods.

It was surprising anybody ever trusted him, for with his snaky body, weasel's face and eyes, card-sharper's hands and hyena's laugh, all set off by a natty check suit, a jaunty soft hat, pointed shoes and smart-alec's walk, Barney, alias Jimmy, seemed blessed with all the attributes and tastes of a born wrong-'un. Yet he could talk himself into and out of anything. That was his salvation. Now, he was presumably doing a bit of snooping for divorces and any other disreputable trade he might find profitable, and, most likely, combining a bit of blackmail with it.

"I was just going out.... I'm busy on a case...."

"It can wait a minute or two. If I waste your time, maybe I'll give you a lift with the case myself. What is it?"

"Confidential. Divorce on the highest level. That's all I'm at liberty to tell you."

"I'll bet it is!"

Barney bared his teeth. They were triangular, like little fangs, as though he'd specially filed them down to points.

"What do you know about Granville Salter, Barney?"

"Don't keep calling me Barney. I tell you, Inspector, it'll do me harm. What about Salter? Never heard of him."

"Come, come, Jimmy. It *is* Jimmy, isn't it? Funnily enough, Salter was murdered and your card was found in his wallet."

"Here, here, here. Come off it. There's scores of my cards all over London, but that's my way of making myself known. You can't pin this on me."

"I'm not trying to, Barney. Beg pardon, Jimmy. I want to know what you were doing for or with Granville Salter. Now, you wouldn't hamper the police on a murder case, would you, Jimmy?"

"Of course not. You know me better than that, Inspector. I really haven't a clue what Salter was wanting. He died too soon."

"You mean …"

"I mean, some pal evidently put him on to me. He came here and asked my line. I told him. Discreet inquiries, to put it in a nutshell. Just before Christmas, it was. He was going away and when he got back maybe he'd have a little job for me to do."

"Such as …?"

Barney pushed his hat to the back of his head, bit the end off a cheap cigar, lit it, and slowly ejected the smoke through all his teeth.

"He wanted me to see if I could find a bloke who vanished after the last war. I said maybe. He asked how much. I said five quid expenses for a start and the rest by results. He said he'd let me know. He didn't. He got killed instead."

"And the name of the man?"

Barney shrugged his shoulders and worked the cigar from the left to the right side of his large jaw.

"Dunno...."

"Come again, Barney. He left a five-pound deposit. I know you of old. Who was it and how much do you know?"

"Have a heart, Inspector. You'd take the food out of my mouth. Rifle the kid's money-box, you would. Oh, all right then. The man's name was Alveston. Hadn't been seen since the last war. Salter knew his regiment and had his photo. That's all. I tried to trace him through the British Legion. They did me proud, but the trail petered out at a place called ... let me see ..."

Barney consulted a small, grubby note-book.

"Barby, in the Midlands. And now, please can I go? I'm hot on a trail and they've a rendezvous in half an hour. You wouldn't stop an honest man earning an honest penny, would you, Inspector?"

"No, Barney, I wouldn't. Only see that it is honest. Thanks for the information. One day, maybe, I'll be able to do the same for you."

"Sez you," rudely retorted Barney Faircluff.

Littlejohn dined on the train home. They seemed to serve the meal as they were passing over the roughest part of the track. The attendants danced grotesquely and capered like macaws, spilling soup and food all over the place and the beer jigged and jumped over the edges of the glasses and slopped over the tablecloths. It was quite a time before he could settle down peaceably and sort out the mass of notes left behind by Granville Salter. They proved, as far as Littlejohn could see, almost useless in the case he had in hand. Dates and details of the two legends which were becoming an obsession in the whole business and, as likely as not, a perfect red-herring. The Salter Treasure and the Headless Jesuit. Granville had scribbled the references and variations on the themes and neatly added in brackets their sources. Not much use in solving the very commonplace murder on which they were engaged. The last sheet of paper, however, was a bit more interesting. It contained a column of names, some of them familiar, in which Salter must have found some clue or who might be able to help in his researches.

Rev. P. Worsnip

B. Hosegood

Plucock

Pennyquick

Madeline Fothergill

Aunt Margaret

Flather

Tom Sly

Devereaux

Mrs. Knapp

Stowell, Trotter and Meek

Mr. Fernihough

Mr. Qualtrough

A formidable list and some of them already wellknown to the Scotland Yard men. Other names were a mystery. Plucock was dead—murdered. And by the side of the mysterious Stowell, Trotter and Meek was a pencil note: "Gone away." Devereaux and Knapp, too, were dismissed briefly: "Dead." The obvious man with a key to the puzzle would be Pennyquick. Littlejohn folded the papers, tucked them safely in his pocket, paid his bill and sauntered, or rather, in view of the still uneven track and the swaying of the train, lunged his way back to his compartment. Almost there, from the corner of his eye he detected something vaguely familiar in the far corner of a third-class compartment. It was a check suit. He peeped through the glass.

Asleep, with his atrocious hat over his eyes, lounged James Cooney, Private Investigator, alias Barney Faircluff!

NINE

RHUBARB WINE

LITTLEJOHN and Cromwell called early at the Cobbold police station on the morning after their day of wandering about the country. In answer to their telephoned request from "The Mitre" hotel in Thorncastle, P.C. Pennyquick had made a quick sally to the local inn and there secured them fresh rooms. This having been eagerly done on an empty stomach, the constable was now enjoying a late breakfast. Confusion reigned in the other parts of the house, for it was washing-day. The constabulary laundry hung on lines in the back garden, clouds of steam billowed from the kitchen and vanished on the wind, and Mrs. Pennyquick could be heard handling wet linen and putting it through the wringing machine. She was singing.

> But my false lover stole the rose,
> And, Oh, he left the thorn with me …

The bobby shovelled cereal beneath his moustache and hoped she wasn't referring to him. Then the doorbell rang and he had to answer it, because his missus couldn't hear it on account of her domestic and musical activities.

"Oh, bother and blimey! Ma! MA!! DOOR!!!"

But, as we've said, she didn't hear him.

Pennyquick was a bit put out at this inopportune visit of his eminent collaborators. He kept saying that to himself by way of encouragement. Eminent collaborators.

"Good morning, gentlemen both," said the constable. He chewed furiously to get rid of his corn flakes and cleared his throat. "Excuse the mess we're in. Washin' day. Hu, hu. And I'm just havin' a late breakfast, having got up early to get your rooms, hu, hu. Come in please. Hu, hu, hu, hu."

There was no mirth, only terrible embarrassment in his laughter, and to add to it …

"Ready for the sossidges, love? Oh …"

Mrs. Pennyquick, carrying a plate of sausages and looking red from much wringing and boiling, ran in and then, seeing the visitors, ran out again with confused cries. Littlejohn followed her to the kitchen.

"Come along, Mrs. Pennyquick. It's only the pair of us. No need to worry."

"To think of it, sir. You callin' and all this mess."

"Work's to be done, Mrs. Pennyquick. Wish we could wash our linen as comfortably as you do. We're in a flat, you know, and all the washing goes out. Better done at home, isn't it?"

"Yes…."

But her heart wasn't in it. She was holding the plate of sausages and wondering how to get them in her husband's inside.

"Give him his breakfast, Mrs. Pennyquick," said Cromwell with his best smile. "A big chap like your husband can't last out on cereals...."

It all came out right and soon the bobby was listening to the adventures of the previous day. He wasn't enjoying his food too well, however. He had one secret sin. He loved, when alone, to drink with his mouth full. He liked to mix hot, sugared tea with his food. Now he had to behave.... He punctuated the stories with monosyllabic outcries to show he was interested, nay, enthusiastic about it all.

"Football team! Hu, hu, hu."

"Mayor's banquet.... A little bit tight.... Oughter be ashamed of yerself, if I may say so, hu, hu, hu."

"Alveston called 'imself Grigg did he? The dirty dog."

And so on. That was for Cromwell, who was, more or less, his equal in rank. For Littlejohn, he remained dutifully quiet, chewing busily and, as he forgot himself, washing down the sausages with his tea. From the room beyond, more mangling sounds....

Littlejohn showed the bobby the list compiled by Salter. Pennyquick propped it against the sugar basin and slowly and ruminantly read it, pausing in his chewing as the words framed themselves on his lips.

"That's a corker, sir," he said at length. "Looks to me as if Mr. Granville was after somethin'. I mean, either off to quiz these people about the treasure or ..."

"Or find out from them how far he was related to Miss Alveston," added Littlejohn.

"Ecksactly, sir."

Pennyquick stabbed the paper with a broad index.

"There's the parson, sir, and Tom Sly, the sexton, with 'Osegood, the warden. And all the old servants at the Hall. Flather's the district nurse. Devereaux was the butler, and Knapp was 'ousekeeper. Both dead. Stowell, Trotter and Meek; they was maids and Miss Fothergill's the old doctor's sister, who still lives here, though he's been dead for years and years. Aunt Margaret: that'll be Miss Margaret, livin' in London, married. And I see I'm in it, too. What did 'e want with me, I wonder …?"

"Did he ask you anything?"

"No. Except 'ow me and the family was gettin' on. Maybe he hadn't got as far as me when he died. He's got pore old Plucock here, too. Now I wonder …"

"Yes. So do I. I think I'd like to call on Plucock's widow, just to find out if Salter talked much with him. That might give us a lead on both deaths."

"Yes, sir. I'm ready when you are. Thank you for waitin'."

"All right, Pennyquick. Let's be off."

The bobby put on his helmet and woollen gloves. Then he opened the kitchen door and was enveloped in steam.

"I'm off, ma."

There was a suitable response from somewhere in the mist, and they went about their business. A borrowed police-car stood at the gate of the police-house and they all bundled themselves in. A tight squeeze for three big men. Cromwell let in the clutch. On their way they unloaded their bags at the "Royal Oak", where a number of habituals were already wetting their whistles. They all seemed suitably impressed, greeting the constable familiarly, just to show the newcomers they were well in.

Carstonwood lies where the marsh runs down to the river and consists of a number of old scattered cottages around the estuary, a church, a pub called "The Black Man", and a pumping-station which controls the complicated system of dykes draining the land.

"The sea!" said Cromwell, like a boy on holiday. And there it was, a long, leaden, dim line a mile or so downstream. Far away you could even see the smoke of coasters and a lighthouse built on piles.

"That's Carstonwood light. There's a lot of sandbanks out there, sir. The channel's called the Carston Deep...."

Pennyquick was displaying his local knowledge with the pride of a native.

"They get good cockles there. You should try 'em while yore here. I'll get the missus.... Turn left, sir. Then right. Police station's oppersite the church."

It was there. A bright, new brick cottage in a tidy railed garden, very different from the rest of the dwellings, which were whitewashed wattle-and-daub places, one-time thatched, by the look of it, now a little self-conscious in grey slate roofs.

A forlorn-looking woman was hanging out more washing on a line. Children's little underclothes and socks, for the most part. She turned as the car approached. A pale, buxom woman, who, in happy days might have had apple-red cheeks. Now she seemed torn with grief and still wore a dazed unbelieving look.

"Mornin', Mr. Pennyquick."

"Mornin', Mrs. Plucock. How are you?"

"Middlin'."

She bravely tilted her chin to face him.

"Children at school?"

"No. It's holidays. . . ."

"I forgot."

"They've just gone to their grandma's down the village. They get so mischievous and a bit in the way on washdays. They'll be back soon and bring my mother with them. She comes a lot now."

"Must be a comfort to you. . . ."

A man from Thorncastle cycled out on temporary duty until the Plucock family could find a house to move into. It was very awkward for them all.

"These are two officers from Scotland Yard, Mrs. Plucock. Down about the death of Mr. Granville. . . ."

"What about my man? Don't he matter?"

"Of course, Mrs. Plucock. Don't take on so. We're doing our best. . . ."

"I know you are.... But since my man went, I get so out of temper. You must excuse me...."

She invited them indoors and they entered the small parlour, stiff and formal with its suite of modern furniture and photographs of the family and innumerable relatives on the walls and sideboard. Over the fireplace, an enlarged snapshot in a frame showing a constable standing beside his bicycle. A tall, thin man, with a long face and aquiline nose. Pennyquick caught the eyes of his colleagues and jerked his head in the direction of the picture. They understood. Littlejohn didn't take a liking to Plucock somehow. He looked a bit too crafty....

Mrs. Plucock passed her apron over some chairs and they sat down, whilst she remained standing, her hands, reddened and furrowed with washing, hanging limp by her sides.

"Was there something ...?"

"Yes, Mrs. Plucock," began Littlejohn. "I'm so sorry to bother you and reap up the past, but I'd like to ask you a question or two which may help us in investigating the death of your husband."

"You're workin' for him as well?"

"Of course."

She sat on the edge of a chair near the door. Outside the washing flapped mournfully in the chill wind.

"What did you …?"

"Did Mr. Granville Salter come here to see your husband while he was in Cobbold recently, Mrs. Plucock?"

"Not that I'd know, sir. I didn't see him."

She replied in a monotone, as though totally dried of any emotion, even the power to weep.

It didn't look as if they were going to get far. Pennyquick coughed awkwardly and Cromwell looked blankly through the window at the neglected garden. Somewhere out at sea a ship hooted dismally.

"Before he met his death, Mrs. Plucock, did your husband say or do anything out of the ordinary?"

The woman hesitated and then, suddenly, something seemed to break within her. Her cheeks flushed and she found rapid words.

"I've been waitin' for that! Nobody asked me. You're the first to be interested in Fred. All the others came and looked busy and clever and said how sorry they was, but never a helpful thing did they ask. Not that I was fit to say anything. I don't know what I'm going to do.… And there's the children.…"

She started to weep, passionately and harshly. Pennyquick crossed to her and put a fatherly arm round her. She looked very young for such a blow.

"There, there, Liz. Don't take on so. We only came to 'elp."

"I know you did, Mr. Pennyquick. I'm sorry. But I've turned things over and over in the night when I couldn't sleep for thinkin' of 'im and the children. I'm glad the gentleman asked, because I want to tell somebody about it and there wasn't anybody.…"

"What did you want to tell, Liz?"

"He changed so...."

"Who did, Liz?"

"Fred. He was settled and happy in his job, though he did want to get on on account of the children. He got upset now and then when some of the men got promotion. Said it wasn't fair. But he soon got over it. But after it happened, he changed. Couldn't talk of anything but the better times soon comin' when we'd have all the money we wanted and leave the police for good. He seemed to get queer about money that was coming to him, and him as always told me everything, kept it all to himself."

"What happened, Liz? What do you mean?"

Pennyquick had taken over the case and it was best so. He'd known Liz since she was a girl cycling every day to school at Cobbold. He'd mended punctures for her....

"It was the vicar, Mr. Pennyquick."

"The vicar?"

"Yes, Mr. Worsnip. He called one night something about a little girl from Carstonwood village they was takin' in at Cobbold vicarage as maid. Wanted to know if she was good charactered. It all started as a joke and ..."

"A joke?"

"Yes, Mr. Pennyquick. Fred used to be a one for jokes, as you know. Sometimes, he carried them a bit too far. But there was no badness in 'im. He just didn't seem able to stop at the right time...."

"Did he play a joke on the vicar, Mrs. Plucock?"

Littlejohn looked up from filling his pipe and asked the question.

"Yes, sir. He gave 'im too much of my rhubarb wine."

"Rhubarb wine, Liz?"

"Yes. I make a lot of it, and with keepin' it gets very heady, Mr. Pennyquick. Well, the night the Rev. Worsnip came, late autumn it was, was very chill and damp, so I asked 'im would 'e like a cup of tea. No, thanks, he says, not to trouble, he wasn't stopping. Then, Fred ups and says will he have a glass of rhubarb wine? And he looks at me, winks and puts his finger on his lips. Well, a wineglassful is enough at a time, but Fred, full of 'is joke, fills a tumbler."

"Good 'eavens, and Mr. Worsnip a strict abstainer!"

"Yes. The funny thing about that wine is, you can drink quite a lot of it sittin' down indoors, but come to get on your feet and the air at you outdoors, it takes your legs proper. Mr. Worsnip drunk the lot and smacked 'is lips and said it was good. 'ome made, says Fred, and wouldn't hurt a baby. Mr. Worsnip says he'll 'ave another glass. I said it wouldn't do, but Fred was at it good and proper and shushes me, givin' the reverend what he asked for,"

"And 'e got drunk?"

"It was all right till he tried to get up. He stood there, such a silly look on his face, and staggered to the door, talkin' to himself and laughing soft like.

And when he opened the door and the fresh air tuck 'im, his legs just went. Fred said he'd see Mr. Worsnip safe 'ome. As he was, he'd never get there 'imself. And there was the reverend, sayin' he was quite fine and me wanting 'im to stay a bit and sober up and have a cup o' tea to clear 'is head and the reverend insistin' he could manage himself. It ended by Fred goin' off with him. Three-mile walk it was, too, and how they did it, I don't know. But that started Fred with his ideas. Whether the vicar told 'im somethin', or whether he come across somethin' on the way home, I don't know. But that night brought trouble to us all. It changed Fred from a 'appy man to a secretive one with queer ways and ideas."

"And have you no idea what it was all about, Mrs. Plucock?"

"No, sir. I thought to go and see the vicar and ask, but I've no time now. And I'm that worried about the children. What's going to 'appen to us all, I don't know."

"Don't you worry and take on, Liz. You got friends, my dear, we'll look after you if nobody else does."

"How did your husband behave, for example, Mrs. Plucock? Did he go anywhere or do anything unusual?"

"He spent little time at home after that. He did used to do a bit in the garden now and then, or take out his gun and shoot us somethin' on the marsh at times, or take out the dog for a stroll. But that all stopped. He said 'e was busy with his duties...."

"Did he do anything indoors? I mean, writing or anything?"

"Yes, sir. He wrote things down in a little penny exercise book. I 'ave it here, but it doesn't make sense."

She opened the top drawer of the sideboard and produced the note-book, a dog-eared, grubby object, and passed it to Littlejohn.

On the first page was a jingle, written out in Plucock's childish, round hand. Littlejohn read it aloud.

Salter Treasure
Coward, let be.
Brave man,
Symbols three.
Hosegood's secret;
He'll never speak,
But you, avenger,
Further seek.
Take up eleven,
Eleven to three,
Headless Jesuit,
Aid thee.

The rest was sheer madness. Poor Plucock had evidently thought the doggerel held a cryptic message and had over many pages broken it up, tested it with keys of various kinds, writing out every two, three, four and five words, juggling the letters in endless combinations and permutations and then, angry, heavily scoring out his efforts and beginning again.

"Where did he get all this, Mrs. Plucock? Do you know?"

"I don't, sir. I think it's a curse that brought him to his death. He used to sit up long after we'd gone to bed and then I'd be awake when he come up, but he took no heed of me, talking to himself and pondering, awake far in the night."

"Poor Fred...."

"May I take this, please? I must see the vicar about it. Maybe, he gave this rhyme to your husband...."

Littlejohn flicked over the rest of the pages. Several were blank, then a list of names. The same, though not as many as Mr. Granville's. The servants,

Hosegood, the vicar, Alveston and, at the end of it, a family tree.

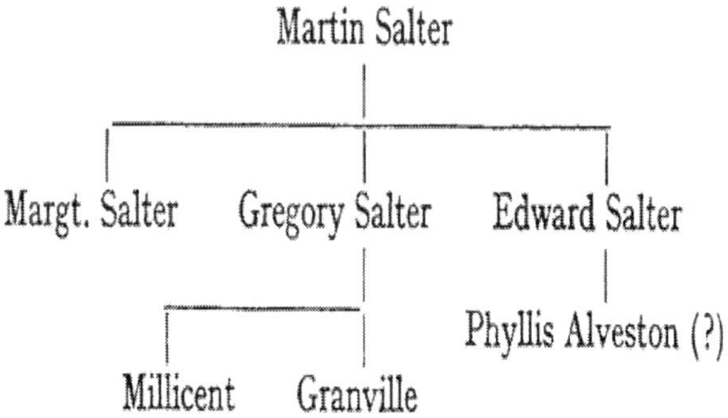

"Why, this thing gives Phyllis Alveston as the child of one Edward Salter, Pennyquick!"

"Rubbish, sir. Why, Mr. Edward was a cripple. All the same, that wouldn't … Still, where's the proof and where did Fred Plucock get that? It's no proof. He might 'ave made it up himself."

"We'd better see the vicar. This is too deep for us. Which of these people is still alive?"

"Margaret only. As I said, married and in London. Edward killed 'imself. Millicent went to America and was torpedoed comin' home in this last war."

On the blue inside cover of the exercise book the dead policeman had drawn a plan, a rough one, of some house or other.

"Recognize this, Pennyquick?" asked Littlejohn.

The constable took a mere glance.

"It's Salter 'All, sir. No doubt about that. See, that's the main door—staircase—gallery—first floor—servants' floor.... Yes, it's the 'All all right."

"So, poor Plucock was yet another victim of the Headless Jesuit tale ...?"

The woman uttered an alarmed cry, half scream, half moan.

"Oh, no, no, no. So that's what poor Fred was after. The Salter Treasure. That's it. He said no more slavin' for me, and good times for the children. What could 'e hope for there? Why, it wouldn't have been 'is, if he'd found it. Curse the Salters.... Curse them all.... They took my Fred...."

"There, there, Liz. Don't take on so. Fred didn't do anythin' wrong. Knowin' Fred, I'm sure he met his death in the course o' duty. He was tryin' to find the treasure so's he could hand it over and get promotion for smart work. That's what it was. I see it all now."

Poor Pennyquick was perspiring heavily in his frantic efforts to comfort his dead comrade's wife and vindicate him.

"Do you think that's what it is, Mr. Pennyquick?"

"Of course I do, Liz. And I shall report on same to the heads in Thorncastle."

In a pathetic gesture to be convincing, Pennyquick took out his black official note-book and started to scribble things in it.

> "P.C. Plucock, invetigiating Salter tressure. Probably murdered in coarse of duty."

In his emotion he forgot how to spell, although normally he was unusually literate, having, to the best of his ability, kept track of his daughters' homework for the High School.

"And do you two gentlemen think the same, sirs?"

"Your husband had the reputation for being a very good officer and of good character. No doubt what Mr. Pennyquick says is quite true, Mrs. Plucock."

Cromwell sagely nodded assent.

The woman fastened on to the theory like someone drowning catching at a lifebuoy. She smiled and tears ran down her cheeks.

"I'm glad it's all cleared up...."

The three policemen looked sadly at each other, wishing it were as easy as that.

"Now I can tell the children their father died bravely, doing his duty. Wore himself out in it, he did, and was killed by those he was on the track of...."

The scene was interrupted by the entrance of a little stout old lady, dressed all in black, gloves, stockings and hat as well. She would have resembled a large cockroach but for her face, a fine, stern old face, with shrivelled apple cheeks and a strong Roman nose. Shyly bringing up the rear were four small children; three, five, seven and nine. They had evidently been enjoying themselves somewhere, for, in spite of their sudden silence, their eyes shone with the pleasure of bringing their grandmother home.

Grandma halted on the mat, carefully placed her umbrella in the corner, and turned an angry face on the three men.

"And what, might I ask, Andrew Pennyquick, is the meanin' o' this? Comin' here upsettin' my Liz, as if she hadn't enough …"

"It's all right, mother. They've just come to talk about Fred. It seems he was killed doin' his duty. Thieves was after the Salter Treasure, and Fred …"

"Tell me later. Not in front of the children. I'm surprised at you, Lizzie. You was brought up better than that. Is this true, Andrew Pennyquick?"

"Yes, Mrs. Hearty."

“Very well, then. I’ll overlook it, though you shouldn’t have upset ’er. All the same, I’m glad you made her cry. Hasn’t had a cry since … Nothin’ like a good cry for easin’ the ’eart o’ grief.… Well, what are you standin’ there for?”

P.C. Pennyquick eyed the old dame with great respect.

“I jest wanted to say, as well, that these two gentlemen ’ave come from Scotland Yard to ’elp us find out about who … well … you know what.…”

He eyed the silent children, now timidly clinging to the old lady’s skirts.

“From where?”

“Scotland Yard, Mrs. Hearty.”

“Never ’eard of it! And what’s gone wrong with you, Andrew Pennyquick, as you need to bring in foreigners from Scotland to do your work for you? Enough to make my poor ’usband turn in his grave.…”

Pennyquick hastily led away his nonplussed collaborators, stopping at the door of the car to explain that the late Sergeant Hearty had, long ago, before his own time, been the Law in the two parishes of Cobbold and Carstonwood and that his widow carried on his good work.

TEN

TWELVE-NOTE SCALE

Miss Madeline Fothergill, sister of the one-time village doctor, lived in a modernized country cottage midway between Cobbold and Carstonwood, and Littlejohn left his colleagues there. The bobby had some routine work to do and Cromwell had in mind getting their belongings settled in at the "Royal Oak" and maybe, over a drink or two, gathering a bit more local gossip about the characters in whom he and Littlejohn were interested.

"See you later...."

The helmet and the bowler hat vanished in the distance.

The old lady's cottage was a pretty one, surrounded by a six-foot hedge of hawthorn and fuchsia. You entered by a gate in a gap carved out of a solid mass of leaves and branches. There was no doubt about who lived there. Instead of calling it after some scene of sentimental recollection or a vulgar suburban joke of a name, the owner had come straight to the point and labelled it *Fothergills.* Littlejohn opened the gate and entered. He made his way through little neat lawns and empty flower-beds, turned over and ready for their spring decorations, following a narrow track to the front door.

Inside, somebody sounded to be tuning the piano. Thin, stringy, confused notes, with no air, yet bearing a strange coherence which fascinated you. A maid opened the door in answer to his ring. The piano-tuning sounded to be going on more furiously than ever.

The girl took his card and bade him sit down. This he had to do on a chair in the hall, for the cottage seemed only to have one large living-room, where the thin twanging was going on, and a kitchen.

"Got the piano-tuner in?" asked Littlejohn, trying to be friendly.

The maid gave him a scorching, pitying look and vanished into the living-room, leaving him sitting there, like Dr. Johnson ingloriously waiting on his patron. The music stopped and the girl returned.

"Miss Fothergill will see you now," she said haughtily. Apparently something he'd said or done had filled her with contempt for him, in spite of his card and the name of Scotland Yard, about which, like the terrible Mrs. Hearty, she'd probably never heard. The girl soon put him right. Before opening the door to admit him to the holy of holies, she whispered to him in tones of reproof.

"That was not the tuner. It was Miss Fothergill playing. She's one of the most famous players of the twelve-note scale in the country. So there!" And she flounced off into the hidden regions behind a curtained door at the other side of the hall.

There was nothing of the lavender lady about Miss Fothergill. She was like the name on the gate. Straight and to the point. Tall, well set-up and heavy, she had a strikingly handsome face, bonneted by a close-cut cap of silky grey hair. She didn't look her age by any means.

She was sitting at the open piano, a fine grand which fitted handsomely in the large, well-lighted room. The place was in comfortable disorder; polished floor with large Indian mats, antique black-oak furniture, good pictures on the walls mixed with one or two charcoal drawings, one of herself, and other odds and ends. Over the large brick fireplace a portrait of what must have been her late brother. His features were remarkably like her own, kindly and benevolent, with a small, grey moustache and humorous blue eyes.

Miss Fothergill was smoking a cigarette. It hung from the corner of her mouth, man-like, and she coughed now and then as the smoke caught her. She rose, Littlejohn's card in her fingers, and shook him by the hand.

"Not often we have Scotland Yard down here. What do you want, Inspector?"

"I'm here about the village murders; young Salter and P.C. Plucock."

"Sit down. Have a cigarette, will you? Yes, of course, light your pipe. Nice to have pipe smoke about again. My brother always smoked a pipe. Well … and where do I come in?"

"Strangely enough, Miss Fothergill, both the murdered men seemed somehow bent on a quest. Something to do with the Salter Treasure, we believe…."

"What! That poppycock! I'm surprised at intelligent men wasting time on that old legend. It's been defunct for a century or more. I can assure you, if there'd been any treasure at the Hall, the greedy money-hunters would have found it. Short of pulling it down stone by stone, all the Salters, all the antiquaries, and all the dotty folk of this district have been after it at one time or another. I thought they'd tired of the nonsense. My brother knew all about the story and, I think, all about those who went after the treasure. Believe me, it's just tomfoolery...."

"Yes, madam. That's as may be...."

"By the way, Inspector, please don't *madam* me. In the first place, I'm a spinster and in the second this isn't a *modiste's* shop. I hate the term.... Just plain Miss Fothergill or nothing at all, if you don't mind."

"Sorry, Miss Fothergill. It's this way. Both Mr. Granville and Plucock left papers behind which apparently had some bearing on this treasure hunt. Your name appeared in a list of persons who they either thought knew something of what they were after or whom they proposed to interview...."

"They did call to see me, both of 'em."

"They did?"

"Yes. I think the reason I was included in the list would be that my brother was, for nearly forty years, medical attendant at the Hall and also a member, a prominent member, of the local antiquarian society. In roundabout ways, both Plucock and young Salter asked me if they might look at my brother's papers. I said no, and that was that."

"Do you mind telling me exactly what happened, Miss Fothergill?"

"Not at all. By the way, it's noon and my coffee time. Care to join me? I don't take lunch."

The haughty maid served the coffee and, finding Littlejohn getting on very well with her mistress, thawed and smiled upon him graciously. Outside, an elderly gardener, with white mutton-chop whiskers, a crafty face and a battered old felt hat, began hammering nails in an empty beehive. Miss Fothergill opened the window.

"Go away and work at the back, please, Sly. We can't hear ourselves speak. Take it to the shed and do it there...."

"Very good, Miss Madeline...."

He shouldered the hive with an ease which belied his age and shambled off.

"Is that Tom Sly?"

"Yes. Why?"

"He's on the list, too."

"Significant. He's the local gravedigger. Where were we?"

"Your brother's papers...."

"Oh, yes. My brother spent such spare time as he had in his later years compiling a history of the Salter family and the Hall. He was intimate with them when they lived there and, as an antiquary, was in a good position to make a scientific job of it. He'd collected a mass of facts and was half-way through the book when he died. One night, just after dinner, he was starting to do some of it, when he just dropped down dead. I've never got over it."

That was apparent. She spoke of her brother in every other sentence. The bond between them must have been fond and firm.

"First came Mr. Granville. He'd heard of my brother's researches and would like, if I'd let him, to have a look at the papers. And, did my brother, by any chance, keep a diary? As a matter of fact, he did. He was a great diarist, but I wasn't going to lend anyone the record of his most intimate thoughts, even though they *were* mixed up with Salter history. I haven't even read them myself."

"Did Mr. Granville deliberately ask for the diary?"

"As a matter of fact, he gave me the impression of being keener on the diary than on the family records. I wasn't letting him have either. I intend to finish my brother's book one day. Then, whoever wants may read it. Unfortunately, Mr. Granville won't be one of them."

"No. The diary business is most interesting, though. Have you any idea why he wanted it? Did he say?"

"No. I'm afraid I was a bit abrupt and didn't even ask. Granville was a nice boy. Big pity. But there are limits to what one can do for people, and this was one."

"What excuse did Granville make for calling, Miss Fothergill?"

"He said he was putting together a family tree and records. That seemed very thin to me, because they've already been very well put together by the local antiquarian society, chiefly by Mr. Qualtrough and Mr. Polydore. They did separate books, too, because they're so jealous of each other. They can't agree and, instead of collaborating and making one fine work, the silly little men worked separately. Mr. Polydore's is by far the better of the two."

"And Granville was having a go as well?"

"No, of course not. He'd some other motive which he didn't disclose. But I knew...."

"You didn't know the motive, though?"

"No."

"I think maybe I can tell you, though in strictest confidence."

"Of course."

Upstairs, the maid was busy turning out the bedrooms. It was certainly a delightful house. Wattle-and-daub, like the rest of the local places, with a thatched roof, as well, only the thatch was new and golden, apparently renewed in the autumn after harvest, when the thatchers had time. The old stone floors had been replaced by wooden ones and broad new windows had been let in the walls in place of the old narrow sashes. Littlejohn wished Letty, his wife, had been there to see it all and meet the owner.

"Well ... I think Granville was in love with Phyllis Alveston."

"Everybody knows that. Why bring that in, Inspector?"

"But, rumour has it that Phyllis was a Salter, born on the wrong side of the blanket. If that is so, she's related to Granville, or rather, was. How nearly related, seems to have been his problem. Mrs. Alveston wouldn't say a word about it. We've discovered that Granville tried hard to make her say and then asked if he could marry Phyllis. The old lady was horrified at the thought. So, young Salter set out to find out for himself. He didn't get very far, I gather, but … and this is where your brother's records come in … he was proposing to question all who might have been about at the time Phyllis was born. Your brother must certainly have been at the confinement…."

"Why? He did attend to the accouchements at the Hall, but if this was an illicit affair … well … All the same, if the family were concerned, I'm sure he'd be called in. They trusted him as one of themselves. That's why … another reason why … if he mentioned the affair in his day-book or diary, it should not be allowed to come to light. I couldn't agree to any searching of his private and professional documents. He wouldn't have wished that."

"Mr. Granville, then, drew a blank with you?"

"He did. And so did Plucock."

"You had Plucock around as well, then?"

"Yes. He called about another thing. He said the vicar had told him to see me about my brother's researches. This time it was another bit of local nonsense. The Headless Jesuit. Maybe, you know all about it. It's common property."

"Yes. But please tell me your own version."

"I've heard my brother talk a lot about it. He used to say there was no foundation in fact for the legend of the priest who was beheaded by Cromwell's men and is said to haunt the place. But, quite definitely, Simister Salter, the worst of the family, a terrible man who was lord of the manor in, I think, the Regency times, used it in a sort of rhyming puzzle to give a clue to something he'd done or hidden at the Hall. That started the hunt for the Treasure again."

"Do you know the rhyming puzzle, Miss Fothergill?"

"I did; but I've forgotten it. A silly thing, not worth recollecting."

"How's this:

Salter Treasure,

Coward, let be …"

"That's it. Where did you get it?"

"Among Plucock's papers. What did he want of you?"

"He said something about hiding-places in the Hall. They'd reason to believe somebody wanted by the police was hiding there. Had I, among my brother's records, any details of the priests' holes and other retreats? It seemed he'd asked the vicar, another old Salter family friend and antiquary, about it and he'd told him my brother had been the expert on such things and maybe I'd be able to help. I sent Plucock packing. Those papers are sacred things to me and not for anyone's idle curiosity."

"But surely … the police …"

"Police, my foot. Plucock's tale didn't ring true. It was all made up. I knew it from the poor way he told it and improvised when I questioned him. No; Plucock was another of the victims of the Treasure Hunt bug."

"So that was the end of that?"

"Except that one night someone broke in and rifled the bureau and my brother's old writing-desk. They didn't get anything, though. I woke and came down and they bolted. They scattered papers about and left untouched a cash-box with a few pounds in it which I kept about. I'd put my brother's papers in a deed box at the bank when I went to London in the autumn and hadn't brought them back. So the intruders got nothing much."

"You talk as if you suspect the robbery was for that, then."

"I do. If not, why leave the money? I don't say it was Granville, or Plucock, though it's hard not to suspect one or the other. The police came from Thorncastle and played around a bit. No fingerprints or clues. They were puzzled, too, because, had it been a tramp, he surely wouldn't have worn gloves. I didn't tell them my suspicions. Don't really know why I'm telling you. But I can talk comfortably to you. That must be it."

"Thank you, Miss Fothergill. And now, will you kindly do something for me?"

"If I can and it's not too outrageous."

"I'm not going to ask you to let me see your brother's diary or papers, but could you possibly look through them all yourself and see if there's anything there which will help?"

"Such as …?"

"Will you make a list of the births in the family recorded over the past, say, fifty years, and any fuller details of them? And will you also copy any references to the Headless Jesuit you might find there?"

"Quite a big job you're giving me. But not quite so big as it might have been. The papers are in scrupulous order, and to go through them, and the diaries, will give me the greatest pleasure. My brother was very dear to me and it will be as though he were back again, speaking with me. Yes, I'll do it."

"I'm very grateful, Miss Fothergill. Would you care to ring me up or send a note to the 'Royal Oak', where we're staying, if you should find anything useful?"

"Certainly."

"By the way, there's another matter you might help with, too, if you can, Miss Fothergill. You must have known the servants at the Hall over the past thirty years or so...."

"Yes. I was a frequent visitor there with my brother, and sometimes alone. Why?"

Littlejohn produced Salter's list again.

"This is Granville's list of people in whom he was interested, presumably in his search for information. Can you tell me what happened to the servants?"

"Yes, more or less. There's Devereaux, the butler. He died in service and is buried in the village. Mrs.

Knapp, the housekeeper, retired to a cottage here. She was a soldier's widow with one child. Knapp … I mean Mrs. Knapp, died many years ago. Her daughter married and still lives here in her mother's old cottage. A plaintive, queer little thing who lost her husband in the war. No children and she lives alone and kept a little toffee shop in the house. Rationing bothered her a lot, and it seemed to drive her off her head. She locked and bolted the door recently and never opened up again. They say she keeps a large stock with which she won't part. Poor thing…."

"Not much use to us, then."

"I don't know. She's always been very nice to me. Maybe I could help if you need me. Just let me know."

"Thank you. Flather?"

"Mrs. Flather was District Nurse until not long ago when she retired. Held the job for untold years. Never heard of or saw Flather. Maybe he ran away on the honeymoon, because she's a tartar. Or maybe there never was a Flather. Reason Granville put her down may have been about the birth business. Perhaps thought she attended. But the ladies at the Hall probably wouldn't have had her about. They had nurses from Thorncastle."

"And the unholy three, there … Stowell, Trotter and Meek?"

"Oh, those! I remember them. Yes, maybe they were there at the time Granville's concerned about. Stowell went away for a better job in London. I gave her a second reference. Trotter … well, she just drifted off somewhere, probably a better job, too. Meek got herself in the family way with somebody or other. She had to leave, but the fellow married her. They went off some place or other. I'd say from your point of view, Inspector, they were no-accounts."

"Many thanks, Miss Fothergill. In the jingle we were mentioning, there's a Hosegood. Now Mr.

Granville also has that name down. Could you throw any light on it?"

"Hosegoods have lived in the village ever since it was a village. The present head of the family is a churchwarden and a poor, mean sort of fish. Ben Hosegood's a tailor and doing badly. I seem to recollect a Hosegood being found dead in the grounds by Simister Salter and getting mixed up in the legends."

"That is so."

"Maybe, Granville was interested in him. Why?"

"I can't say. That's part of the mystery."

"What do you make of it all, Inspector?"

"It seems to me Granville was hunting for Phyllis Alveston's real history and, as a sideline, some clue as to the truth or not of the Treasure story. In the course of his inquiries he crossed the trail of others bent on the same game. Where Plucock comes in, I can't say, but he couldn't have murdered Granville; he was dead already. There are others at large and I hope to unravel this tangle sooner or later and find them. . . .”

“I hope you do. I’ll try my best to help.”

A car could be heard drawing up at the gate and the anxious face of Cromwell next appeared, mixed up with the thick thorn hedge. With unwonted speed he rushed up the path and rang the bell. The maid came and went and came again and then brought Littlejohn to the door to consult his colleague.

“Could you come over to the Hall, sir? Pennyquick just came back to the ‘Royal Oak’ to say there’s been another murder. At the Hall, this time.”

“Right. I’ll just say good-bye to Miss Fothergill. . . .”

Pennyquick was waiting agitatedly in the car.

“This is the limit, sir! Three of ’em on our ’ands now. The village’ll be in an uproar when it gets round. It’s not safe to go out.”

“What’s it all about?”

“The lodgekeeper phoned down to say he found another body—in the Hall, this time. He went over mid-mornin' to have a look round and found the fellow at the foot of the stairs with a broken neck. He wasn't there last night, because the lodge-keeper says he looked all over the place before he turned in after dark."

It was Littlejohn's first visit to the Hall. The great gates, with rampant lions rearing from the tops of their stone posts, stood open and, standing by, a short, stocky man in corduroy trousers and old jacket. They picked him up but he remained silent, apparently stunned by what he had found.

There was a fine elm drive to the Hall, which came suddenly in view standing on a slight eminence with large neglected lawns about it. It was composed chiefly of wood and plaster, a basement of stone holding a strong framework of timber connected by horizontal beams. A gracious manor-house, free from all pretentions and now looking empty and forlorn.

But Littlejohn and his party had no time to admire either the house itself or the remarkable interior. They parked the car and hurried inside to the foot of the main staircase, a great oak structure rising in gentle steps to a gallery round the main hall. At the foot lay the body, just as the caretaker had left it. It was twisted, face downwards, arms and legs sprawling, splayed-out. The back of the head was smashed in by a terrible blow. The corpse was cold and stiff with every appearance of having lain there all night. Probably the crime had been committed not long after the lodge-keeper had locked up and departed.

Pennyquick waited respectfully, watching Littlejohn almost reverently, expecting now to learn exactly how the great ones from Scotland Yard behaved at the very beginning of a crime. Littlejohn stood with his hands in the pockets of his overcoat and his hat thrust back on his head. He didn't seem in the least anxious to turn over the body and see whose it was. Pennyquick felt a bit disappointed.

"Aren't we going to turn 'im over and see who 'e is?" he ventured at length. "Can't say I recognize 'im, as he is, and I think myself he's a stranger...."

"I know him. Saw him yesterday in London," said Littlejohn.

There was no mistaking that suit; it looked fresh from the racecourse!

Littlejohn gently turned over the body and confirmed what he already knew.

It was James Cooney, Investigator, alias, Barney Faircluff, gaolbird.

ELEVEN

THE THIRD VICTIM

THE inquest on Barney Faircluff went off quietly. The police saw to that. But the Coroner, Mr. Lancelot Qualtrough and his clerk, Whatmough, were obviously excited. They knew that Barney, under an assumed name and calling himself a professional investigator, was a crook and was after the Treasure.

"If the craze spreads, someone will be finding the Salter gold, and then we shall have a Crowner's Quest," remarked Mr. Qualtrough gleefully.

"If we don't find it first," added Mr. Whatmough, *sotto voce.*

"What?" asked his master. But there was no reply.

The inquest was adjourned, naturally, but was graced by the appearance of a strange character who looked as though a wash wouldn't come amiss and who bit his nails to the quick. This was Herbert Moss, Barney's clerk and factotum, who, in the absence of other relatives and friends, came to identify the body. He wore a shabby navy-blue suit and a black tie to chime with the occasion and gave his bit of evidence with a practised hand. He it was, in Barney's divorce business, who snooped round doors, keyholes, lighted windows and hotel bedrooms. He was small, fat, and his bloated countenance spoke of titbits of information gathered over pints of beer at bars.

"Don't know what 'e was doin' rahnd 'ere," he said with an exaggerated expression of innocence, when questioned by Littlejohn.

"Come on," chimed in Cromwell. "Don't give us that."

"I don't know. And don't you bully me. I've been a lawyer's clerk, so don't try it on...."

"When?"

"Never you mind. Mr. Cooney dealt wiv this case himself, see?"

"You don't say."

"Yes. Some bloke got 'im checkin' up on a bloke as once lived rahnd 'ere. He must 'ave come across sometin. Set 'im all of a dither. Didn't tell me nothink...."

Littlejohn had turned out the contents of Barney's pockets. He passed a snapshot over to Mr. Moss. It showed Barney wearing a paper cap walking along the promenade of some seaside resort with a girl got up to kill. She also wore similar headgear with the addition of a label on the front of it: "Kiss Me." Mr. Faircluff looked as though he'd already done that several times. They were thoroughly enjoying themselves and had been snapped by a tout.

"Know who that is, Mr. Moss?" said Littlejohn, pointing to the girl.

"Never seen her in my life...."

"Well, well.... I have. Her name's Deborah James and she lives in a flat below the man who hired your boss to trace the bloke as once lived rahnd 'ere, as you call him."

"Nothin' to do wiv me. I was 'is clerk; knew nothin' of his private life."

"Ever seen that before?"

Mr. Moss took the paper in his nail-bitten fingers.

"Poetry," he said and looked nauseated. "Nothin' in the boss's line ... or mine."

"I'll bet it wasn't, but it was in Mr. Cooney's pocketbook. Ever seen it lying about at the office?"

"Nah.... Wot's it orl abaht?"

"We'd like to know that."

The sheet contained in the writing of Granville Salter the same old rhyme:

  Salter Treasure,
Coward, let be.
Brave man,

Symbols three....

With it was a plan of the Salter house. On sheets of paper, both Salter and Barney had been trying their hands at solving the enigma. There was no indication as to how far they'd got.

They let Herbert Moss return to London after he'd claimed his expenses and quarrelled fiercely about them. Cromwell travelled on the same train, but not in Herbert's company.

Ex-Company-Sergeant-Major Bedford was still in his chair, running the flats by remote control, when Cromwell called upon him.

"Miss James at home?" he asked after making himself known.

"Yes."

"How do you know?"

"Tell 'em by their footsteps on the stairs. She's come in and not gone out again."

"You certainly have mastered the art...."

"What's that?"

"Oh, nothing. Mr. Salter's flat still vacant?"

"Yes. 'E paid the rent to month-end. Besides, the police …"

"Of course. We were forgetting the police, weren't we?"

A cat, as large and lazy as his master, sprang down from a great height on the sideboard shelf and started to rub round Cromwell's trousers.

"Get away, cat!"

Cromwell isn't fond of cats and knew of its presence as soon as he entered the room. The creature took a flying leap back on the sideboard and fell asleep.

"Ever go up to Mr. Salter's room, Bedford?"

"Of course. Got to see that all's right now and then. I got a pass-key. Any objections?"

"No. Ever let any deputies go in to see that all's right now and then?"

"Waddyer mean?"

Mr. Bedford was getting rattled. At the back of his mind he sensed that someone was trying to disturb his peace and he resented it.

"I mean, to save your legs, do you ask any of the other lodgers to take a peek in and see that all's right now and then?"

"What you gettin' at? Look 'ere …"

"You look here yourself. This is a murder case, so no messing about. Did you or did you not lend Miss James your key to get in Mr. Salter's rooms?"

"The window was open and it looked like rain. She said …"

"She said she'd do it for you. She even suggested it looked like rain and the window was open, didn't she?"

"Well … nothin' wrong in that. My old leg wounds bother me, and them stairs …"

Whereupon Mr. Bedford rose and took a turn round the room to show how much he limped and how bad he was on his legs.

"Of course. That's all I wanted to know. Now I'll pay Miss James a visit, if you don't mind."

"I don't mind a bit. Do it and welcome. And if there's any bother, don't forget, I let her do it because me legs are bad."

"I won't forget. While I'm up, are there any other rooms you'd like me to see to for you?"

"'Ere, you! I'll report you, I got me friends, see?"

"All right, all right. Don't get rattled. I'm not going to spoil your nice, cushy job."

"Better not. I got good friends as'll …"

But Cromwell was knocking at Deborah James's door.

There were noises of shuffling about inside. A wireless set was playing a soft sentimental song. Someone switched it off. A thick voice called out:

"Who is it?"

"Police."

The shuffling turned to a wild scrimmage.

"Wait a minute."

Deborah James opened the door. She was wearing the same dress as when Littlejohn had talked with her. A worn wrapper covering very little else in the way of clothes, her legs were bare and she had shabby mules on her feet. She had been weeping and her face was red, swollen and bedraggled.

"Come in," she said to Cromwell. "I've been expecting you."

"Why?"

"I saw it in the paper that Barney'd been killed. I guessed sooner or later you'd be here."

"What was Barney to you?"

Cromwell looked round the room. It combined living and sleeping quarters and there seemed to be a small scullery through a door at the far end. The divan bed hadn't been made, there were articles of clothing and newspapers littered all over the shop. A portable wireless-set on the hearthrug and a cheap gramophone tucked in one corner with records scattered round it. A bottle of gin and a glass, too.

Deborah had been drinking, playing sentimental tunes and, in this fashion, weeping and mourning for Barney.

"A friend of mine," she replied in answer to Cromwell's question. Then, for no reason whatever, she seemed to get annoyed.

"I know what you're thinking. You know the sort I am and how I earn my living. But it wasn't that way with me and Barney, see? I know enough about men never to want to see another. But not Barney. He was different.... He was me chum...."

Cromwell showed her the snapshot taken at the seaside. She began to cry again.

"Yes.... Best friend I ever had." She was almost bawling between her tears. "That was just after I met him. We got together on the boat, going for a daytrip to Margate. We'd have been married by now, only Barney had a wife somewhere. She was no good to him. He give me back my self-respect. Made me feel I was a woman again, instead of what others used to think me, judging from the looks they gave me. Now, it's all over. I was just thinkin' of the gas-oven when you came in."

"Don't be silly," said Cromwell. It seemed all he could say. He was just pondering on the strangeness of life. Here was a woman whose self-respect had been restored by a jail-bird, a cheap racing tipster, a shady blackmailing snooper.... And now he'd gone too far and got himself murdered for his pains and left her worse than she was before he found her.

"I don't know what I'm going to do now. He paid for all this, you see. I've been ill and he looked after me. Came every day, he did. Even cleaned up the room and bought me a gramophone. I was just playing the tunes he liked best when you got here. 'Red Sails in the Sunset', 'Waggon Wheels' and 'Pistol-Packin' Momma'...."

And she started bawling again like a lost child.

"So you're on our side?" asked Cromwell.

She stopped her noise and looked at him queerly through her tears.

"What you mean?"

"I mean Barney was murdered and you want us to find out who did it. . . ."

"You bet your life. I'm with you there. Like hell I am."

She had changed from howling to roaring now, like a wounded tigress.

". . . But don't expect me to say anythin' about Barney. He was my pal. I won't have him harmed."

"Of course not. Past harm now, isn't he? Now I want to know what lead up to his going to Cobbold—that's where he was killed—up to Cobbold and meeting trouble. Any ideas?"

"It all started with the fellow upstairs. The one who got killed, too. Salter, he was called."

"What about him?"

"I was a bit neighbourly with Mr. Salter. Quite a gentleman, he was, who'd a bit of money of his own, if you ask me. I used to go up now and then to borrow a drop of milk or, maybe, a bob for the gasmeter."

"I'm listening."

"Well, one day I went up and there he was with the whole place spread about with books and papers and him puzzling over them like somebody solving a crossword puzzle. I asks him what he's at. At first, he didn't want to say. But he was always a lonely chap and, when all's said and done, one has to talk to somebody. He opened out a bit to me."

"What did he tell you?"

"It seems he was in love with a girl at the place you mentioned … what was it called …? I forget."

"Cobbold?"

"That's it. Known her from being kids. But there was a snag to it. She was related to him. How near he didn't know. He wanted to find out. Her mother was a queer one, it seems, and wouldn't tell him. All she said was it couldn't be. He'd have run away with the girl, he said, and risked it, but her mother was sick and she'd nobody else. The girl wouldn't. He said her father had disappeared. All this came out last autumn. He hadn't asked the girl to marry him since then, and when he did and her mother knew, she had a fit. Mr. Salter was workin' to trace if she was really a relative or not."

"It's a funny business to me. Surely, someone else would know."

"That was just it. The secret, if she *was* his relation, was so well kept he didn't know where to start. That's where Barney came in."

"What do you mean?"

"I told Mr. Salter about him. He'd started as a private detective after … after …"

"After he came out?"

"Yes, seeing that you know. He'd been jugged, but said he'd make a clean start.… However, forget it.… Like a drink?"

"No, thanks, get on with what you were saying and drink after."

"I told him about Barney and said maybe he could trace the girl's father. So Mr. Salter set him on it. He told me he'd come to a dead end. Meantime, Mr. Salter had drawn up a list of people who might know somethin' and went off to Cobbold. He got killed."

"I see. What took Barney up to Cobbold after his death?"

"I don't know. . . ."

"Come on, now. That's not all. What did you take from Salter's room after he'd gone? And give to Barney? What about the Headless Jesuit and the Salter Treasure . . .?"

The girl got up and took a drink . . . a good one.

"No stalling. I want to know."

"You seem to know all about it."

"You hunted through Salter's papers with Barney and took out some of them, didn't you, and Barney got killed trying to find out more about them?"

"I may as well tell you the rest. Though you won't think any the worse of Barney for it, will you? I'll take what's comin' to me.... But Barney ..."

The drink was working and tears were again in the offing.

"Well ... Barney told Mr. Salter he'd come up against a stone wall. Mr. Salter said, like as not, the girl's father might have gone back to Cobbold to squeeze his wife. Maybe, he said, he was somewhere in the Hall. There were plenty of secret places to hide in and make yourself comfortable in. With that, he told Barney to cry-off."

"Well?"

"When Barney had gone, I went up for something. I forget what. But I asked about the Hall. Mr. Salter was quite talkative. Told me about the hiding-places, one of which had never been found. Said to contain a treasure. Thousands of pounds.... It was all there in his family papers. He recited a bit of poetry about it from a paper he had. Said that was supposed to be the key to it."

"Then, what?"

"Well.... Then he went off and got himself killed. I told Barney about the treasure. At first, he laughed. Then, after Mr. Salter's murder, he got serious. He said that was why he'd been killed. Somebody else was after it. I made an excuse to old Bedford and got the key of Salter's flat and me and Barney went through the papers. There wasn't much to go on. Just a plan of the Hall and that rhyme business. Barney took them and said he'd have a look into it. Then he got killed as well. You see, after Inspector Littlejohn called to see me and Barney, he felt there wasn't much time left if he was going to find the money. That hurried him on and he got killed for it."

"And that's all you know?"

"What else is there? Only that I hope you get who ever did for Barney and that he swings for it...."

Meanwhile at the Vicarage, Cobbold, Littlejohn, too, was having a difficult time.

The Rev. Penderell Worsnip, M.A., was a distinguished scholar. His work in life, apart from his duties as a priest, was the compiling of a huge Biblical Concordance which would put even Cruden to shame. At the time of the Inspector's visit, Mr. Worsnip had just finished the letter "H" and, as he was seventy-seven years of age, things were getting a bit pressing if he wished to finish his task this side of the grave. He'd already been at it for forty years! The vicar's housekeeper lead Littlejohn into the study, which was the scene of the utmost commotion and confusion.

Mr. Worsnip's desk had long been too small to accommodate or even hold in piles on the top, the immense mass of information he had accumulated. It was, therefore, spread out all over the floor. It looked like a rummage sale. Every bit of the carpet was covered with papers and books, except for paths, left between heaps of welter to allow the vicar to tread and sit comfortably among it. As he worked, he carried a little stool on which he sat deep in research and perusal, jotting down facts and details in pencil and then toddling to his desk to add them in ink to the enormous manuscript reposing there like the Lamb's Book of Life, dog-eared, but pregnant with so much truth.

This morning, the vicar was very excited. He hadn't been able to eat, sleep or drink for eagerness and exaltation. To-day he was beginning the letter "I". The most important chapter of all, for did it not contain "I" itself, and "I AM", and "IAH" and—yes, he must include that, too—"Ierusalem". At least ten years' work, judging from the past progress he'd made. He hoped he'd be spared to finish it all. If not, maybe Mr. Smythe would.... With this, the housekeeper announced Littlejohn. The vicar lifted his tousled white head and gentle, kindly face from the Cruden he was perusing. After all, you can't do without Cruden in a case like this, can you …? He raised his blue childlike eyes from the written page and gathered his thoughts from far away. "In the beginning, I AM," he muttered.

"Can you get in, Inspector? Take the chair by the desk. I must apologize for the state this room's in. My own fault. I never allow anyone but myself to clean it.… But I'm taking your time. What can I do for you?"

"I'm sorry to disturb you, but I wanted your help in the case I'm on. The Salter murder, you know, sir. In fact, three murders to be exact."

"Of course. The murders of Salter, Pennyquick and Smythe. Yes, yes.…"

"No, no. You've got the victims wrong, sir. Salter, Plucock and Cooney, alias Faircluff."

"I beg pardon.… Yes.… My thoughts are wandering. Pray, what do you want of me? I'm busy on my work, you know. To-day I start on 'I' in my concordance. Very important letter, I assure you.

Full of mystic and significant connotations. And so recurrent in the text. Look …"

And he picked up a large Bible in which, with infinite care and patience he had ringed in red every occurrence of the letter in the text.

Littlejohn couldn't help thinking that although some might think the whole business a wild-goose chase, if everybody had something so harmless, occupying, and, maybe, useful in its way, to keep them busy and even dedicated to it, there might be less mischief in the world.

"I called to ask you, sir, if during Mr. Granville Salter's stay in the village immediately prior to his death, he called on you."

The blue eyes lost some of their innocence, and fear slowly dawned in them. The vicar shuffled a pile of papers and, gathering a number of Bibles lying on the floor together, started to stack them in a neat heap.

"He did," he said guardedly.

"May I ask what he wanted to know?"

The vicar wrung his hands.

"No, no, no," he said appealingly. "Not again, please. Not again, sir."

"He called to ask, did he not, about the parentage of Miss Alveston?"

"Yes, he did. He had no right to. I am a priest and much of my knowledge is sacred. I have no right to divulge it, and I told Mr. Granville so."

"You know the answer to the question then, sir?"

"You have no right to ask me. Nothing shall drag information about that matter from me. It came to me under the seal of confidence and I shall not speak of it. I would rather go to prison … rather die. So, Inspector, I'm sorry I cannot help. I could not help Mr. Granville, much as I would have liked to do so."

"Very well, sir. I have no means of forcing you to talk…."

"I am glad you take that attitude, Inspector. Besides, poor Mr. Salter is dead, now, and the information is past doing him any good."

"Yes; but it may bring a murderer to justice if divulged. I ask you again, sir...."

"No, no, no. Please do not tempt me. I have been terribly worried about it and, after wrestling with the problem for long, I have decided that I must not speak."

"There is another matter, too, Mr. Worsnip...."

The vicar sat on his stool like an aged penitent, full of apprehension. Through the window the gravedigger, Tom Sly, arrived with pick and shovel and, after removing the headstone of a grave, began to dig slowly and rhythmically, pausing now and then to spit on his hands and mutter against the difficulty of his task.

"Do you remember, sir, the night you called on P.C. Plucock for a character for your new kitchen maid and he brought you home?"

"I do. I was not well at the time and, as I sat in the constable's cottage, a strange fever came upon me. I grew light-headed and almost delirious and he had to see me home. It was a difficult journey, Inspector, I assure you."

"What did you talk about on the way, sir?"

"I do not recollect. As I said, I was a little delirious. I dimly remember Plucock ... poor Plucock, a good fellow ... bringing me in here. We must have been talking, for as the warmth of the fire revived and refreshed me, I showed him some old Salter papers of which I must have been telling him on the way. I wasn't aware I'd spoken of them or that the poor fellow was interested in such records, but he was apparently very keen on such things. I lent him the manuscripts and he returned them a day or so later. I expect when he came to peruse them he found them very dry."

"You must have been telling him on the way home about the Salter Treasure and the legend of the

Headless Jesuit, sir, for after that, his wife says he couldn't get the ideas out of his mind. In fact, they may have had something to do with his death."

The vicar was most distressed. He rose to his feet and paced feebly along the little paths which cut through all the raw materials of his Concordance.

"Oh, dear. Oh, dear. I am so sorry. Those legends have been a great source of evil in this parish ever since they started to circulate. For generations, men have plotted and schemed and hunted for gold through them, as if, somehow, they forced the fascination of evil upon them."

"The jingle or doggerel about the Headless Jesuit certainly puzzled Plucock. Are you an antiquary, sir?"

"I once was, but my work on my book now takes all my time. I was once President of the Thorncastle Society of Antiquaries, which has concerned itself very actively with the Salter family, its history and legends, but, as I couldn't conscientiously fill my office with all this to do, I resigned. It is now in the hands of a very good man. Mr. Polydore, of Thorncastle, now holds it."

"Not Mr. Qualtrough, then?"

"Oh dear, no. Far too fussy and erratic, although quite a scholar in his way. Does a lot of digging and investigating here and there. He and Mr. Polydore are not on speaking terms. They are rivals and each thinks the other is no good."

Littlejohn bade the good man good-bye and almost before he had crossed the threshold on his way out, Mr. Worsnip was back again to his studies, busily talking in undertones about "I" and all that it implied.

Tom Sly was half-way down the new grave when Littlejohn passed.

"Good day to you," said Littlejohn. "Is it cold down there?"

"Haffernoon to 'ee. No, it bain't cold; I be as warm as a toast."

"Did Mr. Salter call here to see you just before he died?"

"Ar, he did that. But not 'ere. Oi was a-digging in owld Fothergill's garden when 'e up and stopped me wi' his quizzin'."

"What did he want to know?"

The old man bared his toothless gums and spat in the hole.

"Nothin' as oi would be answerin'. Secret, it was, and nothin' makes me tell. Paid to keep moi mouth shut, oi was. And shut oi'll keep it."

"Was it about who were Phyllis Alveston's parents?"

The old man's jaw dropped and he leant on the handle of his spade.

"'Ow do you know, and if you know, why be aaskin' me?"

"And what did you tell him?"

"Nowt. Same as oi'm tellin' yew."

"This is a police job, you know, Tom. Better tell me here than in court."

"Oi care for no courts. They won't make me tell eether." He didn't care, it was true, for he appeared regularly before the local magistrates for being drunk and disorderly and was fined five shillings, which the vicar paid, for there wasn't anyone to beat Tom at gravedigging in the county.

"Very well, Sly. We'll see about that later. You know, of course, that your obstinacy might very well cause the murderer who's at large to escape …?"

"That it won't, and don't yew be tryin' anythin' like that. Don't you dare tell it about in village, else oi'll be in trouble with they women. Terrible lot they be, those women. ALL women be terrible. Glad I bain't married, though not for want of they women troyin'."

"I won't promise anything. You're definitely against the law by the way you're acting. What the law-abiding people do to you's no concern of mine."

"But oi bam't in any way mixed up in these 'ere murders. 'Ow could a babby buried thirty year gone be to do with killin's now?"

"So that's it. A baby buried thirty years since. Secretly, I guess."

"Aye. But don't yew go tellin'. Vicar'll send me to 'ell if 'e gets to know. Us was paid proper to bury 'im with all the proper rites of Holy Church and to keep us mouths shut. Don't yew be tellin'."

Tom Sly slowly climbed from the grave and clutched Littlejohn with his clay-browned fingers.

"Don't yew be tellin'.... Else oi'll ..."

"Else you'll what?"

"Nothin'.... Oi've said enough. Oi'm off."

He scraped his heavy shoes on the grass, shouldered his tools, and made off to the local to drown his indiscretions.

TWELVE

MEDICAL HISTORIES

THE landlord of the "Royal Oak" had been a brewers' drayman before being promoted by his employers to tenant of one of their tied houses, and he was an expert on horses, horse-drawn vehicles, beer, and the nandling of barrels. He was stocky, bald and side-whiskered, and talked in horsey language, just as an ex-sailor might, in retirement, still speak in the jargon of the sea.

"Whoa, sir," he shouted after Littlejohn as the Inspector entered the inn and climbed the steep stairs up to his room. He had just tapped a cask of beer and was busy raising its contents in the pumps at the bar and testing the result at the same time. His buxom wife stood between Mr. Ashberry and the door.

"Stan' o'er," he said to his missus, who made way for him to join Littlejohn. He removed the queer, tall bowler he always wore when out and about the place. "Young feller called with this note from Miss Fothergill. Said it was urgent...."

"Roast beef, Yorkshire puddin', roast and b'iled potaties an' sprouts for your dinner," said the landlady, just by way of greeting the Inspector and assuring him of her careful attentions. "Treacle puddin' to foller...."

"Whoa, missus.... Whoa, there. K ... ymeeee ..." said her husband, tugging at imaginary reins to silence her. "The hinspector's too busy ..."

"That sounds good, Mrs. Ashberry," said Littlejohn, reading his note. Miss Fothergill said she had news and would like to see him as soon as he could call on her.

"I'll be back in time for your excellent meal, Mrs. Ashberry. I'm just off again for a bit...."

The landlady bobbed a real, old-fashioned curtsy.

"Don't let it spile, sir," she said.

"Stiddy, stiddy, Mrs. Hashberry," said her husband to command her silence and respect.

The owner of Fothergill's was playing twelve-note pieces again when the maid admitted the Inspector.

"The pianner-tuners is *not* in," she said cuttingly and went off to announce him.

Miss Fothergill rose to meet him. She was still smoking and was dressed in a cream jumper with a tweed skirt. The former was covered in a pattern of blue hieroglyphics which dazzled you if you looked too long at it; the latter looked as if she'd woven and cut it herself.

"I'm glad you've called, Inspector. I'm off to London to-morrow and want to get this matter over before I go. I'm playing at a concert.... I've news for you. Lots of it. Sit down...."

Littlejohn lowered himself in an arm-chair, the springs of which seemed ready to fly through the material of the seat and on which he had to shuffle himself to and fro to keep safe and comfortable.

"You uncomfortable? Take this and sit on it!"

Miss Fothergill flung a cushion of brick-coloured material embroidered in blue. The pattern represented a distorted human face with a huge eye in the middle of the forehead.

"Like the pattern? Pablo Besso did it and gave it to me. Ever heard of him?"

"I can't say I have, Miss Fothergill…."

"Pity. Great artist…. Symbolist, you know. The design on that cushion is called 'Conscience'. Turn your back on it or sit on it, it's still there. Follow? Well … that's not getting on with our business. I've been through my brother's diaries. Sat up till dawn on two nights. Can't say I feel good after it. All the same, revived myself by a couple of hours' scale-playing. The records show startling things. Quite helpful to you, I should think."

"I'm very grateful for your trouble, Miss Fothergill."

"Not at all. It gave me great pleasure. As I sat there, I could hear his voice speaking to me over the years. It was that which kept me up so late; not your sordid inquiry, for sordid it is."

"Indeed!"

"Yes. You'll appreciate that all this is confidential. I could never be a party to making my brother's professional notes and diary public. You see that, don't you?"

"Of course, madam."

"Don't call me madam. So, whatever I tell you must also be separately discovered by your own investigations. In other words, I shall give you hints; you will follow them up in the proper quarters, say by questioning Mrs. Alveston, the vicar, and Mrs. Lacey, formerly Miss Margaret Salter. Understand?"

"I see your idea, Miss Fothergill. The public part of the information must be given by someone else, although you, too, will tell it to me beforehand?"

"That's it."

"I hope the others will be a bit more helpful than the vicar. I've just tried to enlist his help. He invoked the seal of the church … the confessional almost."

"Worsnip's an old fool! But it's up to you. I shan't let you have my brother's diaries or his day-books. They're back in the bank. You can, as I say, confirm in your own way what I'm going to tell you. You promise?"

"Yes."

"Well, in the first place, Phyllis Alveston was Granville Salter's cousin, not his sister. That's all the same to Mrs. Alveston. She's so religious and orthodox that the idea of cousins marrying would be abhorrent to her. Granville mistook her there."

"Will you please give me a few more details, Miss Fothergill?"

"Yes. Smoke if you wish. I like the smell of tobacco smoke from a pipe. It reminds me of … but there, I'm wasting time. This, briefly, is what happened. Margaret Salter, now Mrs. Lacey, was Granville Salter's aunt. Thirty years ago, she was a very beautiful woman and was much sought after. She was much younger than her brother, Gregory, young Granville's father. She fell in love with a married man and had an affair with him. He returned to France and was killed just before the war ended. He left Margaret expecting his child. A first-class scandal!"

"Yes."

"But it was all hushed up and fate helped in the hushing. Mrs. Alveston, then Mary Ann Trumper, was also enceinte by Alveston, the bailiff to the Salters, and they saw that he married her. Her child and Margaret's were born about the same time. My brother attended at both lyings-in. The Alvestons' child died at birth; Margaret's lived. The Salters arranged an exchange, with the consent of the

Alvestons, of course, and for a consideration in cash. The poor dead mite was baptized by the vicar and buried in a grave dug by Sly. . . .”

“Sly mentioned the burial in a panic which I induced. . . .”

“Getting him drunk might have been as effective, although, as tar as I know, he’s kept his counsel very well.”

“He said the vicar would sack him if he said a word.”

“So that was it. Yes. . . . My brother had all this down in his day-book. The two confinements and attendance later on Miss Margaret and the Alvestons. A nurse from Thorncastle, a very discreet woman, assisted. Now that’s that. I’ve given you enough names to be going on with, and if you can’t drag sufficient from one or the other of them to complete your case, you’re a poor detective.”

"But that, of course, doesn't solve the murders, Miss Fothergill. It explains what Granville Salter was after, but little else."

"Pursue the lines I've indicated. See those people and something about your murders is sure to come out."

"Was the Headless Jesuit mentioned in the diaries?"

"Nothing to speak of. My brother hadn't time to bother his head about such old wives' tales. But there's something else I've got to tell you. You recollect my telling you about poor Polly, Mrs. Knapp's daughter, who keeps a little shop and whom the rationing of sweets and chocolates bothered so much that she went half off her head?"

"Yes...."

"Well, after your visit, I called to see Polly. She was still sitting in the room behind her shop, with the door locked, and when I tried to get in, peeped round the blind like a poor hunted animal. I shouted that I wanted to see her. She's always been a bit fond of me. Used to clean here for me when my brother was alive and we were both as kind as we could be to her. She didn't want to let even me in, but I called out that I'd get in even if I had to sit on the doorstep all day and all night as well."

"And she let you in?"

"Yes. She was terrified. And now, you'd better accept what I tell you as true, and don't go round pestering poor Polly. I won't have that. If you go trying to get at her, she'll go clean mad. She's almost that already … with terror! Do you know what's happened?"

"No."

"Alveston had been in the village, called at her shop, took all her chocolate and tinned goods and told her he'd come back and slit her throat if she told a soul."

"So…. He did land back on his old ground. I thought that was it. He came either after the Salter

Treasure or else to terrorize his wife and get money from her. He's had some bad luck and talked of going off and getting money to emigrate. He came here."

"I'd the devil's own work to get it out of Polly. She cried and begged me not to ask her. But I insisted and the poor thing in her effort to keep the secret got all muzzed-up and blabbed the whole thing before she knew what she was doing. Then she had a fit. Yes, a real fit with terror. I promised I wouldn't betray her and if you dare say a thing that will lead to her or to a hair of her head being damaged, you'll answer to me, Mister Inspector."

"I'll be discreet, Miss Fothergill, I promise you. And I'll see to it that Polly comes to no harm."

"You'd better. And what do you deduce from what I've told you?"

"Alveston came here for money and somehow got involved in an affair which drove him into hiding."

"Exactly. Murder? Was it Plucock or young Salter himself or that terrible little man they've just found at the Hall with his neck broken?"

"We'll have to find that out. He's gone into hiding with Polly's chocolates and tinned stuffs to keep him alive. And he's probably somewhere at the Hall. The place is, I hear, riddled with secret hideouts."

"That's just what I thought, Inspector. And now, it's up to you. Smoke the vermin out and see that he hangs. He deserves that for what he's done to poor Polly, let alone anybody else. And now, I must hustle you away. I've a bag to pack and get the train from Thorncastle to London, so I've not much time. By my return, I hope you've cleansed this village of its plague. It's like living in a place of the dead just at present. Three murders! People are afraid to stir out of doors. Even the hardened topers at the 'Royal Oak' spent half the night seeing each other home, and the last to be left grew suddenly sober and ran for his life all the way to his wife! I keep thinking of poor Polly, cowering indoors afraid to move, too."

"I'll see to it, Miss Fothergill. Thanks very much for all you've done and told me. I hope you have a good trip."

"Trust me for that. And I trust you to respect my confidences. Somehow, I think you will. I've taken a liking to you, Inspector."

"You may depend on me, Miss Fothergill...."

Greatly to the disappointment of the landlady of the "Royal Oak", Littlejohn did not, to use her husband's words, "return to stable for his provender". Instead, after much telephoning, he ate an evening meal with P.C. Pennyquick and his wife. From somewhere or other, best known to himself, the constable had secured some ham, and they ate it with eggs and followed it by Mrs. Pennyquick's mince tarts. Meanwhile, as the result of Littlejohn's talk with Percival at police headquarters in Thorncastle, six policemen were on their way in a police-van to patrol the house and grounds of Salter Hall. If Alveston was still hiding there, they'd best be ready for him.

Over supper, Littlejohn told the bobby and his wife what Miss Fothergill had hinted about Alveston's hanging around the village and raiding poor Polly's stocks of chocolate and tins.

Mrs. Pennyquick, now recovered from her embarrassment at dining with the stranger from London, although she had told her neighbours that he was like one of the family already, grew talkative about the affairs of the village. The Inspector let her talk away, for thereby he might learn again some past history already given by the doctor's records, which, however, he dare not disclose.

"How many were there of the family living at the Hall when you were in service there, Mrs. Pennyquick?"

"I remember old Mr. Martin, Mr. Granville's grandfather, sir. Regular terror 'e was. He'd been in the army and used to give orders like a general in the field. They pretended to do as 'e wanted, just to humour him. He was in a wheel-chair for years. Huntin' accident…."

P.C. Pennyquick chewed his ham vigorously and, his mouth still full, raised his cup. Then, catching his wife's eye, he coughed, lowered it again and vigorously massaged his moustache.

"The Inspector doesn't want to know the 'istory of all the hancestors of the fambly, love. Tell him about Mr. Gregory and the rest…."

"I was comin' to that…."

The corners of Mrs. Pennyquick's mouth drooped a bit and she looked tearful. Three of the girls who lodged away from home in distant parts had gone off after holidays and the fourth was out courting. The silent house had filled Mrs. Pennyquick's heart with melancholy, and both she and the constable were glad to have "company", as they called the guest at their table. In her present tearful mood, the bobby's wife was cut to the heart by the least suggestion of criticism.

"'Ow lovely you've cooked this 'am, mother," said the constable by way of comfort.

"It's delicious, Mrs. Pennyquick," confirmed Littlejohn.

The woman's face brightened.

"Where was I when father interrupted …? Oh, yes. Well, when I was maid there, Mr. Gregory, that's Mr. Granville's father, was the master. A widower for many years he'd been. My lady had died when Miss Millicent was born. Miss Margaret was looking after things.…"

"Mr. Granville's aunt, Mrs. Pennyquick?"

"Yes. Much younger than Mr. Gregory.…"

The constable chewed to empty his mouth, took a swig of tea and slowly winked one eye.

"Very good-lookin', she was. Bit o' scandal about her, too."

"Dad! You no right to talk about such things. You'll 'ave the Inspector thinkin' we're a right bad lot round here...."

"All the same, Mrs. Pennyquick, it might be useful to know."

The good woman was dying to tell it all and seized the chance.

"She had a baby while I was there...."

"Wrong side o' the blanket, as you might say," said Pennyquick through a mouthful of ham, tea and eggs.

"Dad! Don't be vulgar...."

"Well, it was...."

"No need to put it that way. They hushed it up very well, sir. Most people don't know to this day. And them as do, keeps their mouths shut, Miss Margaret was such a nice lady. Married twice after that and very happy, though never had any more children. Mrs. Lacey she is now, and lives in London. Mr. Lacey used to live at Carstonwood and always wanted her. But she married somebody else, a Mr. Sheldon from Thorncastle. Then Mr. Sheldon died, and Mr. Lacey, now past middle-age and never married because of her, comes back and marries her. Quite romantic...."

"You and your rowmances, ma. It's the pictures does it...."

"Now, saucy, not in front of the Inspector."

"What happened to the child, Mrs. Pennyquick?"

The good woman hesitated.

"Well ... it don't do to talk, but I'll tell you what was said at the time. You remember first time you came we said as how Alveston had to marry his missus because there was a child comin'? Well, they was married and it was said the child died and they secretly adopted Miss Margaret's...."

The bobby stopped eating and gazed dumbstruck at his wife.

"You never told *me* that!"

"I never told a soul before. But this is the police and a murder …"

"But I'm the police!!"

"Oh, dad, don't be so awkward. I tell you, I promised not to tell a soul about it and I kept my promise. What good would it have done to tell you? But now … well …"

And that was all the explanation the bobby got. Crestfallen, he resumed his ham and, disregarding his wife's wishes, by way of retaliation drank copiously with his mouth full.

"There was a lot of comin' and goin' at the Hall in those days. Doctor, midwife, and Mr. Gregory runnin' here and there, and Miss Margaret in bed. It was bound to get round and talked about among the servants. Mr. Devereaux, that was the butler, got us all together. 'Now,' he sez, 'now, I don't know what you're all thinkin' or sayin' about matters here these days, but never one of you dare say a word outside. You might land yourselves in jail for slander if you do, and if you don't, well … you'll be dismissed without references and I'll see that nobody in the county employs you again.' That was terrible in those days. Enough to make you starve or go to the poorhouse. We all promised and as far as I know, we all kept us promises, though we never quite knew the truth."

"So, as likely as not, Mrs. Pennyquick, Phyllis Alveston was cousin to poor Granville."

"Yes. That would be enough for Mrs. Alveston to forbid the marriage. Terribly religious and follows the prayer-book word by word. So, she forbid it, like as not. Some set it about that Phyllis was Mr. Gregory's daughter…."

"Wrong side o' the blanket, too," mumbled the bobby.

"Oh, do stop bein' common, dad. It isn't right in front of the Inspector, and you a married man. I think Mr. Granville was tryin' to make sure so he could marry Phyllis when he died.... Poor Mr. Granville...."

And with that the pent-up tears of a day's griefs and partings flowed freely and Littlejohn and the bobby, the latter greatly distressed, for he knew he was partly to blame by drinking with his mouth full, comforted her as best they could.

"You must excuse me, sir. It's all the girls goin' and the 'ouse so quiet...."

"What about a glass o' port wine, luv ... the one Miss Fothergill give me for Christmas ...?"

"All right. P'raps it'll do me good. Give the Inspector one as well.... It'll cheer him up, too."

"Did you have happy times at the Hall in those days, Mrs. Pennyquick?"

"Oh, yes. They was very good to us. Jobs like that didn't come every day. And then Pennyquick come ridin' round on his bike and saw me and, after that, well ... it seemed part of his beat every day.... Three times a day sometimes."

"Now, mother, don't yew be tellin' tales out of school."

"Yes, them was good times. The family was so nice to us, too. When me and Pennyquick was married, they gave us that table."

Mrs. Pennyquick indicated a fine little mahogany wine-table standing in one corner, shining brightly from much elbow-grease and beeswax.

"They always gave for a weddin' present somethin' from the Hall. Like a piece of furniture or an orniment or somethin'. You could choose within reason. They said it would remind us more of the days we spent at the Hall if we took away one of the things we'd cleaned. Rather funny, but very nice. They had some lovely things there. Now they've all gone. Funny how things change. I got that table, there, an' I recollect they even gave Flather, the midwife, somethin' when she got married. It was the rockin'-chair she used to sit in and was very fond of while waitin' for the pains to come on in the childbirths...."

"Right *or* wrong side o' the blankets, as you might say...."

"Dad! Pleese! But the funniest present of all was the Knight of St. John they gave Mrs. Knapp. When I started there, she was housekeeper. Then she married Knapp, as then kept the 'Royal Oak'. 'E died in less than two years from typhoid, the drains there bein' terrible in those days. So, she came back to her old place at the Hall. They gave her, as I was sayin', the little silver figure of the Knight of St. John. It used to stand on the nursery mantelpiece and many's the teeth that I've seen cut on it. Cool to the gums, if you see what I mean. They was quite taken aback when she asked for it, but havin' promised, they let her have it."

"What was funny about that, Mrs. Pennyquick? I guess it took her fancy."

"Yes, but that's not what I mean. When she left the Hall, she went to live with 'er daughter, Polly, who married Duckett, the water-bailiff. He got killed in the war. Well, Mrs. Knapp took her things to Polly's and with them the little silver Knight. Then she died and Polly sold off some of her things. There was an auction at The Grange, an old house where Major Jamieson lived, and so the auctioneer put Polly's things in with them. They do that sometimes, you know...."

"Oh, I remember that, ma. Yes, nine days' wonder that Knight, wasn't it?"

"I was just goin' to tell Mr. Littlejohn that, when you interrupted. Now yew can tell 'im yourself...."

"Aw, come on, ma, you know yo're better at that than me...."

"Very well, then. The things was set out for view, like, before the sale, and the Knight was there, polished up on a table and Polly was hopin' to get a pound or two for it, because it was silver, you see."

"When was this, Mrs. Pennyquick?"

"About two years since. After her mother died."

"Thank you. Please do go on...."

"The things sold nicely. Prices was good at the time, and a lot that wanted to set up house bid high, because, barrin' poor utility furniture, second-'and was all you could get. Then, it came to the figure. The auctioneer was quite casual. Treated it as somethin' and nothin' and so did most else. But not Mr. Qualtrough and Mr. Polydore...."

"Why? Were they there as well?"

"Yes, sir. You see, Mr. Polydore's a big antique man and goes to all the sales of old stuff. There was a lot of it at The Grange. I don't know why old Qualtrough turned up. But they was both mad for the Knight, for some reason. You'd 'ave thought they'd have had more sense and arranged things beforehand instead of biddin' like they did. Almost fightin' for it, they were...."

"And who won?"

The bobby couldn't control himself longer.

"Why, Polydore, o' course. He's a bachelor.... Qualtrough's married. The bachelors 'ave all the money."

"No need to put it that way. Mr. Polydore *is* nicely off. But, Mr. Qualtrough married a young wife and she spends as fast as he earns it, and more. It's the talk of the neighbourhood. By the time it had got over a hundred pounds, he had to give up. He looked ready to kill Mr. Polydore and so did that oily Whatmough fellow who's always with him."

"But a hundred pounds! It's preposterous for a thing like that, unless it's a valuable antique."

"It was old, sure enough, but after it was over, the auctioneer, Sammy Moon, who knows a thing or two about what he's sellin', said it was worth maybe twenty pounds at most as a work of art and less for its weight in silver."

"If you ask me," chipped in the bobby, "it was the old feud. Polydore and Qualtrough hate one another like poison. Both antiquaries and both think they know best. Qualtrough never forgive him for bein' made President of the Thorncastle Antiquaries. They just bid against one another out of spite."

"What do you say the figure was like, Mrs. Pennyquick?"

"A sort of full-length man, with a broad hat and cloak and holdin' a staff in his hand. Like a pilgrim, you might say. I can see it now."

"A Knight of St. John, did you say?"

"Yes, that's what they called it at the Hall. The little silver Knight. He didn't look like a knight, if you ask me. No armour. Not even a sword. Just a sort of staff in his hand. But there was a sash across his breast with 'S.J.' on it. Saint John, you see."

Littlejohn twirled the empty wineglass between his fingers. A sudden excited feeling ran down his spine. As though he'd suddenly struck something very important. Yet, he couldn't quite think what it was. Somewhere in his subconscious ...

“Have another glass of wine, Inspector?”

“Thanks very much, Pennyquick.… I … I …”

“Does sound a bit funny; so much money for a little image sort of thing. But it was true. I …”

Pennyquick was mistaking Littlejohn’s preoccupation for incredulity.

“It’s not that. I just … I’ve got it.… Are you sure, Mrs. Pennyquick, it *was* a knight? Could it have been a priest?”

“Oh, no, sir. It looked more like an ordinary man.…”

“Of course. They didn’t necessarily dress as priests.”

Pennyquick looked at the Inspector and then at the wine. Surely, he could take more than that without …

“It wasn’t St. John the S.J. stood for, Mrs. Pennyquick. It was Society of Jesus. The figure was that of a Jesuit!”

THIRTEEN

THE SECRET OF SALTER HALL

MR. NATHANIEL POLYDORE carried on business in an old, bow-fronted, oak-beamed shop in the Cathedral Close at Thorncastle. Over the window a sign in Gothic lettering, "Nathaniel Polydore & Co., Antiques". It all belonged to Mr. Polydore. There was no Company, but, to him, it looked better; more spacious, more powerful. A wrought-iron sign "Antiques" also swung and creaked over the door.

Littlejohn opened the door, panelled with tiny panes of bottle-glass, and then halted. Even to get farther in the shop required skilled navigation, for it was packed from floor to ceiling with every kind of old furniture, pottery, bronzes, statues, iron-work and brass. The walls were peppered with nails from which hung plaques, jugs, plates, framed miniatures, samplers, pewter utensils, and anything else that would fit in. From hundreds of hooks in the beams dangled lustres, nautical lamps and lanterns, guns, pistols, powderhorns and cages. It was like a cave, unexplored, protected by stalactites and stalagmites and in which every step added risk and danger to the intruder.

There was no warning bell over the door to alarm the owner and you as you entered. Instead, a ferocious, gaily-coloured parrot did sentry duty from a large cage and screeched "Shop!" every time anyone arrived, and purred "Come again!" as they departed.

All activity had been suspended at the time Littlejohn entered. A meek little man, evidently a tourist, and a large fat lady, with "cathedral set" written large upon her, were standing wedged among the junk collection, in a state of suspended animation. In another corner a tall, thin, elderly man, with long white hair departing from the crown in a large tonsure, and dressed in a morning coat and grey trousers, both the worse for wear, and rather soiled linen, was standing before a wireless cabinet. As Littlejohn entered and the parrot gave the alarm—"Shop!!"—the long man turned irritably and gestured for silence. From the radio were emerging the wonderful, fierce closing passages of Beethoven's Fifth Symphony. The long gentleman was evidently at variance with the conductor and drummer concerning the interpretation, too, for he kept raising his palm with fingers outstretched towards the contraption, as though, by some feat of telepathy or television, he hoped to increase the tempo and damp down the drumbeats.

The final chord died away.

"You have been listening to a performance of Beethoven's Fifth …"

Mr. Polydore switched the thing off with a flourish, and then turned to his visitors. That gave you a surprise, for although his hair was snow white, his eyebrows were jet black and thick, and his long ragged moustache, once white, had turned yellow from too much smoking. He took up a cigarette-box before he spoke, passed it round, received no offers, took one himself, lit it, and held it fastidiously between his long, delicate fingers.

"Thank you all," he said in a gentle, refined voice. "I cannot revist Beethoven.... It iv like a fpiritual bath ... washev away the duft of fin and evil.... Refreshev the foul...."

He suffered from what the experts call "lazy tongue". He couldn't get it round the letter "s" and sometimes his speech sounded like a foreign language. Especially when he got excited, for then "ch", "r" and "I" followed suit and he stammered out strange expressions and cast-up words never heard before. Useless to try and transcribe him in print; we can only offer a translation.

"Tempo far too slow ... drums too noisy.... And now to business."

The customers seemed to understand. The little man was too meek to protest, bought a packet of those Japanese paper-balls which, when thrown in water, open out and festoon the glass with gaily-coloured flowers and foliage, paid his shilling, and made off, happy to be released. The large woman nodded as though she understood all about it and was herself in the habit of suspending her daily operations whenever symphonies were played over the radio.

"I quite agree, Mr. Polydaw, but beeeootiful all the same … beeeeeeootiful.…"

"Ah, I see you are one of the few, Mrs. MunroSquire," lisped Mr. Polydore, and put his head on one side by way of questioning the visit.

"Yaw shaw twenty pounds is the least you'll teck faw the leetle cawved ayveries.…"

Mr. Polydore unctuously assured the lady that he was making a loss at the price. Thereupon the lady took from her large handbag a cheque already made out for the amount, passed it over, received a receipt and put it safely away without another word. It was all done in a pantomime of surprise, despair, thankfulness, mutual appreciation and concern. They bade each other good-bye. the parrot bawled Mrs. Munro Squire out, after she had completed a series of knight's moves among the junk to the door, and then Mr. Polydore turned to Littlejohn. The Inspector had been appreciatively handling a chess-set exquisitely carved in red and white ivory, with oriental potentates for chief pieces, foot-soldiers equipped to the last detail for pawns, and great elephants benring castles on their backs for "rooks".

"May I interest you in that, sir …?"

"No, Mr. Polydore. I'm here for something even more rare. I believe you have the Salter Jesuit in your possession."

Mr. Polydore immediately turned pale, his large black eyebrows flew up in horror and he emitted sounds in a strange tongue which sounded like "I don't know what you mean."

Littlejohn scrambled his way through the obstacles in the shop and stood beside the antique dealer. He took out his warrant-card and passed it across.

"I'm from the police, sir."

Mr. Polydore seemed to lose inches in height and gazed about him like one who has lost his bearings.

"I … I …"

"Have you still got the figure, sir?"

Mr. Polydore pulled himself together, thought a little and then decided to co-operate.

"Yes.… You shall see it on one condition …" Littlejohn understood him to say.

"There are no conditions, sir. I want to see it. All the same, if you'll help me, I see no reason why I shouldn't try to meet any sensible wishes. What is the condition?"

"That I and not Qualtrough shall be your collaborator in finding out the secret of the Jesuit."

"What has Qualtrough got to do with it, sir?"

"I'll tell you later. Agreed?"

"Very well."

"Then I'll show you the figure. Please step this way."

They entered a room behind the shop. It was a kind of retiring quarters and workshop. A cosy open grate with a cat warming herself on the rug, a kettle steaming on the hob, a comfortable arm-chair. The rest was almost as confused as the shop. On one side stood a large bench, covered with tools and materials of all kinds. Bottles of varnish, woodworking tackle, jewellers' lenses, apparatus for riveting and repairing pottery. Here the damaged antiques were made good, and, maybe, new stuff made antique.

"Sit down...."

Mr. Polydore took out a bunch of keys and opened a large modern safe tucked away in one corner. From a drawer inside he took a small parcel wrapped in tissue paper and thence he removed an object about eight inches tall and placed it upright on a small table near the Inspector. It tallied with the image described by Mrs. Pennyquick. A kind of pilgrim with cloak and staff. The workmanship was very fine indeed. But Mrs. Pennyquick had told of a broad-brimmed hat. This figure was headless! As though reading Littlejohn's thoughts, Mr. Polydore further unwrapped the tissue paper, took another small object in his fingers and placed it on the shoulders of the decapitated body.

"Ah...."

"So you know all about it, Inspector."

"No, Mr. Polydore, I don't. That's what I'm here for."

"Then, I will do what I can. But first let me tell you about the condition I made. Qualtrough is a charlatan. A so-called antiquary, ever ready to pounce on other people's findings and pass them off as his own. We are not on speaking terms and our relations have been even more strained since I was elected President of the local Antiquarian Society. He opposed me at the election and was defeated. He never forgave me."

"But has this anything to do with the present matter, sir?"

Littlejohn knew all about such small-town rivalries, the petty jealousies of experts in the same field, and the way they try to discount each other's efforts. He'd no time for it at present.

"I'm coming to that. As you have no doubt learned, there is a legend about the Treasure at Salter Hall and one about the Headless Jesuit. These have intrigued local antiquaries for generations and caused no end of theories and surmise. We have always come against the Salters, however. The family would not allow excavations or examinations in the fabric of the Hall during the time they were in residence. They contended that the Treasure myth had been exploded long ago and were not going to be disturbed by everyone poking and prying into their home. Even requests by the various national and local antiquarian societies were refused. When, some years ago, the rhyme of the Headless Jesuit was found in an old book from the Salter library and printed in the Proceedings of our Society, that added a fillip to the matter."

"But what has this to do with the little figure there?"

"I'll tell you. Some years ago, towards the end of the Salter days at the Hall, there was a sale near Carstonwood—at The Grange, an old house of considerable antiquarian importance—and among the objects for auction were a few belongings of an old servant of the Salters. Included in these was the figure you now see. I came across it and inquired about it. I was told it had been given to the old housekeeper at the Hall by the family as a present, and was what might be called an heirloom. I examined it and found, as you see there, the letters 'S.J.' on its chest. Now under the lens it shows plainly that these letters have been chased on afterwards. The type of lettering is not in keeping with the time when the statuette was made. At once, it dawned on me that this might be a clue, *the* clue mentioned in Simister Salter's jingle. It was hollow and might contain information about the Treasure. The idea of the *Headless* Jesuit also flashed on me. 'Headless Jesuit, aid thee.' It meant, take the head *off* the Jesuit and there was the clue."

"I see. And you found something …?"

"Shop!!" screeched the parrot.

Mr. Polydore with gestures of annoyance passed through the door into the shop and could be heard talking to someone. Then he returned. "Goo' byee. Come again," gurgled the parrot.

"Trippers," he said contemptuously. "'How much is that jug?' she says. 'Ten pounds,' I say. Exit."

"But what has Mr. Qualtrough to do with it all?"

"He was also at the sale and, finding me interested in the figure, began to snoop around. I couldn't very well take the thing then. It was only view-day. The little wretch evidently came to the same conclusion that I did. At the sale, he made me pay dearly for my find. Sixty pounds more than it was worth, but I determined he shouldn't get it. I won. And since then, he has made my life a misery. Shortly afterwards, the Salters sold the Hall; Qualtrough persuaded the tenant not to allow anyone to explore the interior. He used his authority as Coroner, and said he forbade any search for Treasure Trove without his consent. The tenant swallowed it and forbade me the place. I had opened the figure and, I think, solved the puzzle, yet I couldn't get near. Qualtrough started making offers for the figure. I showed him the door. The Hall was being used as a private asylum, which made things still more difficult. Then, the asylum closed and I found the trustees wouldn't let me enter. Not only that, Qualtrough, in his rage, had men keeping watch against intruders. He said it was a precaution in his capacity as Coroner. That fellow Whatmough was for ever hanging around and, when he was away, the gatekeepers or other hired men patrolled the place. So, you see, I've never had a chance to put my theories into effect. Now, perhaps, you'll let me, Inspector, if it lies within your powers."

"It certainly does, sir. But, first, I want to know the theories."

"I opened the figure. There was a document inside. I have it here."

From another part of the safe, Mr. Polydore produced a brief-case and thence several sheets of paper from which he selected one. It was a parchment bearing, in a cramped hand, very faded writing.

Mr. Polydore produced another sheet.

"Here is a copy in my own hand."

It was almost as illegible, but the eccentric handwriting had the virtue of being done in good ink.

The account began without date or preamble.

All this winter I have suspected my wife of an illicit love affair and of late days I have had the proof. It is between her and Bacon, my steward. Two days ago, I intercepted a note which Hosegood, our man, was carrying to her from him. They were about to fly together. That night I choked my wife with my necktie and placed her body in the old Jesuit's hole which has been long disused. I then sent for my steward, struck him on the head until he lost his consciousness, and locked him in the hole with my wife's body. I dismissed all the servants but Hosegood, saying I was leaving for London the following day, and for two days listened to the weakening cries and blows of Bacon, now conscious and perishing in his prison.

I had determined to let the false pair of them rot together, but being troubled by my conscience, which I suddenly found I possessed, and having still,

I find, an affection for my faithless wife, I opened up the hiding-place at dead of night and bore her body to the family vault, where, with the help of my faithful Hosegood, I laid her decently in an old coffin, contents of which had mouldered to dust. Having sealed this, I left her.

Bacon I left as he had died, clawing the door and quite ignoring his one-time paramour.

I set this down to solve the mystery of the vanishing of the pair. I wrap it in mystery as is my fashion and if the riddle is never solved the tale will never be known. I first write the rhyme leading to this figure in which I place this document. I convert the pilgrim to a Jesuit by having Hosegood, who served his time to a silversmith, carve on it the letters "S.J." Someone cunning enough may one day discover.

"Take up eleven": walk eleven steps up the main staircase.

"Eleven to three": third panel up from the eleventh stair. This panel has a spring hidden in the bottom left corner. If the spring is rusted, break the panel. Behind is a locked door with a handle. Unlock the door with the key on the ledge of the panel. Pull the handle. The whole nine panels will fall away and the door will be accessible. Enter and God rest you.

Having written this, I shall remove the head of the figure, place it inside and have Hosegood make safe the head on the body again.

Then, I regret to say, as Hosegood knows too much, I must silence him. He is not so faithful as would appear and has poached other things of mine than game. A barrel of shots for the poacher.

Simister Saltaire.

This 27th day of February, 1824.

"Well?" said Mr. Polydore.

"We'd best get to the Hall at once. There may be more in this than a skeleton or two and a dead man's hate."

"You mean the Treasure."

"No. He'd have had that if there were any. Let's go. My car's outside."

At the Hall the police patrol was active and Pennyquick had joined them in his excitement. They greeted Littlejohn gladly. They were all bored.

"Nothing's happened," said the sergeant-in-charge, a huge beefy fellow called Dainty. "Only Mr. Qualtrough called. Said he'd heard of our bein' here and, actin' as Coroner, came to see what was 'appenin'. He's somewhere about the grounds with that chap Whatmough."

The sun was shining through the huge leaded window which lighted the great panelled hall of the house, from which heavy doors to left and to right gave access to the entertaining rooms. To the left of the main staircase, the way led to the servants' quarters. The place was bare and forsaken. The furniture had been removed and, although the caretaker had kept the rooms moderately free from dust, an empty smell pervaded it all, dust, damp and hidden decay.

Someone had erected a large trestle table, probably looted from a potting-shed, and round it were a number of empty boxes, two tumble-down chairs and a kitchen stool. The policemen's bivouac. On the table a number of dirty cups, a vacuum flask, empty sandwich packets, a carrier bag, a fibre case and, majestic in their midst, a constable's helmet.

Littlejohn strolled from room to room. Here and there a few useless oddments left by the previous tenants, but everywhere the melancholy traces of slow deterioration. The house was dying from lack of money, like a great plant from which the water supply had been removed.

"Well, shall we try?" said Littlejohn at length to Mr. Polydore. The gaunt antiquary was impatiently waiting, now and then pausing to examine some odds and ends of carving or a chimney-piece which took his fancy. Given his own way, he would have set about taking the valuable pieces away at top speed. He knew of good markets for them, especially among American connoisseurs. He was not prompted by greed alone; he felt he wanted as much of this old and gracious beauty to fall into appreciative and capable hands as possible before it crumbled or rotted away.

Littlejohn called Pennyquick and Sergeant Dainty to him and slowly climbed the staircase. Of enormous weight and built in what seemed indestructible oak, it had shallow, easy steps, which rose gently, then, turning twice abruptly, gave on to a gallery which surrounded three sides of the hall, and ended in a platform for minstrels.

One, two, three … eleven.

The Inspector stopped and examined the fine, fluted panels which covered the whole wall of the staircase. Once they had shone from the wax and polishing of generations of proud servants; now the bloom had left them and the wood, unprotected, was gradually pitting from the boring of wood-worms.

At the eleventh stair, Littlejohn halted, closely followed by Polydore, who, with burning eyes and twitching fingers seemed eager enough to test his theory and even brush the Inspector aside.

"Here!" he said, pointing to the third panel from the stair in an upward direction. He tapped it with a long, tobacco-stained index and looked all ready to tear the whole lot down in impatience.

Littlejohn examined the panel. Someone had been there already! It was covered in a mass of fingerprints. He turned to Pennyquick.

"Has anyone been tinkering around here?"

"No, sir. Must 'ave been done before we came."

The Inspector felt round the edge of the panel, but there seemed no trace of catch or spring.

"Let me vee. . . ."

Mr. Polydore could contain himself no longer and lapsed into strange tongues. He pushed his companion aside and feverishly began himself to explore the woodwork. Taking out a penknife, he prodded the corner. Then, suddenly, the whole fell away, revealing, as the document had said, a door handle and a large keyhole. But there was no key in the indicated place.

Littlejohn scrutinized the opening.

"Someone has been here, I'm sure...."

"Yev," said Mr. Polydore. "De vwine!!"

He regarded it as his own preserve and his thoughts were turning to his deadly antiquarian rival, Mr. Qualtrough.

"*He'v* veen at it! No key.... It ivn't here. *He'v* daken izh. Ahhhhh!"

He made gnashing noises.

Littlejohn seized the handle and tugged. Slowly and easily a whole bunch of panels opened outwards, bringing with them a thin iron door and revealing beyond, a dark cavern.

"Got your torch with you, Pennyquick?"

"Eh? Oh yes, yes, sir."

Poor Pennyquick's eyes were almost popping from his head and Sergeant Dainty had recoiled in surprise against the heavy carved banisters.

Mr. Polydore was performing a grotesque dance with glee and making little whining noises of pleasure.

"A lamp … a lamp …"

Dainty scuttered downstairs with astonishing agility, rummaged in the fibre case on the table, and produced a large police lamp. He switched on the light and by its glaring beams they found their way into the hidden room, the priest's hole. It was damp and musty, but somehow ventilated, for the air was dank but tolerable. The whole place was of brick, except the floor, which was of solid stone slabs. At one end stood a stone erection which might have been an altar at one time. But they weren't interested in the structure of the place. On the floor lay the body of a thick-set, powerful man. He was face-downwards and the back of his head had been beaten in like an eggshell. His arms were sprawled ahead of him and his heavy shoes were balanced on their toes.

Dainty knelt and turned over the body.

"Alveston!!" almost screamed Pennyquick. "Godelpus...."

He was wearing a sailor's jersey under a reefer jacket, and his features were horrible in death and dirty from lack of proper washing.

The men shivered. The air was as cold as ice and smelled of damp stone and earth.

"My God! My God! Oh, my God!" whimpered Mr. Polydore. "Zhiz will be zhe death of me...."

"That will do!" said Littlejohn and shook him vigorously by the arm.

The antiquary mounted the three stone steps to the door. He clawed the air as though trying to climb an invisible ladder. "I need air …" they understood him to say before he lapsed into incoherence again.

They flashed the lamp around. On the floor in one corner, as though swept away with a brush or someone's foot, lay a mass of bones. A human skeleton. The pitiable remains of the unfortunate Bacon, the victim of the malicious Simister Salter.

Littlejohn knelt by the corpse and felt the hands.

"He's not been dead very long. A matter of a day or so, I'd guess. Better get the doctor along, will you, Dainty, please? And let Superintendent Percival know, as well. Is there a phone handy?"

"At an 'ouse a little way up the road, sir. I'll go on my bike."

There was no trace of any treasure. Naturally, if Simister had known of the hole he'd have moved it long ago. Pennyquick, who had silently followed Mr. Polydore outside, now returned with some old curtains torn from one of the windows, and with these he covered the heap of bones in the corner.

"Who can 'e be, sir?"

"I'll tell you later. Don't cover Alveston till I've felt his pockets."

Gingerly Littlejohn proceeded with his task. He brought to light the usual oddments a tramping man carries around. A large clasp knife, identity papers which confirmed that it was Alveston, although they were in the name of Grigg. Some bars of chocolate, a ration-book, string, a tin-opener, some keys, a pipe, tobacco in a skin pouch, a huge petrol lighter and some matches.

Finally the hip pocket. Pennyquick, a silent spectator, drew a harsh breath, for out came two fatal objects.

The leather sheath of a knife, roughly the size of the weapon used on Granville Salter, and, more ominous still, a policeman's truncheon.

"Plucock's! They must 'ave fought and Alveston tuck Plucock's truncheon and used it on 'im.... The rotten swine.... The dirty rotten swine. Then, he crept up the dyke which passes the garden 'ere and tuck him to the marsh and left 'im to drown in shallow water.... There's 'ardly any water in that dyke, since they made the new cut. He'd get along without being seen."

"So, Plucock came here. He must have been hunting around and come upon Alveston."

Pennyquick shone his lamp on the floor.

"In 'ere," he said. "He must 'ave had it open. Here's a tunic button...."

He picked up the tarnished object and thrust it in Littlejohn's palm.

"Poor old Plucock.... He ..."

Suddenly there was a great commotion outside. A sound of pattering feet and voices raised in shrill vituperation.

"So! You thought you'd steal a march on me. Cheat! Sneak! You ... you ..."

It was Mr. Qualtrough, returned from reconnaissance with his henchman, Whatmough.

Their figures loomed and bobbed about like a shadow-show in the doorway.

"I found it first! I found it first! That had you, didn't it?"

Mr. Polydore executed a little dance of triumph.

"In the King's Name! As Coroner, I hereby claim and impound the treasure.... In the name of His Majesty...."

"Treasure! He, he, he," rollicked Mr. Polydore. "Too late!! Ish all gone...." He was thoroughly enjoying the discomfiture of his enemy. "Ho, ho, ho. He sezh treazha...."

"Be quiet out there," called Littlejohn. But the protagonists were too busy to bother. They were hotly abusing each other, snapping their fingers in each other's faces, squaring like gamecocks.

"Juzht in time to be too late! Pettifoggin liddle Coroner," gloated Mr. Polydore, casting up strange sounds and unknown words.

All the pent-up rage and rivalry of half a lifetime boiled up in the breast of the faithful Whatmough. He pushed aside his master, seized Mr. Polydore roughly by the lapels of his dusty morning coat, and shook him venomously until his false teeth fell out.

"You … you … you … Grrrrrrr …" Whatmough choked.

The combatants, their long legs entwined like serpents, their hands pushing and clawing at each other's faces and hair, tottered wildly for a moment on the upper edge of the three steps and then, losing their balance, they fell with wild cries headlong into the priest's hole. There, still snarling, spitting and scratching like a pair of Kilkenny cats, they continued flailing at each other and, as they both yelled in high-pitched abracadabra, they rubbed one another's noses in the dust of untold years.

FOURTEEN

THE DISGUSTED DOCTOR

WHEN Dr. Macduff took up practice in Cobbold following the death of Dr. Fothergill, he had a rich sense of humour. He laughed at the queer country characters who visited his surgery and called him to their homes; he laughed at the strange set-up of local government, officials, committees and conferences prevailing in the county; he even laughed when he discovered that his professional rival, a successful practitioner who lived between Cobbold and Thorncastle, boasted the name of Macbeth. With the passage of time, however, the fun and spice of life grew thin. And nationalization was the last straw!

Littlejohn had sent Cromwell to ask Dr. Macduff if Mrs. Alveston, who was his patient, could safely be questioned to the full extent about what she knew of Granville Salter, her late husband's movements prior to his death, and anything else relative to the case. The good woman, in a perpetual state of ill-health, due, Littlejohn thought, to nerves alone, was in the habit of dissolving into tears and becoming convulsed with a form of palsy whenever faced with problems or decisions which she didn't want to be mixed up in. Before pressing hard this most important witness, Littlejohn wished to be sure from her doctor that no ill effects would result. He didn't want to kill her with fright or drive her out of her mind!

Dr. Macduff's plate announced evening surgery at 6.30. At 6.45 Cromwell rang the bell of the annexe marked "Surgery" and ornamented with a red lamp over the door. The lamp hadn't been illuminated since Dr. Macduff had been nationalized. He no longer needed to guide or invite patients. They just came. And in dozens....

A bad-tempered elderly housekeeper opened the door.

"Can't you read?" she said, and pointed to a card stuck on the glass with gelatine lozenges. "Come in."

Cromwell offered the dragon his card, but she ignored it.

"I want to see the doctor on a private matter. I'm from the police."

The old lady was unmoved.

"Nobody's favoured now. All treated alike. First come, first served."

Cromwell entered and gingerly took a seat among the twenty or so patients waiting for the doctor. When a bell rang, the next walked into the consulting room. The sergeant looked round. Some obvious habituals, intent on getting all they could for nothing. Two or three patients in bandages; a child with whooping cough, whose mother during paroxysms called the attention of the rest there with great pride as the way he went black in the face.

Another little boy with a frightful squint and a girl with a red tape tied round her sleeve to indicate she'd recently been vaccinated. She showed her decoration to Cromwell who gave her a threepenny bit for being a brave girl.

The bell kept tinkling and the sufferers went in and out of the private room with lightning rapidity. Inside sat the doctor, brooding at his desk. He was elderly, tall and portly. Once he'd been a rugby player and now the muscle had turned to fat. No time to get it back again to firm flesh by golf. All his time was taken up rushing about the countryside giving people free treatment. He scratched his bald head irritably, doodled on his blotter with his pencil, and looked biliously at the stacks of official forms lying all over the desk. Prescriptions, priorities, death certificates, optical chits, forms for free wigs and corsets, dockets for special cases, orders for artificial limbs. Once, he'd had high ideals about healing the sick. A few at a time, of course, and leisure in which to study their cases. Now … He pressed the bell angrily.

Footsteps and the closing of the door.

“Doctor, I’m not feeling well.…”

Macduff didn’t even look up. He knew who it was. Joe Bartie, drunk as a pig last night, with the allowances granted by his grateful government for his eight children, now getting himself in form for another bout at the country’s expense. The doctor drew a pad towards him.

R. Pil. rhoei co. gr. iv.,

or should he give something more drastic to knock the old toper out for a day or two …?

“Right.… Next.…”

A man for spectacles. He couldn’t read but wanted to see the pictures and comic strips in the daily paper. They were all blurred. Green chit for the optician.

A totally bald man who'd been so for years. Now his daughter was getting married. He thought a wig would add a bit of tone to the wedding. Could the doctor …? Next.

"I must have eaten something, doctor.…"

R. Ext. Cascarae Sag. liq.…

Then Cromwell entered. The doctor continued writing.

"Yes …"

Cromwell wondered whether or not to get himself some glasses whilst he was at it. A pair with horn rims like Littlejohn's.

"Card, please.…"

The doctor looked up.

"Hullo. Who are you?"

"Detective-Sergeant Cromwell, New Scotland Yard."

Cromwell produced his warrant card.

"Ah.…"

This was a change!

"I'm here on the local murder case."

"Glad you called. But what can I do for you? Not sick, I hope."

"No, sir. I've called about Mrs. Alveston. Your patient, I believe."

"Yes. But I'm not divulging any details, you know. Whatever else has happened to us, there's still etiquette left."

"To tell you the truth, doctor, we're in a bit of a difficulty with that lady. She knows quite a lot about the case, but as soon as we broach the matter, she has tears and hysterics. We just don't know what to do about it."

"Best thing to do, of course, would be to slap her face. I'm not being brutal or callous, though God knows these days I've enough damned provocation. But I'll tell you frankly, Mrs. Alveston's had a lot of trouble, but it's been of her own making. She enjoys being ill, and, from what I can gather, her endless plaintiveness and querulousness drove her husband away. How her daughter's stuck it all these years, I don't know. She's battened on that girl and, unless the girl's firm, she'll end up an old maid still looking after mother. I attend her twice a week. They say young Granville and Phyllis were in love and the old woman wouldn't hear of it for some unearthly reason. The reason was as plain as the nose on your face. She wanted to keep her daughter to herself...."

"Is that so, sir?"

"Yes...."

Outside you could hear the patients muttering impatiently and shuffling and walking about the waiting-room. Here was a stranger getting better attention.... It wasn't good enough. A man with a cough and a weakness for aniseed mixture, gathered himself together and barked hoarsely in protest.

"... If you take my advice, Sergeant, you'll press your questions. If she weeps, let her. Carry on. If she had nervous convulsions, carry on. She'll come-to.

Let her tire before you. You'll get your answers. Don't say I told you, but there's no danger. Her complaint now is simply a kind of flight from reality, she retreats into it rather than face her problems. That's all I can say. Hope it works. And I wish I could have a pipe and a yarn with you. I'm fond of detective stories, when I get time to read 'em. Well, I must push you off. The waiting-room's full, I guess.... You don't happen to want a wig or corsets whilst you're here? Only say the word...."

They both laughed heartily. First good laugh I've had in weeks, thought Macduff. Must get out more.... However, next.... The man with the cough. The aniseed fiend. Grimly the doctor drew his prescription pad to him....

R. Tinct. capsici m.X.

That 'ud settle him. Warm him up and give him a change....

Cromwell was hurrying across the road to the "Royal Oak". Littlejohn was out. He was sitting on a hard wooden chair in the bakehouse of Mr. Ephraim Davy, who, pipe in mouth, was keeping vigil over his ovens.

Alveston's body had been taken to the mortuary, and with the help of Phyllis, hastily summoned, the news had been broken to his deserted wife. Strangely enough, she had received it well. It seemed as though, having spent so long not knowing where he was or what had become of him, her mind was more at rest now she knew his wanderings and infidelities were over. The inquest on the morrow would be held by Mr. Qualtrough, but unassisted by Mr. Whatmough. The Coroner's assistant, his face lacerated by Mr. Polydore's nails, and his body bruised by the fall, was confined to the house. His antagonist, who had fallen into the priest's hole nethermost, had suffered concussion, a bleeding nose, and the rupture of his top and bottom sets of dentures. He had shut up shop for some time and, with blinds drawn, malevolently converted new furniture into antiques with the help of secret varnishes and a cunning little drill which created false wormholes.

And so, part of the case was solved. It appeared that Alveston, having lost his job and finding himself on the rocks, had returned to his former haunts to wring money from his wife, for the purpose, he had said, of emigrating. Mrs. Alveston, briefly informed of his death, had gone so far as to say that he had called on her once and tried to get money from her. She had none handy and he had said he would come back, and that she'd better have fifty pounds waiting for him to be going on with. She'd been weeping about it when Mr. Granville came in. He'd asked her what it was all about and, having nobody else she could tell, she'd said how Alveston had turned up and what he wanted. At that, Mr. Granville had grown very excited and said he was the very man he'd been seeking. She'd said, maybe Alveston was hiding at the Hall; he knew a lot about it and might be in one of the secret rooms. With that he'd gone off to the Hall, and when he came back wouldn't say anything except that he was seeing Alveston later. That was on the last day of the old year....

So, there it was. It fitted in. It looked as if Salter and Alveston had met and Alveston, for some reason, had killed Salter. It seemed as if Pennyquick's theory about Alveston's killing Plucock was right, too. The constable's baton in the priest's hole bore it out.

And then, someone had killed Alveston.

Two of the murders had, therefore, been provisionally accounted for. Yet, things were as bad as ever because the biggest nut to crack was, who'd killed the killer!

"That's right. Hall ready, now."

"Eh?"

Littlejohn had been sitting brooding over the case until Mr. Davy had completed his vital task of preparing the staff of life for his customers. He'd made it plain to the Inspector that until the bread was out, he couldn't concentrate on anything else.

"Me heart's in me job, sir," he'd declared. "And I can honly do one job at a time. Take a seat, sir, and 'ere's the h'evenin' paper. They won't be long before they're done...."

Mr. Ephraim Davy, having consulted his watch and some dials on the side of the great gas ovens in which his masterpieces had now matured, pulled a lever and the several doors of the contraption opened, revealing row after row of risen loaves, nicely browned on top, standing in tins. A wave of heat leapt from the shelves and suffused the bakehouse, temporarily taking Littlejohn's breath away. Mr. Davy took out a sample on a wooden shovel, tested it and grunted with satisfaction. Then he began to unload them and spread them out to cool. This went on for some time....

"Now, sir. Jest ten minutes. Then another lot...."

Crickets began to chirp in the bricks of the bakery, and a cat sleeping on a sack of flour rose, arched her back and disappeared into an inner room.

Mr. Davy puffed pleasurably at the pipe which never left his mouth. He was in his working clothes, a kind of clean white suit, and if he'd taken a header in his flour bin he couldn't have been more smothered in the raw product of his trade. It was in his hair, eyebrows, moustache, and there were rings of it round his eyes.

"Now, sir!"

"It's about the man you say you saw with Mr. Granville Salter the night he was killed. You're sure he was a small, stocky man?"

Mr. Davy, beneath his coating of flour, managed to convey the impression that he was deeply hurt. The corners of his mouth fell, his powdered eyebrows rose, and his eyes protruded more than ever in his chalky face.

"I'm not in the 'abit of givin' false information to anybody. Police or not police. In this village I'm known for me integrity."

"I'm not doubting what you say for a minute. Don't think that, Mr. Davy. But the Rev. Smythe, the curate, said it was a tall man about the size of Mr. Granville. Could it be that two men met him?"

"No, sir. Certingly not. I was there all the time. S'matter o' fact, I'll tell you somethin'. We was in church by twenty to twelve, singin' hymns to pass the time. I've one weakness, sir, and I see that you indulge the same. I'm a big smoker. Maybe wrong to be so much in the grip o' nicotine, but I'm as you might say, wedded to me pipe. Smoke at work, smoke at play, and, I must admit it, I get up in the night sometimes to 'ave a smoke. Well, a quarter to twelve the cravin' come on me, and as it was my turn to let the New Year in the church, I thought I might as well take a few minutes extry and smoke till twelve. Which I did. I stood in the night at the chapel door and smoked me pipe. I saw all that went on as could be seen, which wasn't much."

"You saw Salter and the stocky man and nobody else?"

"I saw the Rev. Smythe as must have been goin' in church just after I come out. Mr. Salter and the stocky man was there then talkin'. I couldn't see what they was doin'. All I see was shadows. I didn't know it was Salter till I heard what 'ad gone on. Then I knew I seen him."

"And do you think Smythe saw them?"

"Sure. I was quite a distance across the road, but Smythe passed close by. Could hear what they was sayin' if he'd a mind."

"Very well, Mr. Davy. I'm glad you confirmed that. It helps quite a lot."

"Do you know who killed Mr. Granville?"

"I think so. But I'll not commit myself, yet. That'll come later."

"Funny goings on in this village for a long time. I hope you solve it all. Maybe the police can rest then."

"What do you mean?"

"Three murders.… Oh, yes, I hear about Alveston bein' found at the 'All. The place is cursed. First Plucock, then Mr. Granville … and that stranger chap … and now Alveston. That's four!! I've lost count of 'em. Do you know, I saw Plucock goin' in the Hall the day he was killed, too."

"You did?"

"Yes. Deliverin' bread at the lodge. Happened to look up t'wards the big 'ouse and there was Plucock trying the front door. Then he went round the back. Thought nobody saw 'im, but I did. That's Andy Pennyquick's beat, not his, I thinks. And then I forgets all about it till now."

"Well, sir, it's nine and I must be gettin' in my last lot o' loaves. Else I'll be late up and miss me little read before bed."

"Yes, Mr. Davy. I'll be off. Reading anything interesting?"

"Encyclopædia, sir. Nothing like an encyclopædia. I'm readin' mine from cover to cover. Surprisin' what learnin' there is in the world. Trouble is, as soon as I've learned one lot, I forget another lot. All the same it's fascinating, sir. At present I'm up to Navigation. Used to have a little boat in the estuary and did a bit o' fishin' myself, but I never knew there was so much in sailin' a ship.... Marvellous...."

Littlejohn bade him good night and went out into the dark, leaving Mr. Davy still pop-eyed with wonder at the vast deep of human knowledge.

Phyllis Alveston answered Littlejohn's knock at the door when, ten minutes later, he called at their home, having, meanwhile, met Cromwell, who was waiting for him over a pint of beer and gave him the doctor's message. Meg, the sheep-dog, followed closely on her heels and greeted Littlejohn with a great agitation of her rear quarters, for she had no tail with which to signify joy in the usual canine way. It was all settled. Littlejohn was to take the dog when he left. His wife had already fallen-in with the idea and she had written only that day to say that the owner of their Hampstead flat had granted them a concession, they could keep the dog there, although it was contrary to the usual regulations. After all, it was as well to keep in with the police.… Meanwhile, Meg was lodging with the Alvestons, rather against Mrs. Alveston's will. She didn't like dogs, poor woman. She didn't know what she was missing!

Mrs. Alveston was in the sitting-room, in one of the large, uncomfortable-looking arm-chairs, with a rug round her knees. She looked apprehensively at Littlejohn when he entered.

"Good evening, Mrs. Alveston. How are you?"

"Only middlin'; only middlin'.…"

"I can only say how sorry I am about the death of your husband and I hope you will be willing to help us in finding out who was responsible for it.…"

"I'm in a maze, sir. I don't know hardly what I'm doin'. I can't say I shall miss him, after bein' without him all these years. But he was my husband, all the same.... The Lord hath given, the Lord hath taken away; blessed be the name of the Lord."

"Do you feel fit now to talk about him and matters concerning him, Mrs. Alveston?"

"Yes.... But it depends on what you ask me."

She was beginning to tremble a little with the usual nervous spasms from which she suffered, but Littlejohn, forewarned by the doctor, pretended not to notice them.

"Your husband visited you of late?"

"Yes. Two days before Mr. Granville was killed."

"He wanted money from you. Was that all?" Phyllis, who had been standing-by taking it all in, now spoke. "And she kept it all to herself. If she'd told me, maybe I could have done something."

"I told Mr. Granville.... He said he'd help."

"Did he say exactly how he hoped to meet Mr. Alveston again?"

"No. But my husband said he'd be back in a day or two. He never came back though."

"Will you tell me now, why Mr. Granville was here?"

"You might as well tell him, mother. She's told me all about it, Inspector. It doesn't matter now, does it, seeing that Granville's dead ...?"

Phyllis spoke bitterly and in a choking voice, and hurried from the room.

Mrs. Alveston began to weep.

"I'm that poorly, sir. Don't ask me any more tonight, please. I'll tell you all to-morrow."

"I'm sorry, Mrs. Alveston, to-morrow won't do. We've waited far too long. Had you told us all you know, we might have prevented much of the violence in this village...."

Littlejohn faced her squarely. She sobbed a bit and then grew calm.

“All right.”

“Phyllis isn’t your daughter at all, is she? She’s the daughter of Margaret Salter and was changed when your own child died.”

“Yes. Alveston and me promised we’d never tell.”

“You kept to your part of the bargain. Others have told me. Did you receive any consideration in money for it?”

“Yes. The family trust paid us three hundred a year. . . .”

“Three hundred!”

“Yes. Alveston arranged it all. Then, when he left me, I got letters with addresses at post offices, saying I was to send him half or he’d come to the village and tell it all. I couldn’t let him do that for Phyllis’s sake and Miss Margaret’s. So I sent it to the addresses he gave.”

“You posted it off when you went to see your sister?”

“Yes. How did you find out?”

"I guessed it, hearing of your journeys. Why, if he had such a regular income, did he come for more?"

"He said 'e was goin' abroad and wanted another hundred or two."

"And now, will you tell me, please, why Mr. Granville came here at Christmas time?"

"He wanted Phyllis."

"And you wouldn't agree."

"Accordin' to the Prayer Book, a man can't marry 'is cousin. I wasn't bein' no party to a sin. I'd tell him nothing, because I knew if I said she was 'is cousin, they'd wed, whatever I wanted. He thought maybe she was 'is sister. Mr. Gregory havin' a bit of a name and things … untrue things … once havin' been said about Mr. Gregory and me. He said he'd get to the bottom of it another way. That's why he wanted to see Alveston, I'm sure o' that."

"Did Mr. Granville ever mention the Salter Treasure?"

"Yes, in a bit of a joke. Said if 'e found it, the family would soon be in the old home again. He said he'd got some good clues about the treasure if any there was."

"Did he mention what clues?"

"No. But when I said Alveston 'ad been here, Mr. Granville said maybe he was hidin' in the Hall, not wantin' to be seen about the village on account of what he'd once done. Now he's dead I might as well tell you that he 'listed for the first war on account of bein' wrong in his estate accounts by some hundreds. Mr. Gregory found it out, so Alveston fled off. Mr. Gregory never told the police out of regard for me, but Alveston didn't know that. It kept 'im away from the village. Not that 'e wanted to come back to me. There were other women. That I knew. When Alveston come by night, I didn't tell him the police knew nothing of his crimes, so he went off to hide somewhere."

"And Mr. Granville went after him."

"Yes. 'E said, maybe Alveston was hidin' in one of the priests' holes. He'd just found how to get in one of them and would try."

"Did he find Alveston, then?"

"No, sir. But 'e found the hiding hole. Alveston wasn't in it. But somebody had been there of late, because Mr. Granville said he'd found chocolate packets and tins of food there and signs of somebody in it. He also showed me a policeman's truncheon. I asked what it was for. Mr. Granville said maybe Alveston had got it from somewhere and used it for protection...."

"A policeman's baton, eh?"

So, that was why Alveston had killed Granville. He'd found Plucock's truncheon, dropped in the fight in which he died, and accused Alveston of the murder.

"How did Mr. Granville seem when he came here? I mean after he found the hiding-place."

"Very cut-up. He said if Alveston came again, not to let him in. To keep the door locked and not tell Phyllis what had happened."

"I see."

Mrs. Alveston was sobbing again.

"I've been a good mother to Phyllis. She can't say I haven't. Nobody could 'ave been better. I wasn't lettin' her marry in sin. Besides, 'e was far above her station...."

"Hardly, if she was his cousin."

"That didn't matter. It was how she'd been brought up with servants of the Hall and her illegitimate.... Besides, Phyllis could have 'ad plenty better. Good men there was wanted 'er, and would have made her far better husbands."

"Such as?"

"Her own boss's son in Thorncastle would give his eyes for her. Mad about 'er. And a lot of other nice young men from round about in good jobs and not ruined gentry, either. And there's Mr. Smythe, too.

He wants her bad, but she wouldn't even look at the poor man because of Mr. Granville. It was a shame to see poor Mr. Smythe."

"You mean Smythe, the curate here?"

"Who else? A very nice young man, too. You might think he's a bit timid and queer, but that's his nerves. He was a chaplain in the war. Went over with our boys on 'D' day, he did, and won the M.C. for bravery. She might 'ave done worse with a man like that."

"Did Mr. Smythe know she loved Granville?"

"I guess so. He came here and asked me for 'er. Then, he proposed to her and she said there was another. He must have known who it was. All the village knows. To see Granville and Phyllis in the village together was enough."

"Did Smythe think Phyllis was your daughter?"

"I guess so. I never told him anything else."

"Have you seen him lately?"

"Yes. 'E called to-day to say how sorry 'e was. Seemed very cut-up about it. And his nerves terribly bad. Like a ghost, 'e was."

"You've nothing more to tell me, Mrs. Alveston?"

"What more is there? I seem to 'ave told all I know."

"By the way, how did your husband come to know the hiding-places in the Hall?"

"He was a handyman and often did jobs indoors. He looked after a lot of the fabric afore we was married. Said 'e'd found places there as would be useful if ever 'e wanted to disappear."

So Alveston, in the course of his work, had probably found the old priest's hole and used it when he needed it. Old bones for company would mean nothing to a callous man like him.

"Well, thanks very much, Mrs. Alveston. I'm sorry to have troubled and upset you. We have our work to do, you know."

"Yes, I know. I wish Phyllis would come back to me. I feel that poorly...."

Phyllis, her eyes red with weeping, came from the kitchen to let Littlejohn out and, as he bade her goodnight, shook hands with him cordially to show him she still thought him her friend.

FIFTEEN

MISS MARGARET

MRS. HENRY LACEY, née Margaret Salter, lived in a flat in a mews in Kensington. Her husband was one of those invisible powers whose names are rarely heard except in certain closely confined circles. He was a retired diplomat, whose work had been so good during his days at the Foreign Office, that he was retained as unofficial adviser to untrained politicians, who, suddenly finding themselves rocketed into office and with the life and well-being of a whole world in their grasp, turn to find a steady hand to hold and guide them. Henry Lacey spent most of his time on the Continent, where conference after conference held him tied. His wife usually kept him company, but, refusing to spend Christmas anywhere but at home, had paid a flying visit to the little oasis they kept over a stable in London. There, Littlejohn was lucky enough to find her when he called.

Margaret Lacey was tall and, in spite of advancing years and little vigorous exercise, had kept her figure. She must have been a beauty in her youth, for, in the fifties, she retained the clear skin, firm, delicately modelled features, fair complexion and fine blue eyes which had attracted so many to her in her heyday.

A chauffeur in wispy moustache and sideboards, like a South American dancer, who was polishing a flashy car in the former stable under the Lacey flat, didn't even remove his cigarette when Littlejohn asked for her. He just jerked his head to show she was up above and went on with his rubbing. The car didn't belong to the Laceys, who, to the chauffeur's way of thinking, were no-accounts. All breeding and no cash.... Now, his boss, who lived round the corner, in a large house formerly occupied by a lord, had made a cool million in floating companies, and cabinet ministers ate out of his hand....

Littlejohn rapped on the little brass knocker on the green door of the flat. Mrs. Lacey answered it herself and asked him in. The place was modestly furnished in exquisite taste, with odds and ends, bought all over the world during half a lifetime of collecting lovely things.

"I've seen you before, Inspector.... At my nephew's funeral...."

It was quite true. She had been pointed out to the Inspector on the day before, but he preferred a trip to London rather than an interview on the spot at an unsuitable time.

"I called to ask you one or two questions about your nephew, Mrs. Lacey. I had to come to town, so thought it best to call...."

"Yes. I got your message that you'd be coming. What can I do to help? I'm afraid Granville and I didn't meet much. I'm abroad most of the time. Even now, I'd be back in Paris if it hadn't been for poor Granville's death. A shocking business. I hear you've an idea who killed my nephew...."

"We have. Though the motive eludes us still. We think it was Alveston, the former bailiff."

"I never liked him.... Always a surly, insolent man, though good at his job. I give him credit for that. And now he's been killed, too."

"Yes. We've still to find his murderer and we haven't an idea."

"So you think I can help you."

"I imagine so, although some of the questions will be rather painful...."

"Suppose we have a cup of tea. I'm just making one for myself and the kettle's on."

She hurried to the kitchenette and soon returned with a tray of silver and china tea-things.

"Now, Inspector," she said, when they were settled.

"In the first place, Mrs. Lacey, how long is it since you saw your nephew last?"

"Just before Christmas. He wrote to me in Paris asking me certain questions about the family. I replied that I didn't care to write.... Besides, it was a bit complicated. So I'd tell him when I came over for Christmas. That brought him here."

"What were the questions, please?"

"He was in love with Phyllis Alveston and called to ask if she was in any way related to him."

"Why?"

"Her mother would not hear of their marriage and, as there have been rumours about her parentage, Granville wanted the truth."

"And you told him, Mrs. Lacey?"

"No. Do you know the truth?"

"I do, madam. Why didn't you tell him?"

"She is my daughter. Needless to say, she's illegitimate and my husband knows all about it. I tell you that because of what follows."

"Thank you."

"I didn't tell Granville, because there were both Phyllis and Mrs. Alveston to be considered. When the Alvestons adopted my daughter, they became her parents. There was an arrangement, both moral and financial, and it was agreed that the secret should be rigidly kept. If Mrs. Alveston did not choose to tell Granville, I'd no right to do so. I doubt if Phyllis knew, and if she did, I laid no claims whatever to her love or duty. Those belonged to her mother by adoption. It cost me a lot to take such an attitude, because nothing would have pleased me better than for them to wed, cousins though they were. Granville was a very decent boy.… But, I wanted to see Mrs. Alveston before breaking the secret. And, as Granville was staying with her at Christmas, it was naturally a bit awkward. I let it wait, intending to write to the Alvestons later."

"I follow."

"He was killed before I could do so."

"What motive could Alveston have had for killing Mr. Granville?"

"I'm sure I don't know."

"I have my own theory. Alveston was hiding at the Hall. He thought the police were after him for embezzlement of the family funds in days past. He encountered the local constable, Plucock, and, in a scuffle, stunned him and threw him, unconscious, in a ditch to drown. In the fight, the policeman's truncheon was dropped in Alveston's hiding-place. Granville found it and must have accused Alveston. For that, Alveston killed him."

"But why all this skulking in hiding-places?"

"In the first place, Alveston went to Cobbold to wring money from his wife. He had to hide and, knowing the secrets of the Hall, concealed himself in a priest's hole there."

"Ah … I see.…"

"Plucock, the constable, had become obsessed by a treasure said to be hidden there. The secret of the Headless Jesuit...."

"Yes. A great thrill in our young days."

"He must have been prowling about the house when Alveston emerged from his hideout."

"Granville talked about the priest's hole when he was here. He said it was a kind of sideline he'd encountered in his searches in family records for some trace of Phyllis's birth. He had the little jingle, said to have been written by Simister Salter with him. I was able to give him a clue. You see, my husband is a bit keener witted than our family and when I mentioned it once, in fun, he suggested that one number might be stairs on the staircase and the other panels.... I told Granville and he wrote it down."

"That accounts for a lot. He evidently tried out the solution, succeeded, and discovered Alveston's hiding-place with the truncheon in it. He must have left the note with his papers, because another fellow, you remember him no doubt—the little private investigator who was found killed in the Hall—also disturbed Alveston and met his fate. The victim, Barney Faircluff, had been rummaging among Mr. Granville's papers and must have found your clue, too."

"Oh, dear! What tragedy from such a simple thing."

"Have you yourself heard or seen Alveston lately, Mrs. Lacey?"

"I was coming to that. The Alvestons received three hundred a year for Phyllis until she married, from a family trust. When Alveston ran away, his wife tells me, she sent half the money to him after he'd written and demanded it as the price of keeping silent. Then, that wasn't enough. He wanted it all. She sent it and had to open her little business to make out. That seemed to satisfy him for quite a while. . . ."

"He was in a profitable business for a long time and, I guess, was quite well-off. Then, he started drinking and fell lower and lower. He lost his business, but his competence got him a job … quite a good one … with a Corporation. His drinking lost him that eventually. He then decided to go abroad."

"When was that, Inspector?"

"In the late autumn, as far as I can find out. When he got short of cash, he went to Cobbold and began to pester his wife."

"And me, too…."

"You mean …?"

"He tried blackmailing me. It was late autumn, too. A letter from him was forwarded to me in Paris. He said unless I sent him five hundred pounds, he'd tell my husband about Phyllis. I was foolish enough to reply that my husband already knew. I then told my husband and had great difficulty in persuading him not to inform the police. I got another letter from Alveston. He said he'd tell all the village, then. I burned it. I didn't even tell Henry. He got so cross. I wish I had, now."

"Did you hear any further?"

"No. By that time, things were happening to him in Cobbold, apparently. I inquired if he'd been seen there. He hadn't, however."

"Who did you ask?"

"The curate, Mr. Smythe...."

"Smythe! You know him well, then?"

"Of course. He's my regular correspondent and source of information."

"But surely, Mr. Worsnip, as an old friend ...?"

"No, no. In his dotage. Smythe is indirectly connected with the family. He's the son of Meek, who used to be our tweeny ... the maid who had to leave because she got herself into trouble and the man deserted her."

"And the trouble was Mr. Smythe ...?"

Mrs. Lacey laughed.

"If you want to call him that. You see, Inspector, I'd been through all that agony myself. I befriended Meek. Got her rooms far enough away and, when her baby was born, I looked after him. He was put in a good home for babies and, later, I kept an eye on him and, as he proved a very clever lad, I sent him to college. He did well and, as the living at Cobbold is, or was, one of our family perquisites, I got him made curate there. Meek married a very decent fellow later and went to Australia."

"And you and Smythe remained very firm friends, Mrs. Lacey?"

"Yes. He's devoted to me. Might be my own son. I couldn't have children after Phyllis was born, so I suppose I've lavished mother-love on my foundling a little."

"You know, of course, Mrs. Lacey, that Smythe's in love with Phyllis Alveston, too. That's what her mother told me."

"Yes. Poor boy. He knew she and Granville were fond of one another, too. It was rather hard on him."

"He didn't know, of course, who Phyllis was?"

"I'm afraid he did...."

"You told him?"

"Yes. Some time ago, under promise of the strictest secrecy. I could trust him implicitly...."

"But why?"

"He was always worried about his parentage. He asked me over and over again.... In the end, I promised to tell him when he graduated. I did. He was terribly distressed. He'd already developed an inferiority complex, in spite of all my efforts. Naturally, of course, not knowing who his father and mother were. I consoled him, and, to show him he wasn't the only one, I told him of Phyllis. He met her later, and fell in love with her. They'd a bond in common ... illegitimacy, you see. I guess he felt that, loving her, if they married it would level things up."

"Did he come to see you much?"

"Well, no. We are away so often. But whenever I crossed home, I let him know and he came up to London for a day or two and saw me."

"He never mentioned Alveston, or showed any great hatred of Granville … or … well, developed signs of bitterness?"

"No. I was very proud when he got decorated in the war. He was always a shy, timid boy, but could brace himself for desperate efforts.… I guess it stood him in good stead when he was with the troops on 'D' day."

The chauffeur had, apparently, cleaned his car and now started the engine. The whole place shook with dull throbbing and then, as the roar increased, you couldn't hear yourself speak. It was as well the Inspector and Mrs. Lacey had finished their talk. He left her getting ready to pack for her return to Paris to-morrow.

Whilst all this was going on, Cromwell, left behind, was paying a visit to one of the casualties of the battle at Salter Hall. Mr. Whatmough lived with his mother in an old black-and-white cottage in one of the many narrow sidestreets of Thorncastle. He had been unable to attend the inquest on Alveston owing to his appearance after the fray. A black eye, scratches on his face and a nose almost twice its already outsize.

Cromwell knocked at the door. A little old woman opened it. She didn't in any way resemble her dark, lanky son. She was grey, with sandy and grey eyebrows, a little pinched face with high cheek-bones, and a hooked nose. She looked like a small witch and might have been expected at any time to seize a besom and become airborne. But she lacked the confidence of a black artist. She was very humble and fawned upon Cromwell as soon as he told her who he was.

"Come in, sir. Come in. I do hope, sir, you've come to do somethin' about the 'orrible thing that scoundrel Polydores 'as done to my boy. A shame it is, and him so ’armless ’imself. Wouldn’t ’urt a fly, sir, and so good to his poor old mother. Come in, sir.”

The windows were small and the room was dark. You could only see about a yard from the windows, and where the large fire in the old grate cast a glow about itself. By the fireside were seated another strange pair. A little man with a totally bald head and a face like Punch and a little woman who, with the exception of a large, hairy mole on her chin, was a replica of Mrs. Whatmough.

“This is me sister and brother-in-law, sir. They’re all we’ve got left of the family. A great comfort to me in me time of trouble, sir.”

To prove what a comfort he was, Punch, otherwise Mr. Enoch Tyle, leapt to his feet and in a shrill voice began to get very angry.

“Someone is goin’ to sit up for this, sir. I don’t care ’ow wealthy and influential that rascally Polydores is … I’ll ’ave ’im before the Law. He shall pay, sir. He shall pay if it costs me every penny I've got. I'll even sell my shop…."

"Ow … ow … ow …" moaned his wife, as though she already saw what was left of their small and unprofitable grocery business being sold up. "Ow … ow … ow … It ought to be his master, Mr. Qualtroughs, 'oo pays. He was injured in the course o' duty…."

"Be quiet, Nellie," hissed Mr. Tyle. "Leave all to me. I'm a business man. I *know.*"

"But I see it in the teacups," protested his partner. "I see it in the tea-leaves as Mortimer was comin' into money and weddin'-bells in a month, so …"

The thought of losing her boy as a result of her sister's soothsaying was too much for Mrs. Whatmough. She started to howl, as well.

"Weddin' bells! Ow, ow, ow…. Me boy. I don't want to lose me boy to a schemin' woman. He's the joy of me old age. Such a clever boy, sir…. Such a clever boy…."

“Could I see him, please?” said Cromwell, thoroughly fed-up with the scene and half suffocated from the hot, airless atmosphere into the bargain.

“The doctor said ’is nerves was bad and to stop in bed a day or so. It’s that Polydores ...”

“Leave ’im to me.... Leave ’im to me.... I’ll make ’im sit up. I’ll make ’im bounce! Every penny he’s got I’ll ’ave out of ’im in damages for this.... Nobody’s goin’ to do damage to a relation of Enoch Tyle’s without bein’ made to suffer....”

Punch’s voice rose like the cawing of an old crow. It caused a disturbance upstairs.

“Hey! Hey, there. What’s goin’ on down there ...?”

Mr. Whatmough, from his couch of pain, was getting angry.

His mother rushed to the foot of the staircase which mounted aloft from the living-room.

“All right, Mortimer. All right, love. It’s a Mr. Cromwells called from the p’leece. Wants to see you....”

“Well, why the ’ell ’asn’t he been sent up? Kicking up all that row. What will he think you are, all of you?”

“Don’t swear so, Mortimer. You wasn’t brought up that way. ’E wasn’t brought up that way, I’m sure, Mr. Cromwells, sir, but that Polydores ’as made his nerves that bad....”

“I’ll swear if I want. What’s he waitin’ for? Send him up.”

“Would you be so kind as to go up, sir? Good of you to call at our ’umble ’ome to see my boy. He’s a good, clever boy. Rose from office-boy with Mr. Qualtroughs to be his right-hand man. Mr. Qualtroughs depends on ’im, sir. I don’t know ’ow he’s doin’ without ’im. And an inquest on that there Alvestons to-day, too.”

And the couple by the fireside chanted like a dismal Greek chorus.

“I’ll knock ’is money out of that wicked Polydores, if it costs ...”

"Ow … ow … ow …"

"What the 'ell …?" fluting from upstairs. "Shut up crying and send 'im up…."

Cromwell mounted the stairs and, guided by the old lady who hovered in the background like a wraith, turned into the best bedroom.

"No need for you, mother. This is private."

"All right, Mortimer love. Did you take your medicine as the doctor said? And the 'erbs your aunt Nellie brewed you? Do you want anything? Are you comfortable …?"

"Oh, yes, yes, yes. Can't I be left alone?"

Whatmough was best left alone. He was an awful sight. Added to the disfigurements of his by no means prepossessing face inflicted by Mr. Polydore, Mortimer was angry and dishevelled. His lanky hair stood on end and the elegant moustache which he took such a pride in fixing and twisting to two long points, one on each side, had been combed out and now looked like a piece of bushy black knitting stuck on his upper lip. He was sitting up in bed the better to denounce the causes of the turmoil and had gathered the patchwork counterpane round his shoulders. He looked like Joseph in his coat of many colours after a bad night out.

"Well?" he shouted at Cromwell.

Whatmough hadn't recovered from the shock and humiliation of being bested by Mr. Polydore, but what was worse, he had been laid up and prevented by his doctor from attending an inquest, and that on Alveston.

Mr. Qualtrough, to add to Mortimer's heap of misery, had been too busy with his affairs even to inquire or call about the health of his underling. In fact, he had been more chirpy and talkative in court than ever before, revelling in the freedom of being without his watchdog. And the last drop in this bitter cup had been the report of Uncle Enoch, who had been sent to the inquest, that Flitcroft, the hated rival of Whatmough and his junior in the office, had assisted Mr. Qualtrough in his place.

"I'll make that Polydores pay for all this," Uncle Enoch had said by way of consolation.

"Oh shut up," came the ungrateful reply.

"Hope you're feeling better," said Cromwell when they were alone and the door closed.

"No, I'm not. I'm bad. I'll kill Polydore for this. I'll wreck his shop. I'll … I'll …"

"Now, now, now, Mr. Whatmough. Calm yourself. You'll soon be out and about again."

"I won't soon be out and about. This is going to be a long job. I'll make Polydore suffer for this. Unprovoked attack, it was.…"

"All right, then. Do as you like. But answer me a question or two first."

"What? I hope it's about the assault. You're not letting it rest there? And what's up with Mr. Qualtrough? Hasn't even been to see me. And me as good as saved 'is life. If it hadn't been for me,

Polydore would 'ave … I hope you've got a note of that. Attempted murder by Polydore…."

"Come along, now…. You remember some time since, saying you saw the Headless Jesuit at the Hall …?"

"And was laughed at. If that's all they can do … Besides, that's beside the point. It's me, now. Polydore did the crime…. You can see how desperate he is. Stop at nothing…. He did 'em. After the treasure…."

"What do you know about the treasure?"

"It should have been in the hiding-place where we found Polydore. He's had it. That's why he tried to kill me. Knew it was the Coroner's by right…."

"The Jesuit we were talking about…."

"I did see him. No imagination…. Runnin' across the lawn, he was…."

"What did he look like?"

"A Jesuit, of course."

"What does a Jesuit look like? I've never seen one to know him."

"They're monks. This one was a monk."

"You mean he had on a sort of monk's gown and girdle?"

"It was dusk.... I couldn't see the belt, if there was one. How could I? It was dusk, I tell you. But, as he ran, I could see sort of skirts flapping...."

"A sort of cassock?"

"I don't know. Like a monk."

"But you said he was headless...."

"I couldn't see his head."

"Perhaps he'd sunk it on his breast so as not to be recognized."

"Could have been ... I don't know. My nerves are bad. I hope that's all you've got to ask. I'm not fit ... I'm ..."

"Just one more. When was this?"

"Night before I told you and you all laughed...."

"You mean the day of the Granville Salter inquest?"

"Yes."

Alveston wasn't dead then, according to medical evidence and Barney Faircluff hadn't then been killed, either.

"Talkin' of inquests, to-day, were you there at Alveston's?"

"Yes."

"How did it go?"

"Adjourned, of course...."

Whatmough flailed the air impatiently, tore at the patchwork quilt and clawed at the throat of his nightshirt.

"I don't mean that ... I don't mean that.... How was it conducted?"

"All right. No complaints. The Coroner had another clerk with him...."

"Flitcroft! Blast 'im. Blast Polydore.... Blast everybody...."

And with that, he sank in the bed and turned his face to the wall. From below a shrill voice:

"Are you all right, Mortimer ...?"

Cromwell descended hastily and made for the door.

"He doesn't seem so well.... Maybe a dose of medicine...."

"Me pore boy...."

Mrs. Whatmough hastily tramped up the stairs.

By the fireside the Tyles were still brooding. Mrs. Tyle was deep in the dregs of another cup of tea.

"Money's comin' to Mortimer.... Money.... An' weddin'-bells in a month...."

"To 'ell with weddings...."

"They's a funeral here, too, afore long."

"That's more like. It'll be that Polydores. He'll fold up and die when I've done with him...."

"Good afternoon," said Cromwell.

"Good afternoon," barked Mr. Tyle. "See you in court when the time comes...."

“Phew!” said Cromwell to himself as he got the right side of the closed door between himself and the motley crew at the Whatmoughs’. He gulped in lungfuls of fresh air.

Upstairs he caught sight of the curtains moving and round the edge appeared the face of Mrs. Whatmough watching him depart. It gave him quite a shock, for her eyes were full of hate.

SIXTEEN

MRS. PAWKER GIVES NOTICE

THE Rev. Augustus Smythe, known to the schoolboys as Gussie, was not at his lodgings when Littlejohn called to see him just before dinner on his return from London.

"'E's gone off to Thorncastle," said Mrs. Pawker, Smythe's landlady. "Spends a lot o' time there nowadays, if you ask me. It's not right, it isn't, with the old vicar in his dotage and so much to do in the parish. Them atheists and communists wants watchin'. Wot is parsons for but to keep the banner of the Lord flying? And if they aren't there, who's …?"

"Excuse me, Mrs. Pawker, but would you mind asking him when he comes in, if he'll kindly call at the police station; I want a word with him?"

"Oh dear! I 'ope 'e's not been doin' somethin' wrong. They's enough wrong been done in this village already...."

"No; nothing wrong. Just a word, that's all."

"Wot a relief. A nice man. I never 'ad a better lodger. Never. So considerate, like. But 'e's sweet on Phyllis Alveston and never off the doorstep of the place she works at in Thorncastle. Poor chance he's stood so far, with the gentry in competition. Now, maybe, things'll be better for 'im. We're only young once, are we?"

"That's true. Thank you...."

Littlejohn was going to say good-bye, but Mrs. Pawker had been washing other people's small-clothes all day and was now ironing them. This had kept her indoors and she'd missed her tour round the village and her talk to her cronies. The gossip was all bottled up inside her and Littlejohn looked a nice man. She wasn't going to give in so easily. She ignored his gestures of departure.

"As I was sayin', he's a nice young man. Not that Miss Phyllis isn't a nice young woman. A good pair they'll make, I say. But Phyllis is a bit of a jumped-up one, if you know what I mean, sir. Most other girls in the village as 'ad laid-up mothers, would 'ave done for them and kept the 'ouse nice at nights when they'd done they's work. But not Miss Phyllis. Oh no. A daily 'elp is what they 'ave. All the work, and when Miss Phyllis goes out o' nights, somebody pops in now and then to see Mrs. Alveston doesn't want anythin'. That's what I been doin' for nigh on twenty years. Ever since Phyllis was a child. And I'm gettin' fed-up with it. 'S matter of fact, I give me notice to-day."

"You *do* for Mrs. Alveston, Mrs. Pawker?"

"*Did,* you mean, although they asked me to consider me decision. But they's plenty of other good jobs where they don't deceive them as helps 'em."

"Deceive?"

"Yes.... But come in, if you like, sir. No use standing out in the dark and cold...."

She led Littlejohn into her cottage. A neat two up and two down place, clean as a new pin.

"Sit down, sir.... I was just goin' to brew. Will ye take a cup, sir?"

"Thank you, Mrs. Pawker."

Mrs. Pawker's ironing was hanging on a clotheshorse and there were piles of it on chairs and in a basket. The room was choc-a-block with old-fashioned furniture. The walls were like a photographic exhibition. The late Pawker, a roadman, had been knocked down and killed by a dray in the course of duty, leaving his wife with five children to bring up, which she did most gallantly. Now they'd all married and were scattered. The walls were covered with little framed photographs of the weddings of the three male and two female Pawkers and then followed the results of such events, seventeen grandchildren, displayed on the walls in various stages of evolution, from lying flat and naked on their bellies and alone, to gathered together in their respective droves with parents standing proudly in the groups. The last picture showed the eldest grandson in R.A.F. uniform with a buxom wife and two kids of his own. To add an air of legitimacy to the whole exhibition, there was, over the fireplace, in the seat of honour, a huge framed enlargement of Mr. and Mrs. Pawker, Senior, taken on their wedding day, she in white with a huge hat sprouting flowers, and he, looking like someone taken from cold-storage, in an antique billycock, white tie, dickey and high collar, and what looked like his father's mourning suit. There was an astonished look on the face of the progenitor of the enormous framed brood which faced him, as though he'd somehow started something he was powerless to stop.

"'Ere we are.... Good and 'ot and strong, sir."

"Thank you, Mrs. Pawker. Don't let me stop you ironing. We can talk as you work."

Oh, no. None of that for Mrs. Pawker. No half-measures. The gossip was going to be full to the brim and overflowing. She sat heavily down in the armchair facing Littlejohn, took a good swig of tea, and relaxed, which mainly consisted of allowing her enormous bosom to rest on her knees.

"You're discontented with the Alvestons at present?"

"I am that. Come wot may, all weathers and all times, I've stuck by 'em. Even when me rheumatics nearly crippled me, I went. Not that Mrs. Alveston couldn't 'ave done a bit more for 'erself. Let 'erself go when Alveston left 'er. With a 'usband like 'im, she oughter bucked-up when he went ... yes, an' set about and found another. When my old man was killed, I'd several offers meself from nice men in Thorncastle, till I told 'em about my five. Well … you couldn't expect …"

"What's wrong at the Alvestons'?"

"The people as I does for usually treats me as one of the fambly. Takes me into their confidenks, like. That's 'ow it was at the Alvestons' till lately. Now she's started holdin' back on me, deceivin' me, that's what she's done. Deceived me."

Mrs. Pawker took another draught of tea and exhaled loudly to show her approval of it.

"I've known Mary Ann Alveston ever since she come to the village. About fifteen she'd be then. Her dad came as postman from somewheres in Kent, I think. Lame, 'e was, and got about with a stick. Well, for one thing, that's gone."

"What's gone, Mrs. Pawker?"

"The stick. It was allus there in the 'all stand. Sort o' curio. It must 'ave wore down a lot with Bill Trumper usin' it so much, so he put about three inches o' lead pipe on the end instead of the ferrule thing, like. A day or two since, it was missin' from the stand. 'Where's yore pore father's stick? It's gone,' I sez to Mrs. Alveston. 'I'm sure I can't say,' sez 'er ladyship, 'igh and mighty. O'course she knew! Else she'd'ave been in a tear about it. She treasured that stick. Reminded 'er of the ole man. But to talk to me and 'old out on me like that! I knew 'er when 'er and 'er dad 'adn't two ha'pennies to rub together.... But that's not all."

Littlejohn sipped his tea. It was a strong brew, the kind a spoon would almost stand upright in. It left a slightly metallic coating in the mouth and throat.

"... All them tinned things, too. Durin' the war when things was so bad to get ... and after, too, for that matter ... I allus got 'er what I got meself. Sorry for them, I was, with all this rationin' and queuein'. I laid-in a shelf o' sardines, tinned beefs, stewed steaks, and the like. Well, they've half of 'em gone...."

"You don't say, Mrs. Pawker?"

"Yes, they 'ave. I allus said to 'er: 'Be careful o' those tins,' I sez. 'They's worse times comin'. So keep as many as you can. Wot with this government, and strikes, and whatnots, we's all starve afore we've done. So, you keep them tins...'"

"Quite right, too."

"Well, a good dozen of 'em's gone. Corned beef, sardines, tinned mackerel.... And the Snooks left behind. I wouldn't 'ave minded the Snooks...."

"Where have they gone, Mrs. Pawker?"

"All in good time...."

She was enjoying it. She sipped her tea and added to it an even more horrible, standing brew from the teapot. It was as black as ink.

"More tea? No? Well, as I was sayin', the tins went and when I asks 'Whatever's 'appened to that shelf o' goods I got you?' her ladyship up and sez some they'd ate and some must 'ave been took. Took! 'Oo could 'ave took 'em? Me, I expect, or Andy Pennyquick, 'as is allus in and out o' the Alvestons' since the murders, or maybe, Mister Granville or the Reverend Smythe.… Took! She give ’em away, and I know ’oo to.”

The climax was coming! Littlejohn sipped his unholy brew. He had to admit that it perked him up. It acted like a tonic on his nerves, otherwise this long-winded harangue would have …

“I knew ’oo. She tuck ’em to Alveston herself.”

“But she’s bedridden.…”

“Bedridden when it suits ’er. It don’t stop ’er goin’ to see her sister now and then. An’ it don’t stop ’er gettin’ up when nobody’s about and in the dark o’ night, goin’ over to the Hall to give my tinned stuff to that good-for-nothin’ as is hidin’ there from justice. Ever since Alveston come back to the village, she’s been all of a twitter, worryin’ and wonderin’. And then, when ’is vittles give out, she gives ’im my tins … *and* tells me lies. Deceived me, that’s what she done. So I give notice.…”

"But how do you know she went to the Hall herself? He may have called for them."

"Not 'im. She went. Now as we knows 'oo done for Plucock and Mr. Granville.... Oh, we know; it's got out.... Now we know as Alveston did it, no wonder 'e daren't show 'is nose. She went to 'im."

"How do you know?"

"Well, in the first place, she must 'a gone through the field-path behind 'er cottage to the 'all. That dirtied 'er boots. So she cleaned 'em herself."

"Well, what of that?"

"I allus cleans the boots there, first thing. Includin' Miss Phyllis's. Nobody uses the cleanin' tackle but me. It's in a wood box. I know when anybody's bin at that box. I'm a tidy woman. I leaves it all neat; tins, brushes, cloths, all apple-pie, like. Somebody mixed 'em all up. And, it wasn't Phyllis, becos I asked 'er and she said no, why should she?"

"I see...."

"And that's not all. Two nights since I went over to the Alvestons' house with the laundry. Nobody was downstairs, so I thought Miss Phyllis must be out. So I lets myself in with me key. I allus 'ave a key on account of the old lady bein' in bed. I lets meself in. Missus must be asleep, I thinks. It was so quiet. I just went up quietly to see she's all right and lo and be'old the bed's empty! She's gone out. And 'er with a bad 'eart. Whatever else she's got or whatever else the doctor sez, 'er heart's bad. I know it. She'd gone to the 'all with some more tins of mine. That's what she done. I left the washin' and off. Next day, I sez nothin'. Neither did me lady. That's the last straw, I thinks, I'm off. So I gives me notice and tells 'er I got me pride. What do I mean? she sez. You knows very well, I sez, and with that I takes me apron and I leaves there and then."

Littlejohn sat very quietly thinking and still sipping his tea.

"Let me warm up yore tea, sir...."

"Eh? No thanks, Mrs. Pawker. That'll do very nicely. And now, I mustn't keep you from your work any longer. I'm grateful for the tea and the chat. It's been very nice."

Two nights since. That was the time, according to medical evidence, that Alveston had been killed. And his wife had been up and about....

"What time would that be when you called and found Mrs. Alveston out?"

"I listened to the nine o'clock news and then went straight."

"Between a quarter and half-past nine, then?"

"Yes. Why?"

"What does she usually wear when she goes out?"

"Nearly allus 'as a black dress on an' a black coat. Very partial to black. Suits 'er melancholy, too, I guess."

"And a hat?"

"A 'at when she goes to her sister's. But maybe she'd put 'er shawl over 'er head if nobody was seein' her; it bein' a bit cold."

"What kind of shawl?"

"Black, knitted, woolly one. Why?"

"It's interesting, that's all.... Good night, Mrs. Pawker, and thank you again."

At the "Royal Oak" he met Cromwell and they ate a rather belated meal, exchanging notes and information as they did so.

"Mrs. Alveston! Up and about and taking food to Alveston! That's a corker and a lucky thing you called at Pawker's."

"Yes. Probably that's who Whatmough saw, too. He said a black sort of cassock, didn't you tell me? And no head. Mrs. Alveston was in black skirts and a shawl, maybe crouching her head in her shoulders on account of the cold. She'd evidently been a time or two and Whatmough must have spotted her."

"Yeeees. Maybe. That could account for it."

"And the heavy postman's stick, loaded, to all intents and purposes with a good, solid block of lead piping. The weapon which killed Alveston wasn't found."

"You don't mean to say …?"

"Mrs. Alveston? Hardly. I was just playing with theories. We've cleared the ground about Plucock, Salter and Barney Faircluff. That leaves us to find the murderer of Alveston. And we're about as near to that as we were when we started.… Come on. Let's call on the Pennyquicks. I've arranged for Smythe to be there when he gets back from town. He's out pursuing the lovely Phyllis in Thorncastle at present.…"

The arrival of the two Scotland Yard men at the police-house relieved the tension. It had been growing all day and now was likely to cause an eruption. Over the Christmas holidays as she watched the comings and goings, the flirtations, and the pairings-off of the young of the village, Mrs.

Pennyquick had been seized with maternal apprehension. Four daughters, the eldest twenty-three, the youngest sixteen, and not one of them had yet "got off". It was high time. Mrs. Pennyquick, knowing there weren't any better-looking girls in the county than her own, began to question her intelligence and conscience. It was a great worry; almost a family disgrace. In fact, a personal affront to herself by the eligible males of the county. Her husband didn't agree. There he sat among his daughters, smiling a soft, self-satisfied sort of grin, and they chaffed and waited on him and cheeked him and said he was the only man they loved. And when she mentioned her apprehension to him, he just laughed and said something about their having their heads screwed on right and knowing what they wanted and not being manmad. He sounded proud of it all!

Mrs. Pennyquick sat beside the fire, darning a pair of huge, rough, grey constabulary socks. Her husband was sitting at the table making a report and heavy weather. An old ink-pot stood before him and he kept dipping his pen nervously in it and shaking back into the bottle what he'd taken from it. Now and then he missed his mark and shook it on the table. Then he mopped it up surreptitiously with his handkerchief, thinking she hadn't seen him. He wouldn't go and do his writing in his office, as he called the front room. He preferred her presence beside him. Just like an old coat, she told herself, having seen something to that effect in a lurid love-story in a woman's magazine. Now and then, she'd interrupt his labours. "The Millses girl has got engaged to a nice young man from Carstonwood" or "The Kershaw girl's weddin'll soon be 'ere, now. Choral, it's goin' to be. Wreath and veil...." All the time with her own girls in mind, of course, and hoping he'd sense the reproach in her tone. Instead, he'd got to pretending not to hear. His lips moved as he wrote.... "I beg to suggest that the Inspector be sent to Willow Bank Farm. Previous to Christmas they had a lot more pigs than they now have. I suspect …"

"Does that sound right, mother? 'Than they now 'ave?' Don't seem to chime somehow.…"

"Of course, you wasn't listenin' to what I was sayin'. Might as well be a lump o' wood for all you care.…"

Pennyquick's eyes opened wide. Whatever was the matter?

The constable had removed his tunic and was clad in a blazer, with large, verticle purple and green stripes. A pre-war relic of the Cobbold Bowling Club. Old Major Duff, the President—killed later by a bomb when visiting London—had insisted on blazers. The diffident bobby had withheld from such splendour as long as he dared and then had won one in the annual tournament!

The door-bell rang. Hastily Pennyquick removed and hid the purple and green panoply, and scuffled into his official jacket.

When Littlejohn and Cromwell entered, the Pennyquicks looked the perfect candidates for the Dunmow Flitch for marital bliss. In fact, seeing him there with his distinguished colleagues, as he loved to call them, Mrs. Bobby almost shed tears. She was so proud of him and treated him so bad! She smiled at him and, passing into the kitchen to brew more tea and find how many mince tarts were left in the tin, she patted his arm affectionately.

They had hardly had time to tell the constable how matters were progressing and arrange to check certain people's alibis on the night of Alveston's death, before Smythe arrived. He looked pale and cold and a little alarmed.

"You wanted to see me, Inspector?"

"Sit down, Mr. Smythe. The wife's makin' some tea. You look as if you'd do with a cup, sir."

The curate drew a chair up to the fire and glanced uneasily at the official gathering.

Littlejohn, in particular, looked very grim.

"I wanted to ask, Mr. Smythe, why you told me the man you saw with Mr. Granville Salter on the night he was killed, was about the same build as Mr. Salter. We've reason to believe he was a smaller, stocky man. What do you say?"

"I … I …"

Smythe had good features, but a nervous twitch and the downward look of the troubled disturbed and distorted them. He looked as though life were a perpetual ordeal, unrelieved by any happiness or relaxation. He sat there, his body tense, balancing awkwardly on the edge of the chair. The mamby-pamby curate at the tea meeting … except that he'd won the M.C. for bravery in the war and was generally admired and supported by the fellows in his regiment.

“I wanted to try and explain that. It was dark, you see, and I may have been mistaken. I was in rather a hurry and just gave them a casual glance.

“Mr. Davy, who was standing across the road and saw you, says the other man was small and stockily built. If he was visible from over the road, surely you could do better than that a mere yard or two away.”

“I’m afraid ...”

“I suggest, Mr. Smythe, you are trying to cover someone. The man you saw was Alveston and being a friend of Mrs. Alveston and a close admirer of her daughter, you hid the truth to prevent their having any further sorrow or trouble. Now, if that is the case, tell me at once.... We know it was Alveston who was there and killed Salter. I want your evidence straight, please, before the thing has to be sorted out in court.”

“Very well.... I’m sorry. I did tell you a lie. But I thought it justified at the time. I wanted to protect my friends. They've had quite enough trouble as it is."

"Very well, sir. We'll forget it."

"I made a point of speaking to you at the hotel in Thorncastle just in case Alveston came into the picture."

"You've caused us a few wild-goose chases by it, too, Mr. Smythe. You weren't by any means at your best that night. You not only lied, but behaved very strangely for a priest."

"What do you mean?"

"Dancing on Sunday …?"

Smythe smiled sheepishly.

"I was so upset. I forgot what day it was. I was having an evening off. My friends were as surprised as I was when I went on the dance-floor…."

Mrs. Pennyquick brought in the tea and tarts and they all fell-to.

"By the way, Mr. Smythe," said Littlejohn when the good lady had cleared-up and was washing the dishes in the kitchen. “By the way, have you been to Salter Hall recently?”

“No. I haven’t been near for weeks. I must go now. My landlady’ll wonder where I am.”

He rose, put on his coat and gloves, looking self-conscious all the time. His nerves were in shocking condition, but when he looked you full in the face his eyes seemed alight with some hidden purpose. It might have been religious; on the other hand …

“Is that all? If so, I’ll wish you all good night. And thank you so much for the tea and excellent tarts. . . .”

He called to Mrs. Pennyquick through the kitchen doorway and repeated his thanks and praise for the food and drink. Pennyquick went with him to the door and let him out.

“Somethin’s troubling young Smythe. Don’t know what’s the matter with him these days. Must be love …” he muttered almost to himself as he returned, screwing up his eyes at the light of the room.

“Smythe knows more than he’ll tell,” said Littlejohn. “I hate to say it, but he’s heading for trouble.”

SEVENTEEN

FAKE ALIBI

LITTLEJOHN and Cromwell stood for a moment at the door of the "Royal Oak" and sniffed the air. The wind had changed and now a mist was blowing in from the sea. In the distance a steamer hooted persistently, and the bell on the marsh, which rang at such times as this to guide those who might be lost on the paths and roads between the dangerous swamps of the estuary, clanged dismally.

"All the better for a bit of temporary obscurity," said Cromwell, almost as dismally as the bell. "Stop people gaping at us round curtains and over hedges every time we pass. This place is gettin' on my nerves...."

They parted on their respective errands. Littlejohn to question Mrs. Alveston again; Cromwell to see Smythe, care of Mrs. Pawker.

"You again.… Oh, dear.…"

Mrs. Alveston was sitting in the kitchen in an armchair before the fire. Phyllis had gone to work and, thanks to the infidelity of Mrs. Pawker, had had to see her mother up and dressed before she left. Something had changed in Mrs. Alveston. She seemed more settled and serene, as though, knowing at last the fate of her husband, she had given up her fretting and resigned herself to authentic widowhood.

"What do you want again, sir? Isn't it settled yet?"

"I'm afraid not yet, Mrs. Alveston. We haven't found out who killed your husband, you know. Have you any idea who might have done it?"

Mrs. Alveston started and looked at him with eyes full of fear.

"Why should I know? I didn't do it. How could I? Me in bed and not fit to turn into the street, let alone go to the Hall."

"All the same, Mrs. Alveston, you were out on the night your husband met his death. We know that...."

"How do you know? I was locked in and nobody came. I was in bed...."

"No. You were out. The door was locked, but you were out. You see, Mrs. Alveston, someone called and found the house empty."

She began to weep and moan.

"I'm a poor, lonely old woman with nobody to take my part. It's not fair of you to take advantage of me like this. I couldn't have gone to the Hall...."

"Now, Mrs. Alveston, please. We know you were out and can produce witnesses in court to prove it. You don't want the trouble and disgrace of a public inquiry, do you? Better tell me all about it. It will be for the best...."

"Well … I did go out. Phyllis was in town working late on a rush job and I was in alone. I was lonely and troubled and … and … I went over to see Mrs. Pawker…."

"Come, Mrs. Alveston. That won't do. You didn't go to see Mrs. Pawker because she was out. She called here with the laundry and found the place empty."

"So that was who called…. That was when the laundry came…. I wondered …"

"Better tell me the truth, then, and be done with it. It will be best in the end. You see, we always check alibis, Mrs. Alveston."

She moaned again and rocked herself from side to side.

"Oh, dear. Will it never end …?"

"Not till the truth comes out and we won't stop until it does. Look, Mrs. Alveston, you're a religious woman. You ought to tell the truth, you know. It will save those you love from a lot of pain and trouble and ease your own conscience. You'll never rest with lies on your mind."

"You're right, sir. I guess that's best. It's all simple. My husband was starvin'. He daren't go for food and he had none with him. When he came here by night at first, I gave him bread and some tins and some chocolate. But it didn't last long. He came round two days later and, not being able to find a way in, left a note. It just said, 'No food; starving, you know where.' Phyllis found it but I wouldn't tell her what it was. She thought maybe it was a joke. But I knew it wasn't. After dark, and when she was out, I took the field path and left him food at the Hall. I couldn't get in the first time, so left it on the back doorstep, hoping.... He must 'ave found it. On the night he died, I went again.... I found 'im dead, sir.... Dead on the stairs with the door of the priest's hole gapin' wide. I didn't know what to do. The good Lord must have upheld me then, for since, in nightmares, I've seem 'im there by the light of my torch and woke screamin'...."

She was all-in at the thought of it.

"Have you any brandy in the house, Mrs. Alveston?"

She told him where to find it, and he gave her a dose.

"Feel like telling the rest now?"

"There's little else to tell.... I didn't know what to do. I couldn't take 'im and I couldn't leave him so. So I pushed 'im in the room and shut the door.... How I got 'ome, I don't know. Somebody guided my steps, must 'ave done. When I got in, I went to bed and there I must 'ave gone all unconscious, for, when I came-to, it was mornin' ... and Phyllis there with a cup o' tea. You've slept well, mother, she sez. Little she knew."

"But why didn't you let us know?"

"I ... I ... I don't know. I was so ill. I'm so ill now. Please don't ask me any more...."

Littlejohn looked hard at her. She was still hiding something.

"Now, Mrs. Alveston, the truth, please. You didn't tell us because you saw someone there, someone you wanted to shield, didn't you ...?"

"I ... I ... Ahhhhh ..."

And with that she fainted.

Cromwell found Mr. Smythe writing in his bedroom.

"Go hup," Mrs. Pawker had said, for she was now an ally of the police and, after her long gossip with the 'big man from London' the night before, she felt she was part of the Law itself.

Smythe occupied the best bedroom in which the whole Pawker brood had been born and nurtured. The place was jam-full of furniture. A large bed with brass knobs, the connubial one, in which the curate nightly plunged, lost himself and swam desperately in a vast sea of feathers. A washstand with a marble top and enormous jug and basin, a dressing-table with the glass draped in lace curtains tied back with bows like a little window, a voluminous wardrobe which, at one time, maybe, held the clothes of all the tribe of Pawker. And a small, rickety table, at which Mr. Smythe was now precariously sitting, writing an address for the multiple purpose of the Cobbold Youth Club, the Carstonwood Christian Endeavour and the Thorncastle Watchers' Guild.

"Oh," he said, raising his head and looking fearfully at Cromwell, as though the devil himself had suddenly materialized and challenged him to a spiritual throw or two.

"Oh...."

"Mornin', sir," said Cromwell cheerfully.

Mr. Smythe looked as if he'd do with a bit of good cheer and the kindly sergeant determined to do his best.

"Sorry to disturb you, sir. Won't take much of your time. Nice morning...."

The curate looked through the casement at the two-foot visibility.

"Yes," he replied, with enthusiasm.

"I've just called to ask where you were, sir, on the night Alveston met his death."

Mr. Smythe staggered to his feet and grasped the air for support. His face grew contorted with terrible twitchings and he looked ready to faint.

"Here, here, sir. Steady on.... It's not so bad as that. I'm only seeking your help...."

"I was at Mrs. Alveston's...."

The curate cast it up hastily as though in another minute he might be unable to get it out.

"In that case, sir, I'll just have to ask you to cross the road to the good lady's house. Inspector Littlejohn's there with her now and we can discuss it all together."

Smythe looked thunderstruck. This was more than he'd expected. He'd thought his word would be taken and that would be the end of it.

"But I can't.... She's not well.... I'm just in the middle of ..."

"Will you please get your hat, sir?"

When they arrived at the cottage, Littlejohn was giving more brandy to Mrs. Alveston.

"What have you done to her? Really ... this is the limit. I shall complain.... The poor woman...."

Smythe was now beside himself. Timid about his own affairs, he had within himself a great fund of moral indignation at the suffering of others. It seemed to bubble from every pore of his body. He looked ready for violence.

"Sit down, sir. She's only fainted. She's been telling me what happened on the night of her husband's death and it's been a bit too much for her.... She's coming round...."

"You've wrung it out of her.... It's a lie. You can't believe what an overwrought woman says. She wasn't there...."

Littlejohn sat back on his haunches and looked Smythe full in the face.

"How did you know she told me she was there? Were you there yourself . . . ?"

Mrs. Alveston, being gently assisted to her chair from the ground where she had slumped, suddenly recovered.

"I didn't tell him. Don't tell, Mr. Smythe. . . . Don't tell. . . ."

"You were there, too, Mr. Smythe, weren't you? Come along. The truth. . . ."

"I . . . I . . . Yes. . . ."

The curate hung his head and Mrs. Alveston began to rock to and fro again, moaning.

"And you took the loaded stick with you from the hall, didn't you, sir? You found Mrs. Alveston struggling with her husband and you hit him hard with it and then both of you tried to hide the body. Mrs. Alveston's fond of you. . . ."

Both Smythe and Mrs. Alveston looked petrified. Open mouthed, neither could speak at first.

"But … but … He was dead when we got there.… I swear it."

"It's true, sir. True. I went first and Mr. Smythe come on me as I kneeled beside Alveston. He brought me 'ome … after we'd hid it in the room … nearly carried me, he did, and put me to bed.… Mr. Smythe wouldn't do such a thing.… He's too good … too much of a Christian.…"

Littlejohn believed them, too.

"Tell me what happened, then."

"It's as Mrs. Alveston said, Inspector.…"

Smythe had grown suddenly calm and grim at the idea of getting it all off his mind.

"I called here that night to see that Mrs. Alveston was all right. To tell the truth, sir, Phyllis … er … Miss Alveston rang the vicarage and asked if I'd mind calling to see things were right here. She was working late. When I got to the gate, I saw Mrs. Alveston disappearing through the back garden. It only leads to one place. I guessed at once what she was after. Going to see her husband. I tried the front door of the house, instinctively to make quite sure it *was* her. It hadn't locked properly. I ran upstairs, but the place was empty. I knew the danger and, knowing of the heavy stick, picked it up. I lost it in the confusion on the way back. I followed, but she must have moved fast, for when I got to the Hall she was there already, bending over the dead body of her husband on the stairs...."

"How did you get in?"

"The front door was loose...."

"Had Mrs. Alveston any weapon?"

"No. You're not suggesting ... I ... I ... It's monstrous.... A weak woman like her...."

"I'm suggesting nothing. Only making sure. Mrs. Alveston, you said your husband was starving. Had he no food there at all but what you supplied?"

"No, sir. Not a bit."

"But our inquiries show he got tinned goods and chocolate from Polly … Polly … what's her name?"

"Polly Duckett, you mean, as keeps the shop down the road?"

"That's it."

"Who told you that? Poor Polly's a bit simple. She must have made up the tale. She never … Why, he daren't have shown himself there. He was almost too scared to stir out of the Hall."

"All the same, I have it on good authority, he got supplies from her."

"Well, he was starvin' first time I took him food. What with people prowlin' the grounds and the police out for 'im, he daren't risk it."

"Very well. That will be all for the present, but, please, neither of you leave the village until I say so."

"But I have the Carstonwood Christian Endeavour to speak to this afternoon. I can't let them down…."

"They'll have to endeavour on their own, sir," said Cromwell.

"No, no. You can go, sir. You're on parole, though," cut in Littlejohn.

"Thank you so much, Inspector. You have my word. And I'll look after Mrs. Alveston, too. I'll do all I can to help you."

"I'm sure you will, sir."

At the police station that evening they found Pennyquick making a list of licences due for collection. He was having his busy time with the local dogs. From the kitchen came the sound of singing again.

Oh, good old Jeff has gone to rest,
We know that he is free.
Disturb him not, but let him rest,
Way down in Tennesseeeeeeee.

The constable raised his eyes to heaven in apology.

"You know Polly Duckett, don't you, Pennyquick?"

"Yes, sir. Poor girl. When her 'usband was killed in the war, she went right off her head. And her carryin' his child. Born dead, it was...."

"Does she ever open her shop, now?"

"At odd times, I think. You see, she 'as rather bad do's now and then. Seized with fits o' melancholy and stays in bed. The shop's shut then for days."

"What does she sell?"

"Eh? Oh! ... Sort o' general stores it was. Quite a nice little business ... enough to keep 'er goin', like, till Jim was killed. Then, she got behavin' so strange, people stopped goin'. She's little to sell now and I guess she'd give it up, only, you see, sir, cottages are impossible to get and, if she gave up this place, blest if I know where she'd get another roof over her 'ead."

The singing in the kitchen had ceased and was followed by the ominous hush which told that Mrs. Pennyquick had heard the arrival of visitors and was either listening-in to what was going on in the next room, or, with her usual good-heartedness, preparing yet more hospitality for her visitors. She soon appeared, flushed a bit and rather shy, bearing a large tray of sandwiches and tea.

"This is really awfully kind of you, Mrs. Pennyquick. It's not fair of us eating your rations like this. . . ."

"We've plenty just at present. The girls' rations, left behind. . . ."

"A proper old law-breaker, is ma," chuckled Pennyquick. "A proper disgrace to the Force, she is. . . ."

"You mind yer own business, Andrew Pennyquick. If I didn't look after the food, you'd soon 'ave somethin' 'arsh to say when you come in off the beat.... Proper old eater out of house and home, is my 'usband, sir.... Sugar?"

"We've just been talking about poor Polly Duckett, Mrs. Pennyquick. Sad case."

"Very sad. A nice girl when she was little. 'Ead full o' lovely curls and as nice in 'er ways.... Now ...

Quite wrong in 'er head some days and gets queer notions. Can't sort out 'er rationed goods at all. Points and sweets coupons ... well ... 'er suppliers gave it up as a bad job long since, and now she doesn't sell points stuff and sweets any more...."

"Just a minute, Mrs. Pennyquick. I'll tell you and your husband, in greatest confidence, that I was informed she supplied a lot of tinned goods and chocolates to Alveston when he was in hiding. He frightened her to death and made her give them to him."

"That's all wrong, sir. Whoever told you that, wasn't right. Why, she hasn't hardly any goods at all in the shop now. Besides, if Alveston came out at night, he'd never get in. She shutters up and you never saw how many bolts and bars on the doors...."

"Does she ever stir out, Mrs. Pennyquick?"

"Now and then. But she mostly shuns people. I'm one of the few she'll let in the 'ouse. You see, sir, I had to look after her when her poor dead baby was born. She'd nobody else and, one day, Andrew—that's my 'usband—Andrew, passin' the shop, heard groans from inside and come and brought me. She'll do anythin' for me since."

"Will she be up at this time?"

"Nearin' ten. Maybe. She often sits by the embers, thinkin' of happier days, no doubt. One day, they'll have to take 'er away if she goes on as at present. Quite a good-looking girl, too. Ought to get 'erself another man and start afresh."

"Mind if we go across and try? Perhaps she'd let us in if you were with us."

"I don't mind. . . ."

Mrs. Pennyquick put on a heavy coat and a little navy-blue beret, given to her at Christmas by one of her girls. Her husband solemnly put on his tunic, helmet and belt, tested his torch, and away they all went.

Polly Duckett's place lay just through the village on the main road to the Hall. A wooden bungalow affair, with a large window and a kind of veranda, beneath which the former owner had once spread little tables and chairs and sold soft drinks and ice cream. Polly had let this appendage fall into decay, like much of the rest of the place.

With the help of the constable's lamp, they found their way to the hut. There were lights on downstairs and the chimney was smoking. The bobby rapped vigorously on the door. There were noises inside and then feet approached the door. Nobody spoke, but Polly sounded to be shooting more bolts and bars to hold the door better and protect herself.

"Polly.... It's me. Martha Pennyquick. I want to see you."

A pause. Then an excited and pleasant contralto voice answered.

"It's so late, Martha. Won't it do mornings? I'm almost goin' to bed."

"My husband's here, too, Polly, and the gentlemen from London. They want to ask you somethin'...."

"Oh! ..."

A gasp of terror, which seemed to awake some other occupant of the place to action. Heavy feet joined those of the owner of the shack, a muffled argument, and then a man's voice.

"What ye want with Polly at this hour? Can't you leave 'er in peace? Be off with you all, and see her proper in the light o' day...."

"Sid Chapell!" gasped the bobby in astonished tones, and his wife clicked her tongue against her teeth.

"Yes, it's me, Andrew Pennyquick, and not ashamed of it either. It's you as ought to be ashamed, disturbin' respectable folk at this hour o' night."

"Whatever yore doin' there, Sid, this is important. It's a serious matter about the death o' Alveston. Open up, lad."

The door was slowly opened after a perfect pandemonium of chains and bars being loosed and there, silhouetted by the lamplight, stood a slim, scared-looking woman with a huge, corduroy-clad countryman standing protectively by.

"Can we come in?"

The procession at a signal moved indoors.

But first, Sid had something to say. He was a shy man of few words, but with an air of solemn integrity about him.

"This ain't fair …" he was beginning to say.

Pennyquick looked a bit tickled, now that the strain had been removed.

"Doin' a bit o' courtin', Sid?"

"An' wot if I am? It's not a police matter, is it? Everybody 'ud a known long since, only Polly wouldn't …"

"It didn't seem right, Martha, with me 'usband hardly cold in his grave, but Sid was so perseverin'…."

She was quite a good-looking, dark girl, rather haggard, however, from grief and worry, and bewildered from lack of proper care. She addressed herself to Mrs. Pennyquick, ignoring the rest.

"Rubbish, Polly. You want a nice man to mind you, my girl. And Sid's the one for it. You've pined long enough. It's time you seeked the better things o' life again. Your mournin's over. Time for Sid to set things right."

"You reely think so, Martha?"

"Of course...."

She smiled as though a load had been removed and Sid, the cause of it all, grew hot and stood first on one foot and then on the other.

"An' now, maybe, when you've all done, Polly an' me can talk proper. Glad you made 'er see sense, Mrs. Pennyquick. I've a nice cottage and garden all of me own and four pounds a week. Since me owld mother died, I've been terrible lonely...."

"Ahem.... Well ... wot about our business?" interrupted Pennyquick.

"I just want to ask you, Mrs. Duckett, if you saw Alveston during his recent stay here and if you gave him any tinned stuff and chocolate. . . ."

"'Ere, wot's all this? Polly wouldn't . . ."

Sid was getting a bit nettled.

"You don't interfere, Sid. Inspector Littlejohn just wants to know. No offence intended. Let the Inspector and Polly talk, if you please, Sid. . . ."

"No, he never, sir. . . . I never see him at all. And as for tins and sweets—no. I run out of them long since. I got all mixed up in me points and the wholesalers said until I got 'em fixed, they wouldn't send any more."

"I'll fix 'em," said Sid. "Though when we're wed, which won't be long, they'll be no more servin' pounds o' butter and quarters o' tea for Missis Sid Chapell. There won't that. . . ."

"Tell me, Mrs. Duckett, have you had a visit from Miss Fothergill lately?"

"No. Haven't seen her for weeks, sir."

"H'm. Well … that's all, thanks. Sorry to disturb you…."

"That's all right, sir. And you do think it'll be all right, Martha? They won't talk about me as a bad lot in the village?"

"Bad lot! *You,* Polly. O' course they won't. You teck and wed Sid 'ere as soon as vicar'll put up the banns for ye. Bad lot, indeed! Ought to be ashamed to think sich things."

And with that Mrs. Pennyquick kissed Polly. The bobby, thinking something was expected of him as well, wrung Sid heartily and silently by the hand and, with that, they left them to their secret courting.

EIGHTEEN

A WARRANT AT LAST

THEY were all back at the Pennyquicks' and the bobby's wife had made yet another load of sandwiches and tea.

"I'm 'ungry, luv," Pennyquick had said when they got back and as his wife, knowing the best way to a bobby's heart, had further stocks in the larder, she did her best to appease him.

It was eleven o'clock, but they all felt too excited to part.

"What was all that about Miss Fothergill, sir?" asked the perplexed constable.

"She told me Polly had said Alveston had been round and taken her supplies and told her he'd murder her if she split on him. She also said I must take her word and not pester Polly for confirmation, because she'd enough trouble as it was and any further strain would drive her mad."

"Now why could she 'a done that, sir?" muttered Pennyquick through a mouthful of bread and ham.

Cromwell took from his pocket a pipe, the exact replica of Littlejohn's own new one. He'd been fortunate enough to find one in Thorncastle. He filled up from a pouch containing his chief's blend of tobacco and lit up with slow, thoughtful puffs. Things were beginning to move at last! He hoped they wouldn't be long, for he was heartily fed up with Cobbold and all in it, present company excepted, of course. He drank his good cup of tea, wondering if it would all be settled before the London pantomime season ended. He'd promised the wife and kids....

"It seems to me," Littlejohn was saying, "I've taken Miss Fothergill a bit too much on trust. She gave me a lot of information which, coming as she said from her brother's records and hence professional secrets,

I mustn't divulge. But why lie to me about Alveston and the tinned goods?"

Cromwell removed his pipe and emitted a cloud of smoke.

"Could it be that up to then, we didn't know that Alveston was in the neighbourhood and that was her way of telling us. Suppose she'd seen him, why not tell us direct? Why lead us to him by a cock-and-bull story about Polly Duckett?"

Pennyquick hastily emptied his mouth of his eighth sandwich.

"'Ow if she was protectin' Mrs. Alveston? She's always befriended Mrs. Alveston, sir. You see, Miss Fothergill went up to the 'all quite a lot in the old days, and Mary Ann Alveston's the last o' the old staff, except my missus. That's so, ain't it, ma?"

He shouted the last sentence loudly and thus brought his wife back to the room from the kitchen where she was still busy.

"What was you sayin'?"

"Miss Fothergill was a great friend o' Mrs. Alveston. Sort o' befriended her in her trouble?"

"Yes. The Fothergills 'ad very 'appy days at the Hall. That was, until their trouble.... Poor Dr. Fothergill."

"What are you talkin' about, ma?"

"Didn't you know, Andrew? I thought you'd know all there was to know about this village."

"Now, don't yew start bein' sarcastical, ma. This is very serious...."

The bobby gravely regarded his better half, who returned his stare rebelliously.

"Servants in a big house of'en get to know more than those as we used to call our betters. And if some policemen would tell their wives a bit more, instead of keepin' their business to themselves, they might get to know more...."

With this, Mrs. Pennyquick gave first her husband and then Littlejohn and Cromwell an artful feminine smile. The bobby looked to be growing hot and cold with shame.

"Don't talk like that in front of strangers … or rather friends from Scotland Yard, ma. It's not right."

"Well, it's not right you goin' here, there and everywhere seekin' information and clues, when all the time they're under your own roof!"

Poor Pennyquick looked at his wife in dumb amazement. He'd never seen her like this before. He absently took up another ham sandwich and slowly fed it under his large moustache.

"I could 'ave told you a lot about Dr. Fothergill and his sister. And now that Mr. Granville and Alveston's dead and I'm free to tell things I overheard once and swore to Knapp on me Bible I'd never speak so long as they was alive, I can say somethin' about Phyllis Alveston as well."

"Well … Get on with it, ma. Wot 'ave you to tell?"

Pennyquick sounded kind and tolerant; the husband humouring his missus.

"It's funny how you was tellin' me in bed last night as you'd found Phyllis's mother. I knew all that meself. But I was surprised you paid so little attention to 'er father. 'A married man as went to the war and got killed,' you said. That was just a story by the family to 'ush up the scandal. Phyllis Alveston bore the right name, because Alveston was her real father. Miss Margaret Salter was 'er mother!"

The constable threw up his hands and looked ready to make allowances on account of the late hour.

"Now look 'ere, ma...."

"Please let her go on, Andrew ..." said Littlejohn.

The bobby grew red with pride. To his dying day he'd remember that hour. Littlejohn had called him by his Christian name! Things were indeed looking up!

"I'd better begin at the beginnin'. You must admit, sir, that whatever plots you find on the pictures or in the underworlds of London, our villages is just as good. So, there! In 'is young days, Alveston was quite a good-looking lad, fond of the girls and with takin' ways with him. He used to take Miss Margaret out ridin'. Teachin' her, he said, or that's what he was supposed to do. She was lovely and he must 'ave lost his head and made love to 'er. She was, at the time, a bit of a wild thing. Much given to readin' what was then called modern and advanced novels, but which our girls now say isn't much, but flat and dull. Any way, they was quite an influence then and forbidden to nice young ladies. Alveston must 'ave swept 'er off her feet. Phyllis was the result, an' you know how she came to the Alveston home."

"Is that true, ma, or jest gossip?"

"You've lived with me long enough to know I don't tell lies, Andrew Pennyquick, and I wouldn't pass on gossip about the Family. It's true: every word. Dr. Fothergill was attendin' at the Hall at the time. Miss Margaret never told anyone who the father was, but, at the lyin'-in, she got delirious and spoke it out. I was there and Knapp and Dr. Fothergill. It was then I swore to Knapp. As for Dr. Fothergill … well … he wasn't a young man, but he was fond of Miss Margaret. That was why he stayed a bachelor. You'd only to look at 'is face when she came in the room. He adored 'er."

"Well, well, ma. I never did…."

"When it was all over and the doctor expectin' to be called any time to Mrs. Alveston … Alveston's own wife, mind you … he met Alveston in the great park. The doctor was on 'is horse and with his huntin' crop 'e struck Alveston down with it, and when Alveston got up again, he struck him down again. Three times 'e did it, till Alveston stayed where 'e was on the ground. Then, he left 'im, all covered with blood. I saw it all from the window…."

"You don't say, ma …?"

"A week later, after Alveston's baby was born dead, Dr. Fothergill 'ad been on a late call and, coming home in the dark, somebody set on 'im and beat him up. No doubt who it was. It was Alveston. But only us at the Hall knew, because only us had seen the other fight. And we couldn't say anything on account of Miss Margaret. Poor Dr. Fothergill never got over the rough handlin' they gave 'im. The thing was hushed up, but not long after, he fell dead in his sister's arms...."

They all parted very quietly and, on the way to the inn, Cromwell voiced Littlejohn's own thoughts.

"Miss Fothergill?"

"Yes. She must have seen him hangin' around Mrs. Alveston's and, maybe, carrying off food. So, to make believe Mrs. Alveston wasn't shielding him and in case we came across the tinned food and such and brought it home to the old lady, she concocted the tale about Polly Duckett."

"That would fill the bill. Yes."

"But why did she kill Alveston? Why didn't she leave him to us? Surely, she must have known we'd get him and save her all the trouble."

"She must have had her doubts and feared he'd get away. Wait a minute.... My questions made her take out her brother's papers ... his diary and notes ... and read them through. They must have contained an account of Miss Margaret's tragedy and how the doctor had loved her and how Alveston had beaten him up in the dark and caused his early death from the shock. Then, she saw red, went to the Hall, waited for him and killed him."

"How can we confirm that, though?"

"To-morrow.... Leave it till to-morrow. We'll find a way."

Littlejohn was unwelcome when he called at "Fothergills" early next morning. Felicity Grimes, Miss Fothergill's maid, had all her boxes packed ready for a holiday at home in Dorset and had little time for talk.

"My train's due in half an hour," she said.

"I'll give you a lift to the station," said Littlejohn. "But I must insist on a word with you."

"Well, be quick, then."

"What does Miss Fothergill usually do at nights, Felicity?"

"What's that to do with you? I ain't one to talk behind the back o' my mistress."

"You'd better, please, or else there'll be no train today. I'll have to take you to Thorncastle police station for questioning."

"Oh dear.... And my father'll be at Dorchester to meet-in my train. What do you want to know?"

Littlejohn told Felicity the day and the hour of Alveston's death, without however, mentioning the events.

"I don't recollect...."

"Think again.... You've only ten minutes more and then we'll have to be off, either to Dorchester or Thorncastle."

"She went to Mrs. Alveston's. I remember now."

"How do you remember, Felicity?"

The girl blushed and looked awkward.

"Have you got a boy friend, Felicity?"

"What of it? I can't 'ave him in when the mistress is at home. So, I go and stand with 'im at the back fence on his night off. Keep poppin' in the kitchen to see all's right and I'm not wanted. Nothing wrong with that, is there?"

"No. He must be very fond of you to do his courting that way."

"Oh, I get Saturday or Sunday every week, as well. We do it proper then."

"Oh, do you? And on the night I mentioned, you had the house to yourself and invited him in the kitchen?"

"Yes. I'd made a pie."

"Supper, too. Well, well.... But how did you know Miss Fothergill had gone to Mrs. Alveston's?"

"Dennis saw her goin' up the garden at their house. That's why I let 'im in. I knew they'd be at it for a bit. They were friends and liked a chat."

"Who is this Dennis?"

"Dennis Pratt.... He works at the village branch of the Thorncastle Co-op. Learnin' to be a grocer, he is. Goes to night-school, too."

"Did Miss Fothergill go often to Mrs. Alveston's?"

"On and off. She went three times that week. Told me where she was off the first time. Second time, she let out where she'd been. Third time, Dennis saw her."

"Where is she now?"

"Stayin' in London with friends to give a concert. Must be plannin' a long stay. Took her trunk this time. Never known her do that before. And told me to sheet the furniture. Most unusual, that...."

"Well, come along, Felicity, I'll put your bags in the car and run you all the way to Thorncastle. I'm going there myself."

"Oo.... That'll be lovely. Mind if we just stop at the Co-op on the way? Then I can tell Dennis another good-bye for the present."

They halted at the grocer's and there, Dennis, in his long white apron, jealously eyed Littlejohn for driving his girl about in a nice little police car.

"I don't like it ..." he told Felicity, who smiled, woman-like, but said nothing.

Dennis was a tall, loose-limbed lad with a highly polished, ruddy face, a calf-lick of hair and a pencil behind his ear. His boss, who was a tartar, eyed him malevolently from behind a stack of breakfast cereals and pots of plum jam.

"Yes. Saw 'er with my own eyes going in Alveston's. Didn't go right in, as far as I could see. Sort of sneaked along by the bushes. Not that I was concerned much. I thought it a grand chance for Fel. to get a free 'alf-hour. So I nipped along and rang the door-bell. O.K.?"

"Yes, that's all, Dennis, thanks."

"O.K. Well, so long, Fel. Beseeinyer. Send us a post-card. O.K.? And don't forget what I told yer. I'm not foolin'. O.K.?"

"O.K.," answered Felicity, and with such terms of endearment, they parted. The head grocer thereupon emerged and, as the car gathered speed, Littlejohn, through the driving-mirror, could see him ticking-off his apprentice.

"Dennis is that jealous," said Felicity, eyeing the car with envy. She snuggled down comfortably for the short journey and left Cobbold and the grocer's assistant for ever.

At Thorncastle Percival gave Littlejohn a cordial greeting.

"I'm glad to see you. I got your reports, but I'm glad of a talk. Getting any forrader?"

"Do you know Miss Fothergill, who has a house of the same name at Cobbold?"

"Yes. Knew her brother, too. Used to be village doctor."

"That's the one. She's gone to London to give a concert. Left no address. Can you send out a message to ports and airports? She's not to leave the country, yet."

"Whatever for?"

"I'm afraid she caught up with Alveston before us and killed him."

"No!"

"Everything points that way."

Percival got busy.

Meanwhile Littlejohn, by a sudden inspiration, rang up his wife in Hampstead.

"Do you happen to know any exponents of something called the twelve-note scale, Letty?"

"Good gracious! You're not thinking of taking that up, Tom?"

"No. I want to know if a Miss Fothergill's given any recitals in London lately and, if so, where she's to be found."

"Tall order. All the same, I know Mrs. Askew, in the next block, pretends to be keen. I'll ask her. She'll know, maybe. I'll ring you back."

"Briefly, it amounts to this, Superintendent," said Littlejohn to Percival later, when, visiting the police canteen, they sat together over pints of beer. "Alveston, abroad in the dark at New Year, presumably foraging for food, stumbled across Granville Salter taking a walk. Alveston was in the village, bleeding his wife of money with which he hoped to leave the country. He had been wanted in the past for embezzling Salter funds when he was bailiff. He was hiding out at the Hall in a priest's hole he knew. Whilst he was there, he was surprised by Plucock, who had been told by the village parson in a burst of alcoholic confidence—he'd drunk too much rhubarb wine by mistake!—of the Salter Treasure. Poor Plucock couldn't get the idea of getting rich quick out of his head and was always ferreting around the Hall. He and Alveston came to blows,

Alveston somehow got Plucock's truncheon, knocked him out, and threw him in the dyke, where he drowned."

"So that was it. Poor Plucock...."

A number of officers off duty began to play snooker rather self-consciously with one eye on their chief and the big man from Scotland Yard. They wondered what was on!

"Salter had also been round the Hall treasure-hunting as a pastime and found Alveston's hideout. Alveston was away, but Salter found the truncheon. When he met Alveston he accused him and got a knife in his heart for his pains."

"This made it more than ever necessary for Alveston to keep absolutely hidden. He got word to his wife and told her to bring him food. She was doing that, followed by the Rev. Smythe, who's an interest in her as the mother of Phyllis. He's keen on the girl. She was doing that, as I said, for the last time when she and the parson found Alveston dead. He'd previously come across Barney and killed him, too, to save being caught. Barney must have found him on the prowl. Meanwhile, Miss Fothergill, who was a frequent visitor at Mrs. Alveston's, discovered that the old lady was taking food to the Hall. She suspected why and, to shield Mrs. Alveston in case we found the food, concocted a tale about Alveston's bullying a so-called half-crazy girl who runs a little shop, to keep him in chocolate and tinned goods. In my first interview with Miss Fothergill, I persuaded her to examine her late brother's diary for records of the Salter family. He was their doctor. This she did and, I deduce, discovered his love affair. He loved Margaret Salter, aunt of Granville, and mother of Phyllis Alveston. Alveston himself was the father of the illegitimate child."

"Well, I'm blessed!!"

The shots of the snooker players snapped and clicked as they strode round and round the table and recorded their scores on the marker.

"Good shot, Reg!"

"Yes. There was a quarrel between Alveston and the doctor about it. Alveston after getting a thrashing by Fothergill, waylaid him in the dark and half-killed the doctor. Fothergill never recovered and died not long after from shock. Miss Fothergill was passionately fond of her brother and, coming across this account for the first time, must have gone half mad. Incensed by the murders and knowing from me we'd traced Alveston to the Hall, she waited until Mrs. Alveston was due to leave with fresh supplies for her husband and, hurrying ahead, found him waiting. There's a tool-shed behind the house where Miss Fothergill has a plentiful supply of hammers and crowbars. No doubt she armed herself.

"Well?"

"A warrant, I think. I hope we find her, though she's had long enough in which to escape. Her house is all shut up and the goods sheeted and she's taken away a large trunk of belongings. I wonder if she's managed to give us the slip...."

An officer hurried in and saluted.

"Inspector Littlejohn wanted on the telephone. Mrs. Littlejohn."

Letty had rung up Mrs. Askew.

"She says Miss Fothergill gave a recital two days ago with Bruno Auerhahn at the piano. She was there. They've left for a Continental tour together. Caught the channel boat yesterday. There was a sort of reception after the concert and Miss Fothergill said they were going abroad...."

"Too bad!!"

"What's the matter?"

"She's given us the slip after all."

NINETEEN

THE RELUCTANT FUGITIVE

A FINAL visit to Mrs. Alveston finally clinched Littlejohn's case against Miss Fothergill. He disliked calling on and questioning the invalid woman. She seemed to have been the focus of all the trouble in the place and that, involved as it was with the infidelities of her husband, his crimes, and his final death, had, thought the Inspector, been a large enough burden to bear without a lot of police questioning. All the same …

"You were a friend of Miss Fothergill, I believe," he said to Mrs. Alveston on his last visit.

She was sitting up in an arm-chair. They had managed to obtain another daily help, but she needed watching, having shown a tendency to hide the dust of her labours under the carpets instead of in the bin and to satisfy a voracious appetite by trips to the pantry when nobody was looking, to say nothing of a search for liquid refreshments such as tea, wet or dry, and brandy. So, Mrs. Alveston was keeping an eye on her.

"Yes. I've known her since she was young, sir, She was in the village when I come 'ere with my father, nearly fifty years since. She's been very good to me while I've been in ill 'ealth."

"She called often?"

"Two or three times a week."

"You confided in her much?"

"Well, yes, sir. I've few friends and such as they are, aren't very sympathetic. They often as not talked about pullin' myself together and forgettin' my troubles.... As if I could, with my 'usband gone and me that bad...."

"She was sympathetic, eh?"

"Very. And with 'er knowin' me as a girl, as you might say, I felt I could talk to 'er. Bein' a class above us, she never got spiteful or jealous."

"You told her all about your husband and how unhappy he'd made you?"

"Why … yes. How did you know?"

"Just guessed it. Did she know you were taking food to the Hall and that he was hiding there, Mrs. Alveston?"

"Yes. I told her. She could be trusted, you know. She'd never tell."

"No, I don't suppose she would."

"What did she think of your husband?"

"Not much. Blamed 'im for what he did to me. But I wouldn't let 'er say ill of him. After all, I bore 'is name."

"She called here the week of the crimes?"

"Yes.… What is it you're wantin' to know, sir?"

"Just what she was doing on the nights of that week. I'm checking on all the prominent people who might have had to do with Salter and your late husband."

"She was here three nights...."

"Three!"

"Yes. The night Alveston was killed she was in to see me. Early it was. She offered to take the stuff to the Hall for me. I said 'No'. It was my own business, him bein' my 'usband, however bad he treated me. I wasn't havin' anybody else getting theirselves in trouble on his account. I told 'er so."

"What did she say?"

"Looked queer and said, if that was the way I wanted it ..."

"Had she many friends in the village?"

"No. Once she was friendly with all the county folk, but of late kept herself to herself. I'd think I was about the only one she visited 'ere and stayed with any while."

"Have you seen her since your husband died?"

"Funny enough, no. She's in London, I hear. Mr. Smythe did tell me he went to 'er for help after I'd passed-out when he brought me from the 'all the night we found Alveston. But she was out. . . ."

There was little else for it, but to put in motion the machinery of the law, hunt down Miss Fothergill and question her. In Littlejohn's pocket was the warrant for her arrest and he was ready to put it into effect, if he could find her. If . . .

Miss Fothergill had told her friends that she and her violinist friend, Auerhahn, were crossing to the Continent by boat. Actually, they had booked seats on the Paris 'plane. Thence, Auerhahn would see her off to wherever she wanted to go.

But Miss Fothergill was a reluctant fugitive. Nearing seventy you don't want to be chasing all over the earth out of the way of the police. True, she had a friend in an ideal spot. Pablo Besso, the artist and specialist in Inca work, lived in Lima, but who wanted to end one's days in Peru, with Pablo, who, whilst admiring Miss Fothergill immensely, was a bit of a cad and a shocking bore? Still, one might try it and end up with a final adventure.

When Miss Fothergill confided to Auerhahn that she wished to see Pablo Besso, maybe for the last time, he was not greatly astonished. She was always up to something funny and this was simply her latest. Then his eyes lit up. He offered to take her to Paris and see her off thence, via Lisbon to South America by 'plane. She said she wanted peace and a long rest. They agreed to tell nobody of her ultimate destination. They gave it out that they were off to Paris by boat and booked tickets on the 'plane. Miss Fothergill thought she could trust Bruno Auerhahn....

There was, of course, the problem of money. They only allowed you a few paltry pounds. That was no use when you were off abroad for good. So, Miss Fothergill, who had contacts with strange people, many of them twelve-note addicts, bought diamonds, placed them in a large fancy green bottle, with a glass stopper, poured smelling-salt liquor over them and passed them off as the real thing, carried in her handbag. Enough to keep her going for a while....

Auerhahn, small, bald, dapper and with the look of a rather elderly dirty dog, carefully explained the currency regulations to his travelling companion.

"Maybe, I can do something for you in Paris.... You pay me here and I have friends there who'll see you right."

Miss Fothergill hesitated and then decided against it.

"Pablo will see to all that...."

And there the matter was dropped.

At the airport, the control-of-currency officer took one look at Bruno and nodded to a companion. They led Auerhahn off to be searched. News of his Paris associations had reached them. He was suspected of smuggling out currency. But they found nothing. They turned to his companion....

Miss Fothergill had a lot of music with her. They found it copiously interleaved with five-pound notes. Just a paltry three hundred pounds, but that was quite enough. She was dumbfounded....

"Bruno!" she said, and the look Auerhahn gave her was sufficient. She smote him hard on the bald head with her umbrella and they took him away for first-aid. During the search, Miss Fothergill had been watching her companion. She thought hard and came to many decisions when his perfidy came to light. One of them she put into effect at once.... When they got Bruno to the dressing station, he was still dazedly sniffing at some smelling salts which somehow had found their way into his hand. The customs officer who was keeping an eye on him casually impounded the green bottle and that eventually put Auerhahn out of circulation for some time.

The police half-believed Miss Fothergill's story. She was granted bail. As she left the court, news was passing to and fro that she must be stopped from leaving the country. Miss Fothergill didn't want to leave. At her age it was a gamble.... And now, she felt twenty years older. In fact, finished! She bought a writingpad, envelopes and a pencil. All her luggage was gone and she'd just twenty pounds left in the world. She sat down in St. James's Park and watched the ducks on the pond for a while. They seemed just the same, unperturbed and ageless as in days gone by. Uncle George had once brought her there in a hansom cab and they'd broken bread and thrown it to the birds. A woman nearby had watched hungrily as they did it. Miss Fothergill had been too young then to realize the wretch was starving. A tall gentleman had strolled past, too, and Uncle George had said, "That's Mr. Balfour, Madeline...." Madeline.... Nobody had called her that for twenty years.... Even her cronies of the musical circles called her Miss Fothergill, or sometimes, familiarly, "Fothy". A little girl and a very old man toddled past and began to call and feed the ducks. The sun went in behind a cloud and it grew cold. Miss Fothergill wrote swiftly in a large, characteristic hand.... She sealed the letter, walked slowly to the embankment, taking in the old landmarks, despising the new, thinking how one by one the former things had gone and left her alone. The crowds bustled past, jostled her, made no apologies. It felt terribly cold.... The leafless trees of Parliament Square shook in the breeze; Big Ben struck three quarters.

Miss Fothergill gave the envelope to a boy with half-a-crown.

"Take that in to Scotland Yard ... at once!"

The urchin looked hard at her, snatched the letter and ran on his way as though the furies were behind him. Miss Fothergill followed the path along the Embankment. It hadn't changed much there. A few more memorials and a conglomeration of massive concrete buildings on the Strand side. But the river was just the same. The same smell, the same river craft, Waterloo Bridge quite changed, but the old Shot Tower still there. She wished she could have walked round to London Bridge and crossed it, just as she used to do when she went to meet her brother at St. Thomas's where he was a student. But she was very tired. She entered Charing Cross Underground, taking one look at the Embankment, silhouetted through the entrance against the clean winter sky....

Harry Coop lived for his job. He loved driving his trains. The rattle and the roar, the plunge from the lighted stations into the dark holes burrowing under London, and then the rush into the light again at another halt. The power he controlled by a flick of the wrist! Dashing about in his great monster with hundreds of people at the back of him, tearing or crawling along, just at a twist of Harry's hand. "Old Father Thames keeps rollin' along, over me blinkin' head," he improvised as he rattled under the river from Waterloo to Charing Cross. The brightness of Charing Cross Station shone like a dot in the distance and spread wider and wider as he drew near. He braked gently....

"My Gawd!" yelled Harry, all alone in his cab. He might be one of the best drivers on the Underground, but he wasn't a magician. As he skidded past the platform, struggling to stop the train, he could hear nothing but the protests of the huge machine he was handling. But the faces which flew past ... Terrible! Wide mouths, staring eyes, arms waving, women fainting and having hysterics, people rushing to the mouth of the tunnel from which Harry and his train had appeared.

"I couldn't stop.... You couldn't expect me to stop, could you? 'Umanly impossible.... I couldn't stop."

He kept telling them that, as though they blamed him, and he was still saying it when, weeping harshly and exhausted, they took him home in a taxi to the wife who comforted him.

TWENTY

THE FILE IS CLOSED

"WHO gave you this?"

The constable on duty at New Scotland Yard looked ferociously at the cheeky rascal who thrust the letter in his face at the gate.

"Old dame on Whitehall. . . ."

That was all. He'd done his part and he took to his heels. The police weren't much in his line. He'd opened the envelope on the way, found it contained nothing valuable or thrilling. Only a lot of writing. . . . Probably balmy. He'd read somewhere about the number of letters confessing crimes they hadn't done that people wrote to Scotland Yard every day. He licked the flap of the letter and stuck it up again as best he could.

"Hey," said the bobby. "Who's been openin' this ...?"

But there was nobody to answer.

Littlejohn and Cromwell were in. There wasn't much more to keep them at Cobbold and they'd said good-bye to their friends the Pennyquicks and Percival. Littlejohn turned over the grubby envelope. Another confession, or else somebody with a theory.

"Yours sincerely,

Madeline Fothergill."

"Good Lord!"

Not far away, the ambulance was removing all that was left of her. But Littlejohn didn't know that, yet.

There was not much of it. Three pages of large script; but quite enough.

Dear Inspector,

I think by now you will have reached your conclusions. When I met you, I knew you would sort it all out, however long the road. I should have told you everything at Cobbold and saved us all so much trouble. I can imagine your distress at the thought of arresting a woman for murder, especially one you liked and who quite took a fancy to you, too. I will try to save you that trouble. I haven't as yet quite made up my mind how I will do it.

Briefly, I killed Alveston. He was becoming too dangerous. Already responsible, if not guilty, for three murders, a lifetime's unhappiness for his wife and heaven knows how many other women, it was time he went. Besides, the whole village was scared out of its wits and the peace of the place had gone.

Most important, however, he caused my brother's death. It may sound strange to you, but until Granville's inquiry stimulated me, I hadn't read my brother's journal. I was too afraid to bring back the unhappiness I felt at our parting. I had put it off until I really didn't want to read it. Perhaps I was afraid of what I would find there. When induced to make the effort, I found not only that Alveston had robbed him of the woman he loved, but inflicted upon him the appalling injuries which caused my brother's death. My brother, at least, gave the scoundrel a chance. He beat him with a whip in daylight. Alveston attacked my brother in the dark with a loaded stick and, knocking him down halfconscious, kicked him terribly.... I never knew that until I read the diary. My brother always kept his troubles to himself and tried to share those of others as well.

I had learned from Mrs. Alveston that her husband was about. He was blackmailing her, in addition to the rest. From the diary I learned the secret of the priest's hole and also reached the frenzy which knew no appeasement but the death at my own hands of the wretch who had spoiled the happy life my brother and I had made for ourselves.

I feared you would discover Mrs. Alveston's concealment of her husband and convict her in the end, as an accessory, so I made up the story of Polly Duckett. I knew the time Alveston would be waiting for the food his wife was bringing. To make sure she should not be accused of the crime, I pretended to send a message from Phyllis to Mr. Smythe asking him to call on her at around the time she would leave. He would either detain her or accompany her, I thought. Instead, he was late, but followed her. I had already got to the Hall. I took a small crowbar with me and sat on the stairs in the dark, until he opened the door of the hiding-place. He might not have been there. He might have been on the prowl. In that case, I would have followed Plucock and the little man who was too inquisitive. I was fortunate. Alveston appeared, not from the secret room, but from somewhere below, carrying the limp body of the man in the check suit. I hit him once with all my might. I had only time to hide the body of Alveston's new victim, when Mrs. Alveston and Smythe appeared. I had to leave Alveston for them to find. Until they went I had a few shocks. Especially when they thrust Alveston's body in the priest's hole, the door of which had remained ajar. Luckily, they did not shine a light inside, or they would have found me there with the body of the little man. When they had gone, I emerged and dragged the little man's body to the stairs. Somehow it slithered all the way down. I lost my nerve, closed the door of the priest's hole on Alveston's body and ran for my life.

That is all, Inspector. I am sorry I misled you and wasted so much of your time.

Life is so beautifully ironical, isn't it? I had a perfect plan for getting away to Lima with money enough. Instead of being detained at the port for murder, I was held for a currency offence I hadn't committed. I was granted bail! I am as free as a bird in a cage. In any case, what would a woman of my age be fleeing from justice for? What is there to fly for and from? All I knew, loved and trusted has long since gone.

May I bid you good-bye and wish you well?

Yours sincerely,

Madeline Fothergill

"Exactly as you said," remarked Cromwell after he'd read the letter.

"I wish it hadn't been," said Littlejohn.

He slowly descended to the ground floor and entered a room where, surrounded by a group of admiring officers, sat Meg, the sheep-dog he had adopted and brought home with him. She was ignoring the attentions of all of them and, as Littlejohn entered, her strained expression vanished. Her upper lip crooked in a grin of joy; tailless, she showed her pleasure by agitating the whole hindquarters of her woolly body. The Inspector bent to caress her.

"At least I brought one bit of happiness back from the beastly tragedy of Cobbold," he told them, and together man and dog left for home.

Cover design by Elizabeth Connor

ISBN:

This 2014 edition published by MysteriousPress.com/Head of Zeus

A CIP catalogue record for this book is available from the British Library

ISBN 9781784979317

Head of Zeus Ltd
Clerkenwell House
45-47 Clerkenwell Green
London EC1R 0HT

www.headofzeus.com

THE THOMAS LITTLEJOHN SERIES

FROM MYSTERIOUSPRESS.COM AND HEAD OF ZEUS

GEORGE BELLAIRS
CALAMITY AT HARWOOD

GEORGE BELLAIRS
THE CASE OF THE HEADLESS JESUIT

GEORGE BELLAIRS
THE CASE OF THE
SEVEN
WHISTLERS

GEORGE BELLAIRS
THE CRIME AT
HALFPENNY
BRIDGE
GEORGE BELLAIRS
DEATH IN THE
NIGHT
WATCHES

HEAD of ZEUS

MYSTERIOUSPRESS.COM

MYSTERIOUSPRESS.COM

HEAD of ZEUS

HEAD *of* ZEUS

(212) 587-1011

Monday through Saturday

11:00 a.m. to 7:00 p.m.

FIND OUT MORE AT:

www.mysteriousbookshop.com

FOLLOW US:

@TheMysterious and
Facebook.com/MysteriousBookshop

HEAD *of* ZEUS

30331320R00269

Printed in Great Britain
by Amazon